va............................uctant
I w............................building,
I w............................ from page one,
............................g far into the night."
—Ju........or, *USA Today* bestselling author of
The Good Ghouls' Guide to Getting Even

"I'd so hang out with Merit the vampire. *Some Girls Bite* is
smart . . . and delightful. A must-read."
—Candace Havens, author of *The Demon King and I*

HALL PASS

I flicked on my flashlight and swung the beam into the dark, the arc of light barely penetrating the blackness, even as I squinted to get a better look.

And then I saw them—Scout and Jason behind her, both in uniform and both running toward me as if they were running for their lives. I dropped the beam of the flashlight to the floor to keep from blinding them.

"Scout?" I tried to call out, but fear had frozen my throat. I tried again, and this time managed sound. "Scout!"

They were still far away—the corridor was a deep one—but they were running at sprinter speed . . . and there was something behind them.

Chasing after them was the blonde we'd seen outside on Monday—the girl with the hoodie who had watched us in the memorial garden. She was in jeans, running shoes, and a T-shirt this time, and she ran full-bore after Scout and Jason. But even as she sprinted through the corridor, her expression was somehow vacant, a strange gleam in her eyes the only real sign of life. Her hair was long and wavy, and it flew out behind her as she ran, arms pumping, toward us.

Suddenly she pulled back her hand, then shot it forward as if to throw something at us. When she did, the air and ground rumbled, and this time the impact was strong enough to knock me off my feet. I hit the ground on my knees, palms out in front of me.

By the time I glanced up again, Scout and Jason had reached me. I saw the look of horror on Scout's face. "Get up, Lily!" she implored. *"Run!"*

NORTHEAST COLORADO BOOKMOBILE SVS
WRAY, CO 80758
(970) 332-4715
(800) 306-4715

Praise for Chloe Neill's
Chicagoland Vampire Novels

"With her wonderfully compelling ret...
vampire heroine and her candid world ...
was drawn into Some Girls Bit...
and kept reading ...
—Xen...

NORTHEAST COLORADO BOOKMOBILE SVS
WRAY, CO 80758
(970) 332-2716
(970) 332-4718

FIRESPELL

A NOVEL OF THE DARK ELITE

CHLOE NEILL

3NECBS0081537T

NORTHEAST COLORADO BOOKMOBILE SVS
WRAY , CO 80758
(970) 332-4715
(800) 306-4715

A SIGNET BOOK

SIGNET
Published by New American Library, a division of
Penguin Group (USA) Inc., 375 Hudson Street,
New York, New York 10014, USA
Penguin Group (Canada), 90 Eglinton Avenue East, Suite 700, Toronto,
Ontario M4P 2Y3, Canada (a division of Pearson Penguin Canada Inc.)
Penguin Books Ltd., 80 Strand, London WC2R 0RL, England
Penguin Ireland, 25 St. Stephen's Green, Dublin 2,
Ireland (a division of Penguin Books Ltd.)
Penguin Group (Australia), 250 Camberwell Road, Camberwell, Victoria 3124,
Australia (a division of Pearson Australia Group Pty. Ltd.)
Penguin Books India Pvt. Ltd., 11 Community Centre, Panchsheel Park,
New Delhi - 110 017, India
Penguin Group (NZ), 67 Apollo Drive, Rosedale, North Shore 0632,
New Zealand (a division of Pearson New Zealand Ltd.)
Penguin Books (South Africa) (Pty.) Ltd., 24 Sturdee Avenue,
Rosebank, Johannesburg 2196, South Africa

Penguin Books Ltd., Registered Offices:
80 Strand, London WC2R 0RL, England

First published by Signet, an imprint of New American Library,
a division of Penguin Group (USA) Inc.

First Printing, January 2010
10 9 8 7 6 5 4 3 2 1

Copyright © Chloe Neill, 2010
All rights reserved

 REGISTERED TRADEMARK — MARCA REGISTRADA

Printed in the United States of America

Without limiting the rights under copyright reserved above, no part of this
publication may be reproduced, stored in or introduced into a retrieval
system, or transmitted, in any form, or by any means (electronic, mechanical,
photocopying, recording, or otherwise), without the prior written permission of
both the copyright owner and the above publisher of this book.

PUBLISHER'S NOTE
This is a work of fiction. Names, characters, places, and incidents either are the
product of the author's imagination or are used fictitiously, and any resemblance
to actual persons, living or dead, business establishments, events, or locales is
entirely coincidental.
    The publisher does not have any control over and does not assume any
responsibility for author or third-party Web sites or their content.

If you purchased this book without a cover you should be aware that this book is
stolen property. It was reported as "unsold and destroyed" to the publisher and
neither the author nor the publisher has received any payment for this "stripped
book."

The scanning, uploading, and distribution of this book via the Internet or via any
other means without the permission of the publisher is illegal and punishable by
law. Please purchase only authorized electronic editions, and do not participate
in or encourage electronic piracy of copyrighted materials. Your support of the
author's rights is appreciated.

ACKNOWLEDGMENTS

A special thanks to the Putzy and Murphy families for their hospitality (and patience) during the editing process, and to the always entertaining folks at my online forum (go Team Eel!) for their enthusiasm, humor, and support.

This one is dedicated to Nate.

(He knows why.)

For more information on Chloe or the Novels of the Dark Elite, visit: http://chloeneill.com.

"Chicago—a city where they are always rubbing a lamp, and fetching up the genii, and contriving and achieving new impossibilities."

—Mark Twain

1

They were gathered around a conference table in a high-rise, eight men and women, no one under the age of sixty-five, all of them wealthy beyond measure. And they were here, in the middle of Manhattan, to decide my fate.

I was not quite sixteen and only one month out of my sophomore year of high school. My parents, philosophy professors, had been offered a two-year-long academic sabbatical at a university in Munich, Germany. That's right—two years out of the country, which only really mattered because they decided I'd be better off staying in the United States.

They'd passed along that little nugget one Saturday in June. I'd been preparing to head to my best friend Ashley's house when my parents came into my room and sat down on my bed.

"Lily," Mom said, "we need to talk."

I don't think I'm ruining the surprise by pointing out that nothing good happens when someone starts a speech like that.

My first thought was that something horrible had happened to Ashley. Turned out she was fine; the trauma hit a little closer to home. My parents told me they'd been accepted into the sabbatical program, and that the chance to work in Germany for two years was an amazing opportunity for them.

Then they got quiet and exchanged one of those long, meaningful looks that really didn't bode well for me. They said they didn't want to drag me to Germany with them, that they'd be busy while they were there, and that they wanted me to stay in an American school to have the best chance of going to a great college here. So they'd decided that while they were away, I'd be staying in the States.

I was equal parts bummed and thrilled. Bummed, of course, because they'd be an ocean away while I passed all the big milestones—SAT prep, college visits, prom, completing my vinyl collection of every Smashing Pumpkins track ever released.

Thrilled, because I figured I'd get to stay with Ashley and her parents.

Unfortunately, I was only right about the first part.

My parents had decided it would be best for me to finish high school in Chicago, in a boarding school stuck in the middle of high-rise buildings and concrete—not in Sagamore, my hometown in Upstate New York; not in our tree-lined neighborhood, with my friends and the people and places I knew.

I protested with every argument I could think of.

Flash forward two weeks and 240 miles to the conference table where I sat in a button-up cardigan and pencil skirt I'd never have worn under normal circumstances, the members of the Board of Trustees of St. Sophia's School for Girls staring back at me. They interviewed every girl who wanted to walk their hallowed halls—after all, heaven forbid they let in a girl who didn't meet their standards. But that they traveled to New York to see me seemed a little out of the ordinary.

"I hope you're aware," said one of them, a silver-haired man with tiny round glasses, "that St. Sophia's is a famed academic institution. The school itself has a long and storied history in Chicago, and the Ivy Leagues recruit from its halls."

A woman with a pile of hair atop her head looked at

me and said slowly, as if talking to a child, "You'll have any secondary institution in this country or beyond at your feet, Lily, if you're accepted at St. Sophia's. If you become a St. Sophia's girl."

Okay, but what if I didn't want to be a St. Sophia's girl? What if I wanted to stay home in Sagamore with my friends, not a thousand miles away in some freezing Midwestern city, surrounded by private-school girls who dressed the same, talked the same, bragged about their money?

I didn't want to be a St. Sophia's girl. I wanted to be me, Lily Parker, of the dark hair and eyeliner and fabulous fashion sense.

The powers that be of St. Sophia's were apparently less hesitant. Two weeks after the interview, I got the letter in the mail.

"Congratulations," it said. "We are pleased to inform you that the members of the board of trustees have voted favorably regarding your admission to St. Sophia's School for Girls."

I was less than pleased, but short of running away, which wasn't my style, I was out of options. So two months later, my parents and I trekked to Albany International.

Mom had booked us on the same airline, so we sat in the concourse together, with me between the two of them. Mom wore a shirt and trim trousers, her long dark hair in a low ponytail. My father wore a button-up shirt and khakis, his auburn hair waving over the glasses on his nose. They were heading to JFK to connect to their international flight; I was heading to O'Hare.

We sat silently until they called my plane. Too nervous for tears, I stood and put on my messenger bag. My parents stood, as well, and my mom reached out to put a hand on my cheek. "We love you, Lil. You know that? And that this is what's best?"

I most certainly didn't know this was best. And the weird thing was, I wasn't sure even she believed it, considering how nervous she sounded when she said it. Looking back, I think they both had doubts about the whole thing. They didn't actually say that, of course, but their body language told a different story. When they first told me about their plan, my dad kept touching my mom's knee—not romantically or anything, but like he needed reassurance, like he needed to remind himself that she was there and that things were going to be okay. It made me wonder. I mean, they were headed to Germany for a two-year research sabbatical they'd spent months applying for, but despite what they'd said about the great "opportunity," they didn't seem thrilled about going.

The whole thing was very, very strange.

Anyway, my mom's throwing out, "It's for the best," at the airport wasn't a new thing. She and dad had both been repeating that phrase over the last few weeks like a mantra. I didn't know that it was for the best, but I didn't want a bratty comment to be the last thing I said to them, so I nodded at my mom and faked a smile, and let my dad pull me into a rib-breaking hug.

"You can call us anytime," he said. "Anytime, day or night. Or e-mail. Or text us." He pressed a kiss to the top of my head. "You're our light, Lils," he whispered. "Our light."

I wasn't sure whether I loved him more, or hated him a little, for caring so much and still sending me away.

We said our goodbyes, and I traversed the concourse and took my seat on the plane, with a credit card for emergencies in my wallet, a duffel bag bearing my name in the belly of the jet, and my palm pressed to the window as New York fell behind me.

Goodbye, "New York State of Mind."

Pete Wentz said it best in his song title: "Chicago Is So Two Years Ago."

Two hours and a tiny bag of peanuts later, I was in the 312, greeted by a wind that was fierce and much too cold for an afternoon in early September, Windy City or not. My knee-length skirt, part of my new St. Sophia's uniform, didn't help much against the chill.

I glanced back at the black-and-white cab that had dropped me off in front of the school's enclave on East Erie. The driver pulled away from the curb and merged into traffic, leaving me there on the sidewalk, giant duffel bag in my hands, messenger bag across my shoulder, and downtown Chicago around me.

What stood before me, I thought as I gazed up at St. Sophia's School for Girls, wasn't exactly welcoming.

The board members had told me that St. Sophia's had been a convent in its former life, but it could have just as easily been the setting for a gothic horror movie. Dismal gray stone. Lots of tall, skinny windows, and one giant round one in the middle. Fanged, grinning gargoyles perched at each corner of the steep roof.

I tilted my head as I surveyed the statues. Was it weird that nuns had been guarded by tiny stone monsters? And were they supposed to keep people out . . . or in?

Rising over the main building were the symbols of St. Sophia's—two prickly towers of that same gray stone. Supposedly, some of Chicago's leading ladies wore silver rings inscribed with an outline of the towers, proof that they'd been St. Sophia's girls.

Three months after my parents' revelation, I still had no desire to be a St. Sophia's girl. Besides, if you squinted, the building looked like a pointy-eared monster.

I gnawed the inside of my lip and scanned the other few equally gothic buildings that made up the small campus, all but hidden from the rest of Chicago by a stone wall. A royal blue flag that bore the St. Sophia's crest (complete with tower) rippled in the wind above the arched front door. A Rolls-Royce was parked on the curved driveway below.

This wasn't my kind of place. This wasn't Sagamore. It was far from my school and my neighborhood, far from my favorite vintage clothing store and favorite coffeehouse.

Worse, given the Rolls, I guessed these weren't my kind of people. Well, they *used* to not be my kind of people. If my parents could afford to send me here, we apparently had money I hadn't known about.

"This sucks," I muttered, just in time for the heavy double doors in the middle of the tower to open. A woman—tall, thin, dressed in a no-nonsense suit and sensible heels—stepped into the doorway.

We looked at each other for a moment. Then she moved to the side, holding one of the doors open with her hand.

I guessed that was my cue. Adjusting my messenger bag and duffel, I made my way up the sidewalk.

"Lily Parker?" she asked, one eyebrow arched questioningly, when I got to the stone stairs that lay before the door.

I nodded.

She lifted her gaze and surveyed the school grounds, like an eagle scanning for prey. "Come inside."

I walked up the steps and into the building, the wind ruffling my hair as the giant doors were closed behind me.

The woman moved through the main building quickly, efficiently, and, most noticeably, silently. I didn't get so much as a hello, much less a warm welcome to Chicago. She hadn't spoken a word since she'd beckoned me to follow her.

And follow her I did, through lots of slick limestone corridors lit by the tiny flickering bulbs in old-fashioned wall sconces. The floor and walls were made of the same pale limestone, the ceiling overhead a grid of thick wooden beams, gold symbols painted in the spaces between them. A bee. The flowerlike shape of a fleur-de-lis.

We turned one corner, then another, until we entered a corridor lined with columns. The ceiling changed, rising above us in a series of pointed arches outlined in curved wooden beams, the spaces between them painted the same blue as St. Sophia's flag. Gold stars dotted the blue.

It was impressive—or at least expensive.

I followed her to the end of the hallway, which terminated in a wooden door. A name, MARCELINE D. FOLEY, was written in gold letters in the middle of it.

When she opened the door and stepped inside the office, I assumed she was Marceline D. Foley. I stepped inside behind her.

The room was darkish, a heavy fragrance drifting up from a small oil burner on a side table. A gigantic, circular stained glass window was on the wall opposite the door, and a massive oak desk sat in front of the window.

"Close the door," she said. I dropped my duffel bag to the floor, then did as she'd directed. When I turned around again, she was seated behind the desk, manicured hands clasped before her, her gaze on me.

"I am Marceline Foley, the headmistress of this school," she said. "You've been sent to us for your education, your personal growth, and your development into a young lady. You will become a St. Sophia's girl. As a junior, you will spend two years at this institution. I expect you to use that time wisely—to study, to learn, to network, and to prepare yourself for academically challenging studies at a well-respected university.

"You will have classes from eight twenty a.m. until three twenty p.m., Monday through Friday. You will have dinner at precisely five o'clock and study hall from seven p.m. until nine p.m., Sunday through Thursday. Lights-out at ten o'clock. You will remain on the school grounds during the week, although you may take your exercise off the grounds during your lunch breaks, assuming you do not leave the grounds alone and that you stay near campus. Curfew is promptly at nine p.m. on Friday and Saturday nights. Do you have any questions?"

I shook my head, which was a fib. I had tons of questions, actually, but not the sort I thought she'd appreciate, especially since her PR skills left a lot to be desired. She made St. Sophia's sound less like boarding school and more like prison. Then again, the PR was lost on me, anyway. It's not like I was there by choice.

"Good." Foley pulled open a tiny drawer on the right-hand side of her desk. Out of it she lifted an antique gold skeleton key—the skinny kind with prongs at the end—that was strung from a royal blue ribbon.

"Your room key," she said, and extended her hand. I lifted the ribbon from her palm, wrapping my fingers around the slender bar of metal. "Your books are already in your room. You've been assigned a laptop, which is in your room, as well."

She frowned, then glanced up at me. "This is likely not how you imagined your junior and senior years of high school would be, Ms. Parker. But you will find that you have been bestowed an incredible gift. This is one of the finest high schools in the nation. Being an alumna of St. Sophia's will open doors for you educationally and socially. Your membership in this institution will connect you to a network of women whose influence is international in scope."

I nodded, mostly about that first part. Of course I'd imagined my junior and senior years differently. I'd imagined being at home, with my friends, with my *parents*. But she hadn't actually asked me how I felt about being shipped off to Chicago, so I didn't elaborate.

"I'll show you to your room," she said, rising from her chair and moving toward the door.

I picked up my bag again and followed her.

St. Sophia's looked pretty much the same on the walk to my room as it had on the way to Foley's office—one stone corridor after another. The building was immaculately clean, but kind of empty. Sterile. It was also quieter than I would have expected a high school to be, certainly quieter than the high school I'd left behind. But for the click of Foley's heels on the shining stone floors, the place was graveyard silent. And there was no sign of the usual high school stuff. No trophy cases, no class photos, no lockers, no pep rally posters. Most important, still no sign of students. There were supposed to be two hundred of us. So far, it looked like I was the only St. Sophia's girl in residence.

The corridor suddenly opened into a giant circular space with a domed ceiling, a labyrinth set into the tile on the floor beneath it. This was a serious place. A place for contemplation. A place where nuns once walked quietly, gravely, through the hallways.

And then she pushed open another set of double doors.

The hallway opened into a long room lit by enormous metal chandeliers and the blazing color of dozens of stained glass windows. The walls that weren't covered by windows were lined with books, and the floor was filled by rows and rows of tables.

At the tables sat teenagers. Lots and lots of teenagers, all in stuff that made up the St. Sophia's uniform: navy plaid skirt and some kind of top in the same navy; sweater; hooded sweatshirt; sweater-vest.

They looked like an all-girl army of plaid.

Books and notebooks were spread on the tables before them, laptop computers open and buzzing. Classes didn't start until tomorrow, and these girls were already studying. The trustees were right—these people were serious about their studies.

"Your classmates," Foley quietly said.

She walked through the aisle that split the room into two halves, and I followed behind her, my shoulder beginning to ache under the weight of the duffel bag. Girls watched as I walked past them, heads lifting from books (and notebooks and laptops) to check me out as I passed. I caught the eyes of two of them.

The first was a blonde with wavy hair that cascaded around her shoulders, a black patent leather headband tucked behind her ears. She arched an eyebrow at me as I passed, and two other brunettes at the table leaned toward her to whisper. To gossip. I made a prediction pretty quickly that she was the leader of that pack.

The second girl, who sat with three other plaid cadets a few tables down, was definitely not a member of the blonde's pack. Her hair was also blond, but for the darker ends of her short bob. She wore black nail polish and a small silver ring on one side of her nose.

Given what I'd seen so far, I was surprised Foley let her get away with that, but I liked it.

She lifted her head as I walked by, her green eyes on my browns as I passed.

She smiled. I smiled back.

"This way," Foley ordered. I hustled to follow.

We walked down the aisle to the other end of the room, then into another corridor. A few more turns and a narrow flight of limestone stairs later, Foley stopped beside a wooden door. She bobbed her head at the key around my neck. "Your suite," she said. "Your bedroom is the first on the right. You have three suitemates, and you'll share the common room. Classes begin promptly at eight-twenty tomorrow morning. Your schedule is with your books. I understand you have some interest in the arts?"

"I like to draw," I said. "Sometimes paint."

"Yes, the board forwarded some of the slides of your work. It lends itself to the fantastic—imaginary worlds and unrealistic creatures—but you seem to have some skill. We've placed you in our arts track. You'll start studio classes within the next few weeks, once our instructor has settled in. It is expected that you will devote as much time to your craft as you do to your studies." Apparently having concluded her instructions, she gave me an up-and-down appraisal. "Any questions?"

She'd done it again. She said, "Any questions?" but it sounded a lot more like "I don't have time for nonsense right now."

"No, thank you," I said, and Foley bobbed her head.

"Very good." With that, she turned on her heel and

walked away, her footsteps echoing through the hallway.

I waited until she was gone, then slipped the key into
the lock and turned the knob. The door opened into a
small circular space—the common room. There were
a couch and coffee table in front of a small fireplace, a
cello propped against the opposite wall, and four doors
leading, I assumed, to the bedrooms.

I walked to the door on the far right and slipped the
skeleton key from my neck, then into the lock. When the
tumblers clicked, I pushed open the door and flipped on
the light.

It was small—a tiny but tidy space with one small
window and a twin-sized bed. The bed was covered by
a royal blue bedspread embroidered with an imprint
of the St. Sophia's tower. Across from the bed was a
wooden bureau, atop which sat a two-foot-high stack
of books, a pile of papers, a silver laptop, and an alarm
clock. A narrow wooden door led to a closet.

I closed the door to the suite behind me, then dropped
my bag onto the bed. The room had a few pieces of furniture in it and the school supplies, but otherwise, it was
empty. But for the few things I'd been able to fit into the
duffel, nothing here would remind me of home.

My heart sank at the thought. My parents had actually sent me away to boarding school. They chose Munich and researching some musty philosopher over art
competitions and honors society dinners, the kind of
stuff they usually loved to brag about.

I sat down next to my duffel, pulled the cell phone
from the front pocket of my gray and yellow messenger
bag, flipped it open, and checked the time. It was nearly
five o'clock in Chicago and would have been midnight
in Munich, although they were probably halfway over
the Atlantic right now. I wanted to call them, to hear
their voices, but since that wasn't an option, I pulled up
my mom's cell number and clicked out a text message:
"@ SCHOOL IN ROOM." It wasn't much, but they'd know

I'd arrived safely and, I assumed, would call when they could.

When I flipped the phone closed again, I stared at it for a minute, tears pricking at my eyes. I tried to keep them from spilling over, to keep from crying in the middle of my first hour at St. Sophia's, the first hour into my new life.

They spilled over anyway. I didn't want to be here. Not at this school, not in Chicago. If I didn't think they'd just ship me right back again, I'd have used the credit card my mom gave me for emergencies, charged a ticket, and hopped a plane back to New York.

"This sucks," I said, swiping carefully at my overflowing tears, trying to avoid smearing the black eyeliner around my eyes.

A knock sounded at the door, which opened. I glanced up.

"Are you planning your escape?" asked the girl with the nose ring and black nail polish who stood in my doorway.

2

"Seriously, you look pretty depressed there." She pushed off the door, her thin frame nearly swamped by a plaid skirt and oversized St. Sophia's sweatshirt, her legs clad in tights and sheepskin boots. She was about my height, five foot six or so.

"Thanks for knocking," I said, swiping at what I'm sure was a mess beneath my eyes.

"I do what I can. And you've made a mess," she confirmed. She walked toward me and, without warning, tipped up my chin. She tilted her head and frowned at me, then rubbed her thumbs beneath my eyes. I just looked back at her, amusement in my expression. When she was done, she put her hands on her hips and surveyed her work.

"It's not bad. I like the eyeliner. A little punk. A little goth, but not over the top, and it definitely works with your eyes. You might want to think about waterproof, though." She stuck out her hand. "I'm your suitemate, Scout Green. And you're Lily Parker."

"I am," I said, shaking her hand.

Scout sat down on the bed next to me, then crossed her legs and began to swing a leg. "And what personal tragedy has brought you to our fine institution on this lovely fall day?"

I arched a brow at her. She waved a hand. "It's nothing personal. We tend to get a lot of tragedy cases. Relatives die. Fortunes are made and the parentals get too busy for teen angst. That's my basic story. On the rare but exciting occasion, expulsion from the publics and enough money for the trustees to see 'untapped potential.'" She tilted her head as she looked at me. "You've got a great look, but you don't look quite punk enough to be the expulsion kind."

"My parents are on a research trip," I said. "Twenty-four months in Germany—not that I'm bitter about that—so I was sentenced to lockdown at St. Sophia's."

Scout smiled knowingly. "Unfortunately, Lil, your parents' ditching you for Europe makes you average around here. It's like a home for latchkey kids. Where are you from? Prior to being dropped off in the Windy City, I mean."

"Upstate New York. Sagamore."

"You're a junior?"

I nodded.

"Ditto," Scout said, then uncrossed her legs and patted her hands against her knees. "And that means that if all goes well, we'll have two years together at St. Sophia's School for Girls. We might as well get you acquainted." She rose, and with one hand tucked behind her back and one hand at her waist, did a little bow. "I'm Millicent Carlisle Green."

I bit back a grin. "And that's why you go by 'Scout.'"

"And that's why I go by 'Scout,'" she agreed, grinning back. "First off, on behalf of the denizens of Chicago"— she put a hand against her heart—"welcome to the Windy City. Allow me to introduce you to the wondrous world of snooty American private schooldom." She frowned. "'Schooldom.' Is that a word?"

"Close enough," I said. "Please continue."

She nodded, then swept a hand through the air. "You can see the luxury accommodations that the gazillion dollars in tuition and room and board will buy you." She walked to the bed and, like a hostess on *The Price*

Is Right, caressed the iron frame. "Sleeping quarters of only the highest quality."

"Of course," I solemnly said.

Scout turned on her heel, the skirt swinging at her knees, and pointed at the simple wooden bureau. "The finest of European antiques to hold your baubles and treasures." Then she swept to the window and, with a tug of the blinds, revealed the view. There were a few yards of grass, then the stone wall. Beyond both sat the facing side of a glass and steel building.

"And, of course," Scout continued, "the finest view that new money can buy."

"Only the best for a Parker," I said.

"Now you're getting it," Scout said approvingly. She walked back to the door, then beckoned me to follow. "The common room," she said, turning around to survey it. "Where we'll gossip, read intellectually stimulating classics of literature—"

"Like that?" I asked with a chuckle, pointing at the dog-eared copy of *Vogue* lying on the coffee table.

"*Absolument*," Scout said. "*Vogue* is our guide to current events and international culture."

"And sweet shoes."

"And sweet shoes," she said, then gestured at the cello in the corner. "That's Barnaby's baby. Lesley Barnaby," she added at my lifted brows. "She's number three in our suite, but you won't see much of her. Lesley has four things, and four things only, in her day planner: class, sleeping, studying, and practicing."

"Who's girl number four?" I asked, as Scout led me to the closed door directly across from mine.

Her hand on the doorknob, Scout glanced back at me. "Amie Cherry. She's one of the brat pack."

"The brat pack?"

"Yep. Did you see the blonde with the headband in the study hall?"

I nodded.

"That's Veronica Lively, the junior class's resident alpha girl. Cherry is one of her minions. She was the brunette with short hair. You didn't hear me say this, but Veronica's actually got brains. She might not use them for much beyond kissing Foley's ass, but she's got them. The minions are another story. Mary Katherine, that's minion number two—the brunette with long hair— is former old money. She still has the connections, but that's pretty much all she has.

"Now, Cherry—Cherry has coin. Stacks and stacks of cash. As minions go, Cherry's not nearly as bad as Mary Katherine, and she has the potential to be cool, but she takes Veronica's advice much too seriously." Scout frowned, then glanced up at me. "Do you know what folks in Chicago call St. Sophia's?"

I shook my head.

"St. Spoiled."

"Not much of a stretch, is it?"

"Exactly." With a twist of her wrist, Scout turned the knob and pushed open her bedroom door.

"My God," I said, staring into the space. "There's so much . . . *stuff.*"

Every inch of space in Scout's tiny room, but for the rectangle of bed, was filled with shelves. And those shelves were filled to overflowing. They were double-stacked with books and knickknacks, all organized into tidy collections. There was a shelf of owls—some ceramic, some wood, some made of bits of sticks and twigs. A group of sculpted apples—the same mix of materials. Inkwells. Antique tin boxes. Tiny houses made of paper. Old cameras.

"If your parents donate a wing, you get extra shelves," she said, her voice flat as week-old soda.

"Where did you get all this?" I walked to a shelf and picked up a delicate paper house crafted from a restaurant menu. A door and tiny windows were carefully cut into the facade, and a chimney was pasted to the roof, which was dusted in white glitter. "And when?"

"I've been at St. Sophia's since I was twelve. I've had the time. And I got it anywhere and everywhere," she said, flopping down onto her bed. She sat back on her elbows and crossed one leg over the other. "There's a lot of sweet stuff floating around Chicago. Antiques stores, flea markets, handmade goods, what have you. Sometimes my parents bring me stuff, and I pick up things along the way when I see them over the summer."

I gingerly placed the building back on the shelf, then glanced back at her. "Where are they now? Your parents, I mean."

"Monaco—Monte Carlo. The Yacht Show is in a couple of weeks. There's teak to be polished." She chuckled, but the sound wasn't especially happy. "Not by them, of course—they've moved past doing physical labor—but still."

I made some vague sound of agreement—my nautical excursions were limited to paddleboats at summer camp—and moved past the museum and toward the books. There were lots of books on lots of subjects, all organized by color. It was a rainbow of paper—recipes, encyclopedias, dictionaries, thesauruses, books on typology and design. There were even a few ancient leather books with gold lettering along the spines.

I pulled a design book from the shelf and flipped through it. Letters, in every shape and form, were spread across the pages, from a sturdy capital A to a tiny, curlicued Z.

"I'm sensing a theme here," I said, smiling up at Scout. "You like words. Lists. Letters."

She nodded. "You string some letters together, and you make a word. You string some words together, and you make a sentence, then a paragraph, then a chapter. Words have power."

I snorted, replacing the book on the shelf. "Words have power? That sounds like you're into some Harry Potter juju."

"Now you're just being ridiculous," she said. "So, what does a young Lily Parker do in Sagamore, New York?"

I shrugged. "The usual. I hung out. Went to the mall. Concerts. TiVo *ANTM* and *Man vs. Wild.*"

"Oh, my God, I *love* that show," Scout said. "That guy eats everything."

"And he's hot," I pointed out.

"Seriously hot," she agreed. "Hot guy eats bloody stuff. Who knew that would be a hit?"

"The producer of every vampire movie ever?" I offered.

Scout snorted a laugh. "Well put, Parker. I'm digging the sarcasm."

"I try," I admitted with a grin. It was nice to smile— nice to have something to smile about. Heck, it was nice to feel like this boarding school business might be doable—like I'd be able to make friends and study and go about my high school business in pretty much the same way as I could have in Sagamore.

A shrill sound suddenly filled the air, like the beating of tiny wings.

"Oops, that's me," Scout said, untangling her legs, hopping off the bed, and grabbing a brick-shaped cell phone that was threatening to vibrate its way off one of the shelves and onto the floor. She picked up the phone just before it hit the edge, then unpopped the screen and read its contents.

"Jeez Louise," she said. "You'd think I'd get a break when school starts, but no." Maybe realizing she was muttering in front of an audience, she looked up at me. "Sorry, but I have to go. I have to . . . exercise. Yes," she said matter-of-factly, as if she'd decided on exercise as an excuse, "I have to exercise."

Apparently intent on proving her point, Scout arched her arms over her head and leaned to the right and left, as if stretching for a big run, then stood up and began swiveling her torso, hands at her waist. "Limbering up," she explained.

I arched a dubious brow. "To go exercise."

"Exercise," she repeated, grabbing a black messenger bag from a hook next to her door and maneuvering it over her head. A white skull and crossbones grinned back at me.

"So," I said, "you're exercising in your uniform?"

"Apparently so. Look, you're new, but I like you. And if I guess right, you're a heck of a lot cooler than the rest of the brat pack."

"Thanks, I guess?"

"So I need you to be cool. You didn't see me leave, okay?"

The room was silent as I looked at her, trying to gauge exactly how much trouble she was about to get herself into.

"Is this one of those, 'I'm in over my head' kind of deals, and I'll hear a horrible story tomorrow about your being found strangled in an alley?"

That she took a few seconds to think about her answer made me that much more nervous.

"Probably not *tonight*," she finally said. "But either way, that's not on you. And since we're probably going to be BFFs, you're going to have to trust me on this one."

"BFFs?"

"Of course," she said, and just like that, I had a friend. "But for now, I have to run. We'll talk," she promised. And then she was gone, her bedroom door open, the closing of the hallway door signaling her exit. I looked around her room, noticing the pair of sneakers that sat together beside her bed.

"Exercise, my big toe," I mumbled, and left Scout's museum, closing the door behind me.

It was nearly six o'clock when I walked the few feet back to my room. I glanced at the stack of books and papers on the bureau, admitting to myself that prepping for class tomorrow was probably a solid course of action.

On the other hand, there were bags to be unpacked.

It wasn't a tough choice. I liked to read, but I wasn't going to spend the last few waking hours of my summer vacation with my nose in a book.

I unzipped and unstuffed my duffel bag, cramming undergarments and pajamas and toiletries into the bureau, then hanging the components of my new St. Sophia's wardrobe in the closet. Skirts in the blue and gold of the St. Sophia's plaid. Navy polo shirt. Navy cardigan. Blue button-up shirt, et cetera, et cetera. I also stowed away the few articles of regular clothing I'd brought along: some jeans and skirts, a few favorite T-shirts, a hoodie.

Shoes went into the closet, and knickknacks went to the top of the bureau: a photo of my parents and me together; a ceramic ashtray made by Ashley that read BEST COWGIRL EVER. We didn't smoke, of course, and it was unrecognizable as an ashtray, as it looked more like something you'd discover in the business end of a dirty diaper. But Ashley made it for me at camp when we were eight. Sure, I tortured her about how truly heinous it was, but that's what friends were for, right?

At the moment, Ash was home in Sagamore, probably studying for a bio test, since public school had started two weeks ago. Remembering I hadn't texted her to let her know I'd arrived, I flipped open my phone and snapped shots of my room—the empty walls, the stack of books, the logoed bedspread—then sent them her way.

"UNIMPRESSED RR," she texted back. She'd taken to calling me "Richie Rich" when we found out that I'd be heading to St. Sophia's—and after we'd done plenty of Web research. She figured that life in a froufrou private school would taint me, turn me into some kind of raving Blair Waldorf.

I couldn't let that stand, of course. I sent back, "U MUST RESPECT ME."

She was still apparently unimpressed, since "GO

STUDY" was her answer. I figured she was probably on to something, so I moved back to the stack of books and gave them a look-see.

Civics.

Trig.

British lit.

Art history.

Chemistry.

European history.

"Good thing they're starting me off easy," I muttered, nibbling on my bottom lip as I scanned the textbooks. Add the fact that I was apparently taking a studio class, and it was no wonder Foley scheduled a two-hour study hall every night. I'd be lucky if two hours were enough.

Next to the stack of books was a pile of papers, including a class schedule and the rules of residency at St. Sophia's. There wasn't a building map, which was a little flabbergasting since this place was a maze to get through.

I heard the hallway door open and shut, laughter filling the common room. Thinking I might as well be social, I blew out a breath to calm the butterflies in my stomach, then opened my bedroom door. There were three girls in the room—the blonde I'd seen in the library and her two brunette friends. Given Scout's descriptions, I assumed the blonde was Veronica, the shorter-haired girl was Amie, the third of my new suitemates, and the girl with longer hair was Mary Katherine, she of the limited intelligence.

The blonde had settled herself on the couch, her long, wavy hair spread around her shoulders, her feet in Amie's lap. Mary Katherine sat on the floor in front of them, her arms stretched behind her, her feet crossed at the ankles. They were all in uniform, all in pressed, pleated skirts, tights, and button-down shirts with navy sweater-vests.

A regiment of officers in the army of plaid.

"We have a visitor," said the blonde, one blond brow arched over blue eyes.

Amie, whose pale skin was unmarred by makeup or jewelry except for a pair of pearl earrings, slapped at Veronica's feet. Veronica rolled her eyes, but lifted them, and the brunette stood and walked toward me. "I'm Amie." She bobbed her head toward one of the bedrooms behind us. "I'm over there."

"It's nice to meet you," I said. "I'm Lily."

"Veronica," Amie said, pointing to the blonde, "and Mary Katherine," she added, pointing to the brunette. The girls both offered finger waves.

"You missed the mixer earlier today," Veronica said, stretching out her legs again. "Tea and petits fours in the ballroom. Your chance to meet the rest of your new St. Sophia's chums before classes start tomorrow." Veronica's voice carried the tone of the wealthy, jaded girl who'd seen it all and hadn't been impressed.

"I've only been here a couple of hours," I said, unimpressed by the attitude.

"Yeah, we heard you weren't from Chicago," said Mary Katherine, head tilted up as she scanned my clothes. Given her own navy tights and patent leather flats, and the gleam of her perfectly straight hair, I guessed she wouldn't dig my Chuck Taylors (the board of trustees let us pick our own footware) and choppy haircut.

"Upstate New York," I told her. "Near Syracuse."

"Public school?" Mary Katherine asked, disdain in her voice.

Oh, how fun. Private school really *was* like *Gossip Girl*. "Public school," I confirmed, lips curved into a smile.

Veronica made a sound of irritation. "Jesus, Mary Katherine, be a bitch, why don't you?"

Mary Katherine rolled her eyes, then turned her attention to her cuticles, inspecting her short, perfectly painted red nails. "I just asked a question. You're the one who assumed I was being negative."

"Please excuse the peanut gallery," Amie said with a smile. "Have you met everybody else?"

"I haven't met Lesley," I said. "I met Scout, though."

Mary Katherine made a sarcastic sound. "Good luck there. That girl has *issues*." She stretched out the word dramatically. I got the sense Mary Katherine enjoyed drama.

"M.K.'s just jealous," Veronica said, twirling a lock of hair around one of her fingers, and sliding a glance at the brunette on the floor. "Not every St. Sophia's girl has parents who have the cash to donate an entire building to the school."

I guess Scout hadn't been kidding about the extra shelves.

"Whatever," Mary Katherine said, then crossed her legs and pushed herself up from the floor. "You two can play Welcome Wagon with the new girl. I need to make a phone call."

Veronica rolled her eyes, but swiveled her legs onto the floor and stood up, as well. "M.K.'s dating a U of C boy," she said. "She thinks he hung the moon."

"He's pre-law," Mary Katherine said, heading for the door.

"He's twenty," Amie muttered after Mary Katherine had stepped into the hallway and closed the door behind her. "And she's sixteen."

"Quit being a mother, Amie," Veronica said, straightening her headband. "I'm going back to my room. I suppose I'll see you in the morning." She glanced at me. "I don't want to be bitchy, but a little advice?"

She said it like she was asking for permission, so I nodded, solely out of politeness.

"Mind the company you keep," she said. With that gem, which I assumed was a shot at Scout, she walked to Amie. They exchanged air kisses.

"Nighty night, all," Veronica said, and then she was gone.

When I turned around again, Amie was gone, her bedroom door closing behind her.

"Charming," I muttered, and headed back to my room.

It was earlier than I would have normally gone to sleep, but given the travel, the time change, and the change in circumstances, I was exhausted. Finding the stone-walled and stone-floored room chilly even in the early fall, I exchanged the uniform for flannel pajamas, turned off the light, and climbed into bed.

The room was dark, but far from quiet. The city bustled around me, the thrum of traffic from downtown Chicago creating a backdrop of sound, even on a Sunday night. Although the stone muffled it, I wasn't used to even the low drone of noise. I had been born and bred amongst acres of lawns and overhanging trees—and when the sun went down, the town went silent.

I stared at the ceiling. Tiny yellow-green dots emerged from the darkness. The plaster above me was dotted with glow-in-the-dark stars, I assumed pasted there by a former St. Sophia's girl. As my mind raced, wondering about tomorrow and repeating my to-do list—find my locker, find my classes, manage not to get humiliated in said classes, figure out where Scout had gone—I counted the stars, tried to pick out constellations, and glanced at the clock a dozen times.

I tossed and turned in the bed, trying to find a comfortable position, my brain refusing to still even as I lay exhausted, trying to sleep.

I must have drifted off, as I woke suddenly to a pitch-black room. I must have been awakened by the closing of the hallway door. That sound was immediately followed by the scuffle of tripping in the common room—stuff being knocked around and mumbled curses. I threw off the covers and tiptoed to the door, then pressed my ear to the wood.

"Damn coffee table," Scout muttered, footsteps receding until her bedroom door opened and closed. I glanced at the clock. It was one fifteen in the morning. When the common room was quiet, I put a hand to the doorknob, twisted it, and carefully pulled open the door. The room was dark, but a line of light glowed beneath Scout's door.

I frowned. Where had she been until one fifteen in the morning? Exercise seemed seriously unlikely at this point.

That mystery in hand, I closed the door again and went back to bed, staring at the star-spangled ceiling until sleep finally claimed me.

3

My bedroom was cold and dark when the alarm—which I'd moved next to the bed—went off. Not nearly awake enough to actually sit upright, I fumbled for the OFF button and forced my eyes open. My stomach grumbled, but I didn't think I was up for food. I already had butterflies—the combination of new school, new classes, new girls. Questionable high school cafeteria fare probably wasn't going to help.

After a minute of staring at the ceiling, I glanced over at the nightstand. The red light on my phone flashed, a sign that I had messages waiting. I grabbed it, flipped it open . . . and smiled.

"SAFE & SOUND IN GERMANY," read the text from my mom. "FIGHTING JET LAG."

There was a message from Dad, as well, a little less businesslike (which was pretty much how it worked with them): "HAVE A HOT DOG FOR US! LV U, LILS!"

I smiled, closed the phone again, and put it back on the nightstand. Then I threw off the covers and forced my feet to the floor, the stone cold even beneath socks. I stumbled to the closet and grabbed a robe, then grabbed my toiletries and a towel, already stacked on the bureau, prepped and ready for my inaugural shower.

When I opened my bedroom door, Scout, already in uniform (plaid skirt, sweater, knee-high pair of fuzzy boots), smiled at me from the common room couch. She held up the *Vogue*. "I'll read about skinny chicks in Milan. When you get back, we'll go down to breakfast."

"Sure," I mumbled. But halfway to the hallway door, I stopped and glanced back. "Were you exercising until one fifteen this morning?"

Scout glanced up at me, fingers still pinched around the edge of a half-flipped page. "I'm not admitting whether I was or was not exercising, but if you're asking if I was doing whatever I was doing until one fifteen, then yes."

I opened and closed my mouth as I tried to work out what she'd just said. I settled on, "I see."

"Seriously," she said, "it's important stuff."

"Important like what?"

"Important like, I really can't talk about it."

The room was silent for a few seconds. The set of her jaw and the stubbornness in her eyes said she wasn't going to budge. And since I was standing in front of her in pajamas with a fuzzy brain and teeth that desperately needed introducing to some toothpaste, I let it go.

"Okay," I said, and saw relief in her eyes. I left her with the magazine and headed for the bathroom, but there was no way "exercise" was going to hold me for long. Call it too curious, too nosy. But one day after my arrival in Chicago, she was the closest friend I had. And I wasn't about to lose her to whatever mess she was involved in.

She was on the couch when I returned (much more awake after a good shower and toothbrushing), her legs beneath her, her gaze still on the magazine on her lap.

"FYI," she said, "if you don't hurry, we're going to be left with slurry." She looked up, her countenance solemn. "Trust me on this—you don't want slurry."

Fairly confident she was right—the name being awful enough—I dumped my toiletries in my room and slipped into today's version of the uniform. Plaid skirt. Tights to ward off the chill. Long-sleeved button-up shirt and

V-neck sweater. A pair of ice blue boots that were shorter but equally as fuzzy as Scout's.

I stuffed books and some slender Korean notebooks I'd found in a Manhattan paper store (I had a thing for sweet office supplies) into my bag and grabbed my ribboned room key, then closed the door behind me, slipping the key into the lock and turning it until it clicked.

"You ready?" Scout asked, a pile of books in her arms, her black messenger bag over her shoulder, its skull grinning back at me.

"As I'll ever be," I said, pulling the key's ribbon over my head.

The cafeteria was located in a separate building, but one that looked to be the same age as the convent itself—the same stone, the same gothic architecture. I assumed the modern, windowed hallways that now linked them together were added to assuage parents who didn't want their baby girls wandering around outside in freezing Chicago winters. The nuns, I guessed, had been a little more willing to brave the elements.

But the interior of the cafeteria was surprisingly modern, with a long glass wall overlooking the small lawn behind the building. The yard was tidy, inset with wide, concrete paving stones, tufts of grass rising between them. In the far corner sat a piece of what I assumed was industrial sculpture—a series of round metal bands set atop a metal post. *Ode to a Sundial*, maybe?

Having perused the art, I turned back to the cafeteria itself. The long rectangular room was lined with long rectangular tables of pale wood and matching chairs; the tables were filled with the St. Sophia's army. After ten years of public school diversity, it was weird to see so many girls in the same clothes. But that sameness didn't stifle the excitement in the room. Girls clustered together, chatting, probably excited to be back in school, to be reunited with friends and suitemates.

"Welcome to the jungle," Scout whispered, and led me to a buffet line. Smiling men and women in chef gear—white smocks, tall hats—served eggs, bacon, fruit, toast, and oatmeal. These were not your mom's surly lunch ladies—these folks smiled and chatted behind sneeze guards, which were dotted with cards describing how organic or free-range or un-steroided their particular goods were. Whole Foods must have made a fortune off these people.

My stomach twitching with nerves, I didn't have much appetite for breakfast, organic or not, so I asked for toast and OJ, just enough to settle the butterflies. When I'd grabbed my breakfast, I followed Scout to a table. We took two empty chairs at one end.

"I guess we were early enough to avoid the slurry?" I asked.

Scout nibbled at a chunk of pineapple. "Yes, thank God. Slurry is the combination of everything that doesn't get eaten early in the round—oatmeal, fruit, meat, what have you."

I grimaced at the combination. "That's disgusting."

"If you think that's bad, wait until you see the stew," Scout said, nodding toward a chalkboard menu for the week that hung on the far end of the room. "Stew" made a lot of appearances over the weekend.

Scout raised her glass of orange juice toward the menu. "Welcome to St. Sophia's, Parker. Eat early or go home, that's our motto."

"And how's the new girl this morning?"

We turned our gazes to the end of the table. Veronica stood there, blond hair in a complicated ponytail, arms cradling a load of books, Mary Katherine and Amie behind her. Amie smiled at us. Mary Katherine looked viciously bored.

"She's awake," I reported. That was mostly the truth.

"Mmmm," Veronica said in a bored tone, then glanced at Scout. "I hear you're friends with someone from Montclare. Michael Garcia?"

Scout's jaw clenched. "I know Michael. Why do you ask?"

Veronica glanced over her shoulder at Mary Katherine, who made a sound of disdain. "We spent some time together this summer," she said, glancing at Scout again. "He's cute, don't you think?"

I couldn't tell if they were trying to fix Scout up, or figure out if she was crushing Michael so they could throw his interest in Veronica back at her.

Scout shrugged. "He's a friend," she said. "Cute doesn't really figure into it."

"I'm glad you think so," Veronica said, smiling evilly at Scout, "because I'm thinking about inviting him to the Sneak."

Yep. There it was. I didn't need to know what the "Sneak" was to figure out her game—stealing a boy from under Scout's nose. If I'd had any interest in Michael, it would have been hard for me to avoid clawing that superior look right off Veronica's face. But Scout did good—she played the bigger girl, crossing her arms over her chest, her expression bored. "That's great, Veronica. If you think Michael's interested in you, you should go for it. Really."

Her enthusiasm put a frown on Veronica's face. Veronica was pretty—but the frown was not flattering. Her mouth twisted up and her cheeks turned red, her features compressing into something a little less prissy, and a little more ratlike—definitely not attractive.

"You're bluffing," Veronica said. "Maybe I will ask him."

"Do you have his number?" Scout asked, reaching around for her messenger bag. "I could give it to you."

Veronica practically growled, then turned on her heel and headed for the cafeteria door. Mary Katherine, lip wrinkled in disgust, followed her. Amie looked vaguely apologetic about the outburst, but that didn't stop her from turning tail and following, too.

"Nicely done," I complimented.

"Mmm-hmm," Scout said, straightening in her chair again. "See what I mean? TBD."

I lifted my eyebrows. "TBD?"

"Total brat drama," she said. "TBD is way too much drama for me, especially at seven thirty in the morning."

Drama or not, there were questions to be answered. "So, who's Michael Garcia? And what's Montclare?"

"Montclare is a boys' private high. It's kind of our brother school."

"Are they downtown, too?"

"In a roundabout way. They have more kids than we do—nearly four hundred—and their classrooms are scattered in the buildings around the Loop."

"What's the Loop?"

"It's the part of downtown that's within a loop of the El tracks. That's our subway," she added in an elementary-teacher voice.

"Yes," I responded dryly. "I know what the El is. I've seen *ER*."

Scout snorted. "In that case, you'd better be glad you're hooking up with me so I can give you the truth about Chitown. It's not all hot doctors and medical drama, you know." She waved a hand in the air. "Anyway, Montclare has this big-city immersion–type program. You know, country mouse in Gotham, that kind of thing."

"They clearly don't have a Foley," I said. Given what I knew of her so far, I guessed she wouldn't let us out of her sight long enough to "immerse" ourselves in Chicago.

"No kidding," Scout agreed. She pushed back her chair and picked up her tray. "Now that we've had our fill of food and TBD, let's go find our names." Although I had no clue what she was talking about, I finished my orange juice and followed her.

"Our names?" I asked, as we slid our trays through a window at the end of the buffet line.

"A St. Sophia's tradition," she said. I followed her out of the cafeteria, back into the main building, and then through another link into another gothic building, which, Scout explained, held the school's classrooms.

When we pushed through another set of double doors and into the building, we found ourselves in a knot of plaid-clad girls squealing before three rows of lockers. These weren't your typical high school lockers—the steel kind with dents on the front and chunks of gum and leftover stickers on the inside. These were made of gleaming wood, and there were notches cut out of both the top and bottom lockers, so they fit together like a puzzle.

An expensive puzzle, I guessed. Slurry or not, St. Sophia's wasn't afraid to spend some coin.

"Your name will be on yours," Scout shouted through the din of girls, young and old, who were scanning the nameplates on the lockers to find the cabinet that would house their books and supplies for the next nine months.

Frowning at the mass of squirmy teenagers, I wasn't sure I understood the fuss.

I watched Scout maneuver through the girls, then saw blond hair bobbing up and down above the crowd, one arm in the air, as she (I assumed) tried to get my attention.

Gripping the strap of my messenger bag, I squeezed through the gauntlet to reach Scout. She was beaming, one hand on her hip, one hand splayed against one of the top lockers. A silver nameplate in the midst of all that cherry-hued wood bore a single word: SCOUT.

"It says 'Scout'!" she said, glowing like the proud parent of a newborn.

"That's your name," I reminded her.

Scout shook her head, then ran the tips of her fingers across the silver plaque. "For the first time," she said, her gazing going a little dreamy, "it doesn't say 'Millicent.' And only juniors and seniors get the wooden lockers." She bobbed her head down the hall, where the lockers switched back to white enameled steel with vents across the front—the high school classic.

"So you've upgraded?"

Scout nodded. "I've been here for four years, Lil, squeezing books into one of those tiny little contraptions, waiting for the day I'd get wood"—I made an admittedly juvenile snicker—"and G-Day."

"G-Day?"

"Graduation Day. The first day of my freedom from Foley and St. Sophia's and the brat pack. I've been planning for G-Day for four years." She rapped her knuckles against the locker as girls swarmed around us like a flock of birds. "Four years, Parker, and I've got a silver nameplate. A silver nameplate that means I'm only two years from G-Day."

"You really are a weirdo."

"Better to be myself and a little odd than trying to squeeze into some brat pack mold." Her gaze suddenly darkened. I glanced behind us, just in time to see the brat pack moving through the hall. The younger St. Sophia's girls—awed looks on their faces—moved aside as Veronica, Amie, and Mary Katherine floated down the hall on their cloud of smug. That they were only juniors—still a year from full seniority—didn't seem to matter.

"Better to be yourself," I agreed, then looked back at Scout, who was still massaging her nameplate. "Do I get a locker?"

"Only the best one," she snorted, then pointed down. LILY was inscribed in Roman capital letters on a silver nameplate on the Utah-shaped locker beneath hers (which was shaped more like Mississippi).

"If your stinky gym sock odor invades my locker, you're in deep, Parker." Scout slipped her own ribboned room key from her neck and slid the key into the locker. It popped open, revealing three shelves of the same gleaming wood.

She faked a sniff. "This is the most beautiful thing I have ever seen in my life. Such luxury! Such decadence!"

This time, I snorted out loud. Then, realizing the locker bay was beginning to clear out of students, I poked her in the arm. "Come on, weirdo. We need to get to class."

"You have to stop the compliments, Parker. You're making me blush." She popped extra books into her locker, then shut the door again. That done, she glanced at me. "They probably will be expecting us. Best we can do is honor them with our presence."

"We're a blessing, really."

"Totally," she said, and off we went.

Our lockers arranged (although I hadn't so much as opened mine—there was something comforting about having my books in hand), I used the rest of our short walk through the main corridor of the classroom building to our first class—art history—to drag a little more information out of Scout. Thinking it best to hit the interesting stuff first, I started with Veronica's breakfast-hour ploy.

"So," I said, "since you didn't answer me before, I'm going to try again. Tell me about Michael Garcia."

"He's a friend," Scout said, glancing at the room numbers inscribed on the wooden classroom doors as we passed. "*Just* a friend," she added before I could ask a follow-up. "I don't date guys who go to Montclare. One private school brat in the family is enough."

There was obviously more to that story, but Scout stopped in front of a door, so I assumed we'd run out of time for chatting. Then she glanced back at me. "Do you have a boyfriend back home?"

Well, we were out of time for chatting about *her*, anyway. The door opened before I could respond—although my answer would have been "no." A tall, thin man peered out from the doorway, casting a dour look at me and Scout.

"Ms. Green," he said, "and Ms.—" He lifted his eyebrows expectantly.

"Parker," I filled in.

"Yes, very well. Ms. Parker." He stepped to the side,

holding the door open with his arm. "Please take your seats."

We walked inside. Much like the rest of the buildings, the classroom had stone floors and walls that were dotted with whiteboards. There were only a couple of girls at desks when we came in, but as soon as Scout and I took a seat—Scout in the desk directly behind mine—the room began to fill with students, including, unfortunately, the brat pack. Veronica, Amie, and Mary Katherine took seats in the row beside ours, Amie in the front, Veronica in the middle, Mary Katherine behind them. That order put Veronica in the desk right next to mine. Lucky me.

When every desk was taken, girls began pulling notebooks or laptops from their bags. I'd skipped the laptop today, thinking I had enough to worry about today without adding power outlet locations and midclass system crashes to the list, so I pulled out a notebook, pen, and art history book from my bag and prepared to learn.

The man who'd greeted us, who I assumed was Mr. Hollis, since the name was written in cursive, green letters on the whiteboard, closed the door and walked to the front of the room. He looked pretty much exactly like you'd expect a private school teacher to look: bald, corduroy slacks, button-up shirt, and corduroy blazer with leather patches at the elbows.

Hollis glanced down at his podium, then lifted his gaze and scanned the room. "'What was any art but a mould in which to imprison for a moment the shining elusive element which is life itself?'" He turned and uncapped a marker, then wrote "WILLA CATHER" in capital letters below his name. He faced us again, capping and uncapping the marker in his hands with a rhythmic click. Nervous tic, I guessed.

"What do you think Ms. Cather meant? Anyone?"

"Bueller? Bueller?" whispered a voice behind me. I pushed my lips together to bite back a laugh at Scout's joke as Amie popped a hand into the air.

When Hollis glanced around before calling her name, as if hoping to give someone else a chance, I guessed Amie answered a lot of questions. "Ms. Cherry," he said.

"She's talking about a piece of art capturing a moment in time."

Hollis's expression softened. "Well put, Ms. Cherry. Anyone else?" He glanced around the room, his gaze finally settling on me. "Ms. Parker?"

My stomach dropped, a flush rising on my cheeks as all eyes turned to me. Didn't it just figure that I'd be called on during the first day of class? I was more into drawing than talking about art, but I gave it a shot, my voice weirdly loud in the sudden silence.

"Um, moments change and pass, I guess, and we forget about them—the details, how we felt at that moment. You still have a memory of what happened, but memories aren't exact. But a painting or a poem—those can save the heart of the moment. Capture it, like Amie said. The details. The feelings."

The room was quiet as Hollis debated whether I'd given him a good answer or a pile of nonsense. "Also well put, Ms. Parker," he finally said.

My stomach unknotted a little.

Apparently having fulfilled his interest in seeking our input, Hollis turned back to the whiteboard and began to fill the space—and the rest of the hour-long period—with an introduction to major periods in Western art. Hollis clearly loved his subject matter, and his voice got high-pitched when he was really excited. Unfortunately, he also tended to spit the little foamy bits of stuff that gathered in the corners of his mouth.

That wasn't the kind of thing you wanted to see right after breakfast, but I had at least one other form of entertainment—Mary Katherine had this really complicated method of twirling her hair. I mean, the girl had a *system*. She picked up a lock of dark hair, spun it around her index finger, tugged on the end, then released it.

Then she repeated the process. Twirl. Tug. Drop. Twirl. Tug. Drop. Again and again and again.

It was hypnotizing—so hypnotizing that I nearly jumped when bells rang fifty minutes later, signaling the end of class. Girls scattered at the sound, so I grabbed my stuff and followed Scout into the hallway, which was like a six-lane interstate of St. Sophia's girls hurrying to and fro.

"You've got to figure out how to merge!" Scout said over the din, then disappeared into the throng. I hugged my books to my chest and jumped in.

4

A little more than three hours later, we left art history, trig, and civics behind and headed again for the cafeteria.

"Grab a bag," Scout said when we arrived at the buffet line, and pointed at a tray of paper lunch bags. "We'll eat outside."

I'd been a vegetarian since the day I'd hand-fed a lamb at a petting zoo, only to be served lamb chops a few hours later, so I grabbed a bag labeled VEGGIE WRAP and a bottle of water and followed her.

Scout took a winding route from the cafeteria to the main building, finally pushing open the double doors and heading down the sidewalk. I followed her, the city street full of scurrying people—women in office wear and tennis shoes, men nibbling sandwiches on their way back to the office, tourists with Starbucks cups and glossy shopping bags.

Scout pulled an apple from her bag, then nodded down the street and toward the right. "We can't go far without an escort, but I'll give you the five-dollar block tour while we eat."

"I'm not giving you five dollars."

"You can owe me," she said. "It'll be worth it. Like I said, I've been here since I was twelve. So if you want to know the real deal, the real scoop, you talk to me."

I didn't doubt she knew the real scoop; she'd clearly

been here long enough to understand the St. Sophia's procedures. But given her midnight disappearance, I wasn't sure she'd pass on "the real scoop" to me.

Of course, the most obvious fact about St. Sophia's didn't need explaining. The nuns who built the convent had done a bang-up job of picking real estate—the convent was right in the middle of downtown Chicago. Scout said they'd moved to the spot just after the Chicago Fire of 1871, so the city grew up around them, creating a strip of green amidst skyscrapers, a gothic oasis surrounded by glass, steel, and concrete.

One of those glass, steel, and concrete structures stood directly next door.

"This boxy thing is Burnham National Bank," Scout said, pointing at the building, which looked like a stack of glass boxes placed unevenly atop one another.

"Very modern," I said, unwrapping my own lunch. I took a bite of my wrap, munching sprouts and hummus. It wasn't bad, actually, as wraps went.

"The architecture is modern," she said, taking a bite of her apple, "but the bank is very old-school Chicago. Old-*money* Chicago."

I definitely wasn't old school or old money (unless my parents really did have way more cash than I thought), so I guessed I wasn't going to be visiting the BNB Building any time soon. Still, "Good to know," I said.

We walked to the next building, which was a complete contrast to the bank. This one was a small, squat, squarish thing, the kind of old-fashioned brick building that looked like it had been built by hand in the 1940s. PORTMAN ELECTRIC CO. was chiseled in stone just above the door. The building was pretty in an antique kind of way, but it looked completely out of place in between high-rises and coffee shops and boutique stores.

"The Portman Electric Company Building," Scout said, her gaze on the facade. "It was built during the New Deal when they were trying to keep people employed. It's kind of an antique by Loop standards, but I like it."

She was quiet for a moment. "There's something kind of . . . honest about it. Something real."

A small bronze marker in front of the building read SRF. I nodded toward the sign. "What's 'SRF'?"

"Sterling Research Foundation," she said. "They do some kind of medical research or something."

With no regard for the employees or security guards of the Sterling Research Foundation, Scout made a bee-line for the narrow alley that separated the SRF from the bank. I stuffed the remainder of my lunch back into my paper bag and when Scout signaled the coast was clear, glanced left and right, then speed-walked into the alley.

"Where are we going?" I asked when I reached her.

"A secret spot," she said, bobbing her head toward the end of the passageway. I glanced up, but saw only dirty brick and a set of Dumpsters.

"We aren't going Dumpster diving, are we?" I glanced down at my fuzzy boots and tidy knee-length skirt. " 'Cause I'm really not dressed for it."

"Did you ever read *Nancy Drew*?" Scout suddenly asked.

I blinked as I tried to catch up with the segue. "Of course?"

"Pretend you're Nancy," she said. "We're investigating, kind of." She started into the alley, stepping over a wad of newspaper and avoiding a puddle of liquid of unidentifiable origin.

I pointed at it. "Are we investigating that?"

"Just keep moving," she said, but with a snicker.

We walked through the narrow space until it dead-ended at the stone wall that bounded St. Sophia's.

I frowned at the wall and the grass and gothic buildings that lay beyond it. "We walked around two buildings just to come back to St. Sophia's?"

"Check your left, Einstein."

I did as ordered, and had to blink back surprise. I'd expected to see more alley or bricks, or Dumpsters. But that's not what was there. Instead, the alley gave way to a square of lush, green lawn filled with pillars—narrow pyramids of gray concrete that punctured the grass like a garden of thorns. They varied in height from three feet to five, like a strange gauntlet of stone.

We walked closer. "What is this?"

"It's a memorial garden," she said. "It used to be part of the convent grounds, but the city discovered the nuns didn't actually own this part of the block. Those guys did," she said, pointing at the building that sat behind the bank. "St. Sophia's agreed to put in the stone wall, and the building agreed to keep this place as-is, provided that the St. Sophia's folks promised not to raise a stink about losing it."

"Huh," I said, skimming my fingers across the top of one nubby pillar.

"It's a great place to get lost," she said, and as if on cue, disappeared between the columns.

It took a minute to find her in the forest of them. And when I reached her in the middle, she wasn't alone.

Scout stood stiffly, lips apart, eyes wide, staring at the two boys who stood across from her. They were both in slacks and sweaters, a button-down shirt and tie beneath, an ensemble I assumed was the guy version of the private school uniform. The one on the right had big brown eyes, honey skin, and wavy dark hair curling over his forehead.

The one on the left had dark blond hair and blue eyes. No—not blue exactly, but a shade somewhere between blue and indigo and turquoise, like the color of a ridiculously bright spring sky. They glowed beneath his short hair, dark slashes of eyebrows, and the long lashes that fanned across those crazy eyes.

His eyebrows lifted with interest, but Scout's voice pulled his gaze to her. I, on the other hand, had a little more trouble, and had to drag my gaze away from this boy in the garden.

"What are you doing here?" she asked them, suspicion in her gaze.

The boy with brown eyes shrugged innocently. "Just seeing a little of Chicago."

"I guess that means I didn't miss a meeting," Scout said, her voice dry. "Don't you have class?"

"There wasn't a meeting," he confirmed. "We're on our lunch break, just like you are. We're out for a casual stroll, enjoying this beautiful fall day." He glanced at me and offered a grin. "I'm guessing you're St. Sophia's latest fashion victim? I'm Michael Garcia."

"Lily Parker," I said with a grin. So *this* was the boy Veronica talked about. Or more important, the boy Scout had avoided talking about. Given the warmth in his eyes as he stole glances at Scout, I made a prediction that Veronica wasn't going to win that battle.

"Hello, Lily Parker," Michael said, then bobbed his head toward blue eyes. "This is Jason Shepherd."

"Live and in person," Jason said with a smile, dimples arcing at each corner of his mouth. My heart beat a little bit faster; those dimples were killers. "It's nice to meet you, Lily."

"Ditto," I said, offering back a smile. But not too much of a smile. No sense in playing my entire hand at once.

Jason hitched a thumb behind him. "We go to Montclare. It's down the road. Kind of."

"So I've heard," I said, then looked at Scout, who'd crossed her arms over her chest, the universal sign of skepticism.

"Out for a casual stroll," she repeated, apparently unwilling to let the point go. "A casual stroll that takes you to the garden next door to St. Sophia's? Somehow, I'm just not buying that's a coincidence."

Michael arched an eyebrow and grinned back at her. "That's because you're much too suspicious."

Scout snorted. "I have good reason to be suspicious, Garcia."

Michael's chocolate gaze intensified, and all that intensity was directed at the girl standing next to me.

This was getting pretty entertaining.

"You *imagine* you had a good reason," he told her. "That's not the same thing."

I glanced at Jason, who seemed to be enjoying the mock debate as much as I was. "Should we leave them alone, do you think?"

"It's not a bad idea," he said, brows furrowed in mock concentration. "We could give them a little privacy, let them see where things can go."

"That's a very respectful idea," I said, nodding gravely. "We should give them their space."

Jason winked at me, as Scout—oblivious to our jokes at her expense—pushed forward. "I don't understand why you're arguing with me. You know you have no chance."

Michael clutched at his chest dramatically. "You're killing me, Scout. Really. There's chest pain—a tightness." He faked a groan.

Scout rolled her eyes, but you could see the twitch in her smile. "Call a doctor."

"Come on, Green. Can't a guy just get out and enjoy the weather? It's a beautiful fall day in Chicago. My amigo Jason and I were thinking we should get out and enjoy it before the snow gets here."

"Again, I seriously doubt, Garcia, if you're all that concerned about the weather."

"Okay," Michael said, holding up his hands, "let's pretend you're right. Let's say, hypothetically, that it's no coincidence that our walk brought us next door to St. Sophia's. Let's say we had a personal interest in skipping lunch and showing up on your side of the river."

Scout rolled her eyes and held up a finger. "Oh, bottle it up. I don't have the time."

"You should make time."

"Guys, eleven o'clock," Jason whispered.

Scout snorted at Michael. "I'm amused you think you're important enough to—"

"*Eleven o'clock*," Jason whispered again, this time

fiercely. Scout and Michael suddenly quieted, and both glanced to where Jason had indicated. I resisted the urge to look, which would have made us all completely obvious, but couldn't help it.

I gave it a couple of seconds, then stole a glance over my shoulder. There was a gap in the pillars through which we could see the street behind us, the one that ran parallel to Erie, but behind St. Sophia's. A slim girl in jeans and a snug hoodie, the hood pulled over her head, stood on the sidewalk, her hands tucked into her pockets.

"Who is that?" I whispered.

"No—why is she here?" Jason asked, dimples fading, his gaze on the girl. While her face wasn't visible, her hair was blond—the curly length of it spilling from her hood and across her shoulders. Veronica was the only Chicago blonde I knew, but that couldn't be her. I didn't think she'd be caught dead in jeans and a hoodie, especially not on a uniform day.

Besides, there was something different about this girl. Something unsettling. Something *off*. She was too still, as if frozen while the city moved around her.

"Is she looking for trouble?" Michael asked. His voice was quiet, just above a whisper, and it carried a hint of concern. Like whether she was looking for trouble or not, he expected it.

"In the middle of the day?" Scout whispered. "And here? She's blocks away from the nearest enclave. From *her* enclave."

"What's an enclave?" I quietly asked. Not so quietly that they couldn't hear me, but they ignored me, anyway.

Jason nodded. "Blocks from hers, and much too close to ours."

In the time it took me to glance at Jason and back at the girl again, she was gone. The sidewalk was as empty as if she'd never been there at all.

I looked back and forth from Scout to Michael to

Jason. "Someone want to fill me in?" I was beginning to
guess it was pointless for me to ask questions—as pointless as my trying to goad Scout into telling me where
she'd gone last night—but I couldn't stop asking them.

Scout sighed. "This was supposed to be a tour. Not a
briefing. I'm exhausted."

"We're all tired," Michael said. "It was a long summer."

"Long summer for what?"

"You could say we're part of a community improvement group," Michael said.

It took me a minute to realize that I'd been added
back into the conversation. But the answer wasn't very
satisfying—or informative. I crossed my arms over my
chest. "Community improvement? Like, you clean up
litter?"

"That's actually not a bad analogy," Jason said, his
gaze still on the spot where the girl had been.

"I take it she was a litterbug?" I asked, hitching my
thumb in that direction.

"In a manner of speaking, yes, she was," Scout said,
then put a hand on my arm and tugged. "All right, that's
enough fond reminiscing and conspiracy theories for the
day. We need to get to class. Have fun at school."

"MA is always fun," Jason said. "Good luck at St.
Sophia's."

I nodded as Scout pulled me out of the garden, but I
risked a glance back at Michael and Jason. They stood
side by side, Michael an inch or two taller, their gazes on
us as we headed back to school.

"I have so many questions, I'm not sure where to
start," I said when we were out of their sight and hauling
down the alley, "but let's go for the good, gossipy stuff,
first. You say you aren't dating, but Michael obviously
has a thing for you."

Scout made a snort that sounded a little too dramatic
to be honest. "I didn't just *say* we aren't dating. We are,
in fact, not dating. It's an objective, empirical, testable
fact. I don't date MA guys."

"Uh-huh," I said. While I didn't doubt that she subscribed to that rule, there was more to her statement, more to her and Michael, than she was letting on. But I could pry that out of her later. "And your community service involvement?"

"You heard—we clean up litter."

"Yeah, and I'm totally believing that, too."

That was the last word out of either of us as we slipped through the gap between the buildings, then back onto the sidewalk, and finally back to St. Sophia's. In the nick of time, too, as the bells atop the left tower began to ring just as we hit the front stairs. Thinking we needed to hurry, I nearly ran into Scout when she stopped short in front of the door.

"I know this is unsatisfying," she said, "but you're going to have to trust me on this one, too."

I arched an eyebrow at her. "Will there come a day when you'll trust me?"

Her expression fell. "Honestly, Lil, I hope it doesn't come to that."

Famous last words, those.

There were three more periods to get through—Brit lit, chemistry, and European history—before I completed my first day of classes at St. Sophia's. Maybe it was a good thing I hadn't had much of an appetite for lunch, because listening to teachers drone on about kinetic energy, *Beowulf*, and Thomas Aquinas on a full stomach surely would have put me into a food coma. It was dry enough on an empty stomach.

And wasn't that strange? I loved facts, information, magazine tidbits. But when three, one-hour-long classes were strung together, the learning got a little dullsville.

My attention deficit issue notwithstanding, I made it through my first day of classes, with a lot of unanswered questions about my suitemate and her friends, a good two hours of homework, and a ravenous hunger to show for it.

And speaking of hunger, dinner was pretty much

the same as breakfast—a rush to the front of the line so Scout and I weren't stuck with "dirty rice," which was apparently a combination of rice and everything that didn't get eaten at lunch. I appreciated the school's recycling, but "dirty rice" was a little too green for me. I mean that literally—there were green bits in there I couldn't begin to identify.

On the other hand, it definitely reminded you to be prompt at meal times.

Since we were punctual and it was the first official day of school, the smiling foodies served a mix of Chicago favorites—Chicago-style "red-hot" hot dogs, deep-dish pizza, Italian beef sandwiches, and cheesecake from a place called Eli's.

When we'd gotten food and taken seats, I focused on enjoying my tomato- and cheese-laden slice of Chicago's finest so I wouldn't pester Scout about our meeting with the boys, her "community improvement group," or her midnight outing.

Veronica and her minions spared us a visit, which would have interrupted the ambience of eating pizza off a plastic tray, but they still spent a good chunk of the dinner hour sending us snarky looks from across the room.

"What's with the grudge?" I asked Scout, spearing a chunk of gooey pizza with my fork.

Scout snuck a glance back at the pretty-girl table, then shrugged. "Veronica and I have been here, both of us, since we were twelve. We started on the same day. But she, I don't know, took sides? She decided that to be queen of the brat pack, she needed enemies."

"Very mature," I said.

"It's no skin off my back," Scout said. "Normally, she stays on her side of the cafeteria, and I stay on mine."

"Unless she's in your suite, cavorting with Amie," I pointed out.

"That is true."

"So why this place?" I asked her. "Why did your parents put you here?"

"I'm from Chicago," she said, "born and bred. My parents were trust fund babies—my great-grandfather invented a whirligig for electrical circuits, and my grandparents got the cash when he died. One trickle-down generation later, and my parents ended up with a pretty sweet lifestyle."

"And they opted for boarding school?" I wondered aloud.

She paused contemplatively and pulled a chunk of bread from the roll in her hand. "It's not that they don't love me. I just think they weren't entirely sure what to *do* with me. They grew up in boarding schools, too—when my grandparents got their money, they made some pretty rich friends. They thought boarding school was the best thing you could do for your kids, so they sent my parents, and my parents sent me. Anyway, they have their schedules—Monte Carlo this time of year, Palm Beach that time of year, et cetera, et cetera. Boarding school made it easier for them to travel, to meet their social commitments, such as they were."

I couldn't imagine a life so separate from my family—at least, not before the sabbatical. "Isn't that . . . hard?" I asked her.

Scout blinked at the question. "I've been on my own for a long time. At this point, it just *is*, you know?" I didn't, actually, but I nodded to be supportive.

"I mean, before St. Sophia's, there was a private elementary school and a nanny I talked to more often than my parents. I was kind of a trust fund latchkey kid, I guess. Are you and your parents close?"

I nodded, and I had to fight back an unexpected wash of tears at the sudden sensation of aloneness. Of abandonment. My eyes ached with it, that threshold between crying and not, just before the dam breaks. "Yeah," I said, willing the tears not to fall.

"I'm sorry," Scout said. Her voice was soft, quiet, compassionate.

I shrugged a shoulder. "I've known for a while that

they were leaving. Some of those days I was fine, some days I was wicked pissed." I shrugged. "I'm probably not supposed to be mad about it. I mean, it's not like they went to Germany to get away from me or anything, but it still stings. It still feels like they left me here."

"Well then," Scout said, raising her cup of water, "I suppose you'd better thank your lucky stars that you found me. 'Cause I'm going to be on you like white on rice. I'm a hard friend to shake, Parker."

I grinned through the melancholy and raised my own cup. "To new friendships," I said, and we clinked our cups together.

When dinner was finished, we returned to our rooms to wash up and restock our bags with books and supplies before study hall. I also ditched the tights and switched out my fabulous—but surprisingly uncomfortable— boots for a pair of much more comfy flip-flops. My cell phone vibrated just as I'd slipped my left foot into the second, thick, emerald green flip-flop. I pulled it out of my bag, checked the caller ID, and smiled.

"What's cooking in Germany?" I asked after I opened the phone and pressed it to my ear.

"Nothing at the moment," my father answered, his voice tinny through four thousand miles of transmission wires. "It's late over here. How was school?"

"It was school," I confirmed, a tightness in my chest unclenching at the sound of my dad's voice. I sat down on the edge of the bed and crossed one leg over the other. "Turns out, high school is high school pretty much anywhere you go."

"Except for the uniforms?" he asked.

I smiled. "Except for the uniforms. How was your first day of sabbaticalizing, or whatever?"

"Pretty dull. Mom and I both had meetings with the folks who are funding our work. A lot of ground rules, research protocols, that kind of thing."

I could practically hear the boredom in his voice. My dad wasn't one for administrative details or planning.

He was a big-picture guy, a thinker, a teacher. My mom was the organized one. She probably took notes at the meetings.

"I'm sure it'll get better, Pops. They probably wanna make sure they aren't handing gazillions of research dollars over to some crazy Americans."

"What?" he asked. "We are not so crazy," he said, a thick accent suddenly in his voice, probably an impersonation of some long-dead celebrity. My dad imagined himself to be quite the comedian.

He had quite an imagination.

"Sure, Dad." There was a knock at the door. I looked up as Scout walked in. "Listen, I need to run to study hall. Tell Mom I said hi, and good luck with the actual, you know, research stuff."

"Nighty night, Lils. You take care."

"I will, Dad. Love you."

"Love you, too." I closed the phone and slipped it back into my bag. Scout raised her eyebrows inquisitively.

"My parents are safe and sound in Germany," I told her.

"I'm glad to hear it. Let's go make good on their investment with a couple hours of homework."

The invitation wasn't exactly thrilling, but it's not like we had another choice. Study hall was mandatory, after all.

Study hall took place in the Great Hall, the big room with all the tables where I'd first gotten a glimpse of the plaid army. They were in full attendance tonight, nearly two hundred girls in navy plaid filling fifty-odd four-person tables. We headed through the rows toward a couple of empty seats near the main aisle, which would give us a view of the comings and goings of St. Sophia's finest. They also gave the plaid army a look at us, and look they did, the thwack-thwack of my flip-flops on the limestone floor drawing everyone's attention my way.

That attention included the pair of stern-looking women in thick-soled black shoes and horn-rimmed glasses. Their squarish figures tucked into black shirts and sweaters, they patrolled the perimeter of the room, clipboards in hand.

"Who are they?" I whispered, as we took seats opposite each other.

Scout glanced up as she pulled notebooks and books from her bag. "The dragon ladies. They monitor lights-out, watch us while we study, and generally make sure that nothing fun occurs on their watch."

"Awesome," I said, flipping open my trig book. "I'm a fun hater myself."

"I figured," Scout said without looking up, pen scurrying across a page of her notebook. "You had the look."

One of the roaming dragon ladies walked by our table, her gaze over her glasses and an eyebrow arched at our whispering as she passed. I mouthed, "Sorry," but she scribbled on her clipboard before walking away.

Scout bit back a smile. "Please quit disturbing the entire school, Parker, jeez."

I stuck out my tongue at her, but started my homework.

We worked for an hour before she stretched in her chair, then dropped her chin onto her hand. "I'm bored."

I rubbed my eyes, which were blurring over the tiny print in our European history book. "Do you want me to juggle?"

"You can juggle?"

"Well, not *yet*. But there're books everywhere in here," I pointed out. "There's gotta be a how-to guide somewhere on those shelves."

The girl who sat beside me at the table cleared her throat, her gaze still on the books in front of her. "Really trying to do some work here, ladies. Go play *Gilmore Girls* somewhere else."

The girl was pretty in a supermodel kind of way—in a French way, if that made sense. Long dark hair, big eyes, wide mouth—and she played irritated pretty well, one perfect eyebrow arched in irritation over brown eyes.

"Collette, Collette," Scout said, pointing her own pencil at the girl, then at me. "Don't be bossy. Our new friend Parker, here, will think you're one of the brat pack."

Collette snorted, then slid a glance my way. "As if, Green. I assume you're Parker?"

"Last time I checked," I agreed.

"Then don't make me give you more credit than you deserve, Parker. Some of us take our academic achievements very seriously. If I'm not valedictorian next year, I might not get into Yale. And if I don't get into Yale, I'm going to have a breakdown of monumental proportions. So you and your friend go play clever somewhere else, alrighty? Alrighty," she said with a bob of her head, then turned back to her books.

"She's really smart," Scout said apologetically. "Unfortunately, that hasn't done much for her personality."

Collette flipped a page of her book. "I'm still here."

"*Gilmore Girls*," Scout repeated, then made a sarcastic sound. Apparently done with studying, she glanced carefully around, then pulled a comic book from her bag. She paused to ensure the coast was clear, then sandwiched the comic between the pages of her trig book.

I arched an eyebrow at the move, but she shrugged happily, and went back to working trig problems, occasionally sneaking in a glazed-eyed perusal of a page or two of the comic.

"Weirdo," I muttered, but said it with a grin.

After we'd done our couple of mandatory hours in study hall—not all studying, of course, but at least we were in there—we went back to the suite to make use of our last free hour before the sun officially set on my first day as a St. Sophia's girl. The suite was empty of brat pack members, and Lesley's door was shut, a line of light beneath it. I nudged Scout as we walked toward her room. She followed the direction of my nod, then nodded back.

"Cello's gone," she noted, pointing at the corner of

the common room, which was empty of the instrument parked there when I arrived yesterday.

Music suddenly echoed through the suite, the thick, thrumming notes of a Bach cello concerto pouring from Lesley's room. She played beautifully, and as she moved her bow across the strings, Scout and I stood quietly, reverently, in the common room, our gaze on the closed door before us.

After a couple of minutes, the music stopped, replaced by scuffling on the other side of the door. Without preface, the door opened. A blonde blinked at us from the threshold. She was dressed simply in a fitted T-shirt, cotton A-line skirt, and Mary Janes. Her hair was short and pale blond, a fringe of bangs across her forehead.

"Hi, Lesley," Scout said, hitching a thumb at me. "This is Lily. She's the new girl."

Lesley blinked big blue eyes at me. "Hi," she said, then turned on one heel, walked back into the room, and shut the door behind her.

"And that was Lesley," Scout said, unlocking her own door and flipping on her bedroom light.

I followed, then shut the door behind us again. "Lesley's not much of a talker."

Scout nodded and sat cross-legged on the bed. "That was actually pretty chatty for Barnaby. She's always been quiet. Has a kind of savant vibe? Wicked good on the cello."

"I got goose bumps," I agreed. "That song is really haunting."

Scout nodded again, and had just begun to pull a pillow into her lap when her cell phone rang. She reached up, grabbed it from its home on the shelf, and popped it open.

"When?" she asked after a moment of silence, turning away from me, the phone pressed to her ear. Apparently unhappy with the response she got, she muttered a curse, then sighed haggardly. "We should have known they had something planned when we saw her."

I assumed "her" meant the blonde we'd seen outside at lunch.

More silence ensued as Scout listened to the caller. In the quiet of the room, I could hear a voice, but I couldn't understand the words. The tone was low, so I guessed the caller was a boy. Michael Garcia, maybe?

"Okay," she said. "I will." She closed the phone with a snap and paused before glancing back at me.

"Time to run?"

Scout nodded. And this time, there was a tightness around her eyes. It didn't thrill me that the tightness looked like fear.

My heart clenched sympathetically. "Do you need backup? Someone else to help clean up the litter?"

Scout smiled, a little of the twinkle back in her eyes. "I'd love it, actually. But community improvement isn't ready for you, Parker." She grabbed a jacket and her skull-and-crossbones bag, and we both left her room. Scout headed for a secret rendezvous; I wasn't entirely sure where I was going.

"Don't wait up," she said with a wink, then opened the door and headed out into the hallway.

Don't count on it, I thought, having made the decision. This time, I wasn't going to let her get away with mumbled excuses and a secret nighttime trip—at least not solo.

This time, I was going, too.

She'd closed the door behind her. I cracked it open and watched her slip down the hallway.

"Time to play Nancy Drew," I murmured, then slipped off my noisy flip-flops, picked them up, and followed her.

5

She was disappearing around the corner as I closed the door to the common room. The hallway was empty and silent but for her footsteps, the limestone floor and walls glowing beneath the golden light of the sconces.

Scout headed toward the stairs, which she took at a trot. I hung back until I was sure she wouldn't see me as she rounded the second flight of stairs, then followed her down. When she reached the first floor, she headed through the Great Hall, which, even after the required study period, still held a handful of apparently ambitious teenagers. Unfortunately, the aisle between the tables was straight and empty, so if Scout turned around, my cover was blown.

I took a breath and started walking. I made it halfway without incident when, suddenly, Scout paused. I dumped into the closest chair and bent down, faking an adjustment to my flip-flop. When she turned around again and resumed her progression through the room, I stood up, then hustled to squeak through the double doors before they closed behind her.

I just made it through, then flattened myself against the wall of the hallway that led to the domed center of the main building. I peeked around the corner; Scout was hurrying across the tiled labyrinth. I gnawed my lip as I considered my options. This part of playing the new Nancy Drew was tricky—the room was gigantic and empty, at least in the middle, so there weren't many places to hide.

Without cover, I decided I'd have to wait her out. I watched her cross the labyrinth and move into the hallway opposite mine, then pause before a door. She looked around, probably to see whether she was alone (we're all wrong sometimes), then slipped the ribboned key from her neck and slid the key into the lock.

The click of tumblers echoed across the room. She winced at the sound, but placed a hand on the door, took a final look around, and disappeared. When she was gone, I jogged across the labyrinth to the other side, then pressed my ear to the door she'd closed behind her. After the sound of her footsteps receded, I twisted the doorknob, found that it was still unlocked and—heart beating like a bass drum in my chest—edged it open.

It was another hallway.

I blew out the breath I'd been holding.

A hallway wasn't much to get stressed out about. Frankly, the chasing was getting a little repetitive. Hallway. Room. Hallway. Room. I reminded myself that there was a greater purpose here—spying on the girl who'd adopted me as a best friend.

Okay, put that way, it didn't sound so noble.

Morally questionable or not, I still had a job to do. I walked inside and closed the door behind me. I didn't see Scout, but I watched her elongated shadow shrink around the corner as she moved. I followed her through the hallway, and then down another set of stairs into what I guessed was the basement, although it didn't look much different from the first floor, all limestone and golden light and iron sconces. The ceiling was different, though. Instead of the vaults and domes on the first floor, the ceiling here was lower, flatter, and covered in patterned plaster. It looked like a lot of work for a basement.

The stairs led to another hall. I followed the sound of footsteps, but only made it five or six feet before I heard another sound—the clank and grate of metal on metal. I froze and swallowed down the lump of fear that suddenly tightened my throat. I wanted to call her name, to scream it out, but I couldn't seem to draw breath to make a sound. I forced myself to take another step forward, then another, nearly jumping out of my skin when that bone-chilling gnash of metal echoed through the hallway again.

Oh, screw this, I thought, and forced my lungs to work. "Scout?" I called out. "Are you okay?"

When I got no response, I rounded the corner. The hallway dead-ended in a giant metal door . . . and she was nowhere to be seen.

"Frick," I muttered. I glanced around, saw nothing else that would help, and moved closer so I could give the door a good look-see.

It was ginormous. At least eight feet high, with an arch in the top, it was outlined in brass rivets and joints. In the middle was a giant flywheel, and beneath the flywheel was a security bar that must have been four or five inches of solid steel. It was in its unlocked position. That explained the metal sounds I'd heard earlier.

I wasn't sure I wanted to know what that door was keeping out of St. Sophia's, but Scout was in there. Sure, we hadn't known each other long, and I wasn't up on all the comings and goings of her community improvement group, but this seemed like trouble . . . and help was the least I could offer my new suitemate.

After all, what were they going to do—kick me out?

"Sagamore, here I come," I whispered, and put my hands on the flywheel. I tugged, but the door wouldn't open. I turned the flywheel, clockwise first, then counterclockwise, but the movement had no effect—at least, not on this side of the door.

Frowning, I scanned the door from top to bottom, looking for another way in—a keyhole, a numeric pad, anything that would have gotten it open and gotten me inside.

But there was nothing. So much for my rescue mission.

I considered my options.

One: I could head back upstairs, tuck into bed, and forget about the fact that my new best friend was somewhere behind a giant locked door in an old convent in downtown Chicago.

Two: I could wait for her to come back, then offer whatever help I could.

I nibbled the edge of my lip for a moment and glanced back at the hallway from which I'd come, my passage back to safety. But I was here, *now*, and she was in there, getting into God only knew what kind of trouble.

So I sat down on the floor, pulled up my knees, and prepared to wait.

I don't know when I fell asleep, but I jolted awake at the sound of footsteps on the other side of the door. I jumped up from my spot, the flip-flops I'd pulled off earlier still in my hand, my only weapon. As I faced down the door with only a few inches of green foam as protection, it occurred to me that there might be a stranger—and not Scout—on the other side of the door.

My heart raced hammerlike in my chest, my fingers clenched into the foam of my flip-flops. Suddenly the flywheel began to turn, the spokes rotating clockwise with a metallic scrape as someone sought entrance to the convent basement. Seconds later, oh so slowly, the door began to open, hundreds of pounds of metal rotating toward me.

"Don't come any closer!" I called out. "I have a weapon."

Scout's voice echoed from the other side of the door. "Don't use it! And get out of the way!"

It wasn't hard to obey, since I'd been bluffing. I stepped aside, and as soon as the crack in the door was big enough to squeeze through, she slipped through it, chest heaving as she sucked in air.

She muttered a curse and pressed her hands to the

door. "I'm going to rail on you in a minute for following me, but in the meantime, *help me close this thing*!"

Although my head was spinning with ideas about what, exactly, she'd left on the other side of the door, I stepped beside her. With both pairs of hands on the door, arms and legs outstretched, we pushed it closed. The door was as heavy as it was high, and I wondered how she'd gotten it open in the first place.

When the door was shut, Scout spun the flywheel, then reached down to slide the steel bar back into its home. We both jumped back when a crash echoed from the other side, the door shaking on its giant brass hinges in response.

Eyes wide, I stared over at her. "What the hell was *that*?"

"Litter," Scout said, staring at the closed door, as if making sure that whatever had been chasing her wasn't going to breach it.

When the door was still and the hallway was silent, Scout turned and looked at me, her bob of blond hair in shambles around her face, jacket hanging from one shoulder . . . and fury in her expression.

"What in the hell do you think you're doing down here?" She pushed at the hair from her face, then pulled up the loose shoulder of her jacket.

"Exercising?"

Scout put her hands on her hips, obviously dubious.

"I was afraid you were in trouble."

"You were nosy," she countered. "I asked you to trust me on this."

"Trusting you about a secret liaison is one thing. Trusting you about your safety is something else." I bobbed my head toward the door. "Call it community improvement if you want, but it seems pretty apparent that you're involved in something nasty. I'm not going to just stand by and watch you get hurt."

"You're not my mother."

"Nope," I agreed. "But I'm your new BFF."

Her expression softened.

"I don't need all the details," I said, holding up my hands, "but I am going to need to know what the hell was on the other side of that door."

As if on cue, a crash sounded again, and the door jumped on its hinges.

"We get it already!" she yelled. "Crawl back into your hole." She grabbed my arm and began to pull me down the hall and away from the ominous door. "Let's go."

I tugged back, and when she dropped my arm, slipped the flip-flops back onto my feet. She was trucking down the hall, and I had to skip to keep up with her. "Is it an axe murderer?"

"Yeah," she said dryly. "It's an axe murderer."

Most of the walk back was quiet. Scout and I didn't chat much, and both the main building and the Great Hall were dark and empty of students. The moonlight, tinted red and blue, that streamed through the stained glass windows was the only light along the way.

As we moved through the corridors, Scout managed not to look back to see whether the basement door had been breached or whether some nasty thing was on our trail. I, on the other hand, kept stealing glances over my shoulder, afraid to look, but more afraid that something would sneak up behind us if I didn't. That the corridors were peacefully quiet didn't stop my imagination, which made shapes in the shadows beneath the desks of the Great Hall when we passed through it.

Exactly what had been behind that door? I decided I couldn't hold in the question any longer. "Angry drug dealer?" I asked her. "Mental institution escapee? Robot overlord?"

"I'm not aware if robots have taken us over yet." Her tone was dry.

"Flesh-eating zombie monster?"

"Zombies are a myth."

"So you say," I muttered. "Just answer me this: Are you in cahoots with those Montclare guys?"

"What is a 'cahoot,' exactly?"

"Scout."

"I was exercising. Great workout. I got my heart rate up, and I got into the zone." Her elbow bent, she pumped one arm as if lifting a dumbbell.

When we opened the door to the building that held our dorm rooms, I pulled her to a stop. She didn't look happy about that.

"You were being chased," I told her. "Something behind that door was after you, and whatever it was hit the door after we closed it."

"Just be glad we got the door closed."

"Scout," I said. "*Seriously*. What's going on?"

"Look, Lily, there are things going on at this school—just because things seem normal doesn't mean they are. Things are rarely what they seem."

Things hardly seemed normal, from late-night disappearances, to the coincidental meeting of the boys next door, to this. And all of it within my first twenty-four hours in Chicago. "Exactly what does that mean, 'rarely what they seem'?"

She arched an eyebrow at me. "You said you had a weapon." She scanned me up and down. "Exactly what weapon was that? Flip-flops?"

I held up a foot and dangled my thick, emerald green flip-flop in front of her. "Hey, I could have beaned a pursuer on the head with this thing. It weighs like ten pounds, and I guarantee you he would have thought twice before invading St. Sophia's."

"Yeah, I'm sure that would hold them off." At my arch expression, she held up her hands. "Fine. Fine. Let's say, for the sake of argument, that I'm in a club for gifted kids. Of a sort."

"A club for gifted kids. Like, what kind of gifted?" Gifted at fibbing came immediately to mind.

"Generally gifted?"

The room was silent as I waited in vain for her to elaborate on that answer.

"That's all you're going to tell me?"

"That's as much as I *can* tell you," she said, "and I've already said too much. I wish I could fill you in, but I really, really can't. Not because I don't trust you," she said, holding up a defensive hand. "It's just not something I'm allowed to do."

"You aren't allowed to tell me, or anyone else, that something big and loud and powerful is hanging out beneath a big-ass metal door in the basement? And that you go down there willingly?"

She nodded matter-of-factly. "That's pretty much it."

I blew out a breath and shook my head. "You're insane. This whole place is insane."

"St. Sophia's has a lot to offer."

"Other than nighttime escapades and maniacs behind giant cellar doors?"

"Oh, those aren't even the highlights, Lil." Scout turned and resumed the trek back home.

When we reached the suite, Scout walked toward her room, but then paused to glance back at me.

"Whatever you're involved in," I told her, "I'm not afraid." (My fingers were totally crossed on that one.) "And if you need me, I'm here."

I could tell she was tired, but there was a happy glint in her eyes. "You rock pretty hard, Parker."

I grinned at her. "I know. It's one of my better qualities."

6

Whatever the St. Sophia's "highlights" were, they weren't revealed during the next couple days of school. I still wasn't entirely sure what Scout was doing at night, but I didn't see any strange bruises or scratches or broken bones. Since she wasn't limping, I kept my mouth shut about her disappearances . . . and whatever was going on in the corridors beneath the school.

On the other hand, the dark circles beneath her eyes showed that she was still going somewhere at night, that *something* was going on, regardless of how oblivious the rest of the school was. I didn't pester her, mostly because I'd weighed the benefit of pestering her (nil, given how stubborn she was) against the potential cost (hurting our newfound friendship). We were still getting to know each other, and I didn't want that kind of tension between us . . . even though her secret was still between us.

However, there was still one skill I knew I could bring to the Scout Green mystery game—I was patient, and I could wait her out. I could tell it bothered her to keep it bottled up, so I guessed it wouldn't take much longer before she spilled.

That mystery notwithstanding, things were moving along pretty much par for the course, or at least what I learned was par for the course by St. Sophia's standards. That meant studying, studying, and more studying. I managed to squeeze in some nerdly fun with Scout—a little sketching, checking out her comic book stash, walking the block over the lunch hour—and I'd had a few rushed conversations with my parents. (Everything seemed to be going fine in Deutschland.) But mostly, there was studying . . . at least until my first Thursday at St. Sophia's.

I'd been in European history when it happened. Without preface, in the middle of class, the door opened. Mary Katherine walked in, her hair in a long, thick braid that lay across one shoulder, a gray scarf of thick, felted wool knots wrapped around her neck.

She handed Peters, our surly history teacher, a note. Peters gave her a sour look—the fate of European peasants being the most important thing on his mind—but he took it anyway, read it over, and passed it back to M.K.

"Lily Parker," he said.

I sat up straight.

Peters tried to arch one eyebrow. But he couldn't quite manage it, so it just looked like an comfortable squint. "You're wanted in the headmistress's office."

I frowned, but bobbed my head in acknowledgment, grabbed the stuff on my desk with one hand and the strap of my bag from the other, and stood up. M.K., arms crossed, rolled her eyes as she waited for me. She was halfway to the door by the time I got to the front of the room.

"Nice shoes," she said when we'd closed the classroom door and had begun walking down the hall. She walked in front of me, the note between her fingers.

I glanced down at today's ensemble—button-up shirt, St. Sophia's hoodie, navy tights, and yellow boots in quilted patent leather—as I situated my messenger bag diagonally across my chest. The boots were loud and not everyone's style, but they were also vintage and made by a very chichi designer, so I wasn't sure if she was being sarcastic. I assumed, since they were pretty fabulous, that she was being sincere.

"Thanks," I said. "They're vintage." Unfortunately, the owner of the thrift shop in old, downtown Sagamore knew they'd been vintage, too. Three months of hard-saved allowance disappeared in a five-minute trans-action.

"I know," she said. "They're Puccinis."

Her voice was mildly condescending, as if I couldn't possibly have been savvy enough to know that they were Puccinis when I bought them. Three months of allowance knew better.

That gem was the only thing Mary Katherine said as we walked through the Great Hall, crossed the labyrinth, and turned into the administrative wing. It was the same walk I'd taken when I'd met Foley at the door a few days ago, except in reverse . . . and presumably under different circumstances this time around.

When we reached the office, M.K. put her hand on the doorknob, but turned to face me before opening it. "You'll need a hall pass before you go back," she sniped. She opened the door and after I walked inside, closed it behind me. Friendly girl.

Foley's office looked the same as it had a few days ago, except that she wasn't in the room this time. Her heavy oak desk was empty of stuff—no pencil cups, no flowers, no lamp—but for the royal blue folder that lay in the exact middle, its edges parallel with the edges of the desk, as if placed just so.

I walked closer. Holding my bag back with a hand, I leaned forward to take a closer look. LILY PARKER was typed in neat letters across the folder's tab.

A folder bearing my name in an otherwise empty room. It practically begged to be opened.

I glanced behind me. When I was sure I was alone, I reached out a hand to open it, but snatched it back when a grinding scrape echoed through the room.

I stood straight again as the bookshelf on one side of Foley's office began to pivot forward. Foley, tall and trim, every hair in place, navy suit perfectly tailored, stepped through the opening, then pushed the bookshelf back into place.

"Can I ask what's behind the hidden door?"

"You could ask," she said, walking around the massive desk, "but that does not mean I'd provide an answer to you, Ms. Parker." Elegantly, she lowered herself into the chair, glanced at the folder for a moment, then lifted her gaze, regarding me with an arched brow.

I responded with what I hoped was a bland and completely innocent smile. Sure, I'd *wanted* to look, but it's not like I'd actually had time to *do* anything.

Apparently satisfied, she lowered her gaze again and, with a single finger, flipped open the folder. "Have a seat," she said without looking up.

I dropped into the chair in front of her desk and piled my stuff—books and bag—on my lap.

"You've been here three days," Foley said, linking her fingers together on top of her desk. "I have asked you here to inquire as to how you've settled in." She looked at me expectantly. I guessed that was my cue.

"Things are fine."

"Mmm-hmm. And your relationships with your classmates? Are you integrating well into the St. Sophia's community? Into Ms. Green's suite?

Interesting, I thought, that it was "Ms. Green's suite," and not Amie's or Lesley's suite. But my answer was the same regardless. "Yes. Scout and I get along pretty well."

"And Ms. Cherry? Ms. Barnaby?"

"Sure," I said, thinking a vague answer would at least save my having to answer questions about the brat pack's attitude toward newcomers.

Foley nodded. "I encourage you to expand your circle of classmates, to meet as many of the girls in your class as you can, and to make as many connections as possible. For better or worse, your success will be measured not only by what you can learn, by what you can be tested on, but on whom you know."

"Sure," I dutifully said again.

"And your classes? How are your academics progressing?"

I was only in the fourth day of my St. Sophia's education—three and a half pop-quiz- and final-exam-free days behind me—so there wasn't much to gauge "progressing" against. So I stuck to my plan of giving teenagerly vague answers; being a teenager, I figured I was entitled. "They're fine."

She made a sound of half interest, then glanced down at the folder again. "Once you've settled into your academic schedule, you'll have an opportunity to experience our extracurricular activities and, given your interest in the arts, our art studio." Foley flipped the folder closed, then crossed her hands upon it, sealing its secrets inside. "Lily, I'm going to speak frankly."

I lifted my eyebrows invitationally.

"Given the nature of your arrival here and of your previous tenure in public school, I was not entirely confident you would find the fit at St. Sophia's to be . . . comfortable."

I arched an eyebrow. "Comfortable," I repeated, in a tone as flat and dry as I could make it.

"Yes," Foley unapologetically repeated. "Comfortable. You arrived here not by choice, but because of the wishes of your parents, and despite your having no other connections to Chicago. I can only imagine how difficult it is for you to be here in light of your current separation from your parents. But I am acquainted with Mark and Susan, and we truly believe in their research."

That stopped me cold. "You know my parents?"

There was a hitch in her expression, a hitch that was quickly covered by the look of arrogant blandness she usually wore. "You were unaware that I was acquainted with your parents?"

All I could do was nod. The only thing my parents told me about St. Sophia's was that it was an excellent school with great academics, blah blah blah. The fact that my parents knew Foley—yeah. They'd kind of forgotten to mention that.

"I must admit," Foley said, "I'm surprised."

That made two of us, I thought.

"St. Sophia's is an excellent institution, without doubt. But you are far from home and your connections in Sagamore. I'd assumed, frankly, that your parents chose St. Sophia's on the basis of our relationship."

She wasn't just acquainted with my parents—they had a *relationship*? "How do you know my parents?"

"Well . . . ," she said, drawing out her one-word response while she traced her fingers along the edges of the folder. The move seemed odd for her—too coy. I figured she was stalling for time. After a long, quiet moment, she glanced up at me. "We had a professional connection," she finally said. "Similar research interests."

I frowned. "Research interests? In philosophy?"

"Philosophy," she flatly repeated.

I nodded, but something in her tone made my stomach drop. "Philosophy," I said again, as if repeating it would answer the question in her voice. "Are you sure you knew my parents?"

"I am well acquainted with your parents, Ms. Parker. We're professional colleagues of a sort." There was caution in her tone, as if she were treading around something, something she wasn't sure she wanted to tell me.

I dropped my gaze to the gleaming yellow of my boots. I needed a minute to process all this—the fact that Foley had known my parents, that they'd known her, and that maybe—just maybe—their decision to send me here hadn't just been an academic choice.

"My parents," I said, "are teachers. Professors, both of them. They teach philosophy at Hartnett College. It's in Sagamore."

Foley frowned. "And they never mentioned their genetic work?"

"Genetic work?" I asked, the confusion obvious in my voice. "What genetic work?"

"Their lab work. Their genetic studies. The longevity studies."

I was done, I decided—done with this meeting, done listening to this woman's lies about my parents. Or worse, I was done listening to things I hadn't known about the people I'd been closest too.

Things they hadn't told me?

I rose, lifting my books and shouldering my bag. "I need to get back to class."

Foley arched an eyebrow, but allowed me to rise and gather my things, then head for the door. "Ms. Parker," she said, and I glanced back. She pulled a small pad of paper from a desk drawer, scribbled something on the top page, and tore off the sheet.

"You'll need a hall pass to return to class," she said, handing the paper out to me.

I nodded, walked back, and took the paper from her fingers. But I didn't look at her again until I was back at the door, note in hand.

"I know my parents," I told her, as much for her benefit as mine. "I know them."

All my doubts notwithstanding, I let that stand as the last word, opened the door, and left.

I didn't remember much of the walk back through one stone corridor after another, through the Great Hall and the passageway to the classroom building. Even the architecture was a blur, my mind occupied with the meeting with Foley, the questions she'd raised.

Had she been confused? Had she read some other file, instead of mine? Had the board of trustees dramatized my background in order to accept me at St. Sophia's?

Or had my parents been lying to me? Had they kept the true nature of their jobs, their employment, from me? And if so, why hide something like that? Why tell your daughter that you taught philosophy if you had a completely different kind of research agenda?

What had Foley said? Something about longevity and

genetics? That wasn't even in the same ballpark as philosophy. That was science, anatomy, lab work.

I'd been to Hartnett with my parents, had walked through the corridors of the religion and philosophy department, had waved at their colleagues. I'd colored on the floor of my mother's office on days when my babysitter was sick, and played hide-and-seek in the hallways at night while my parents worked late.

Of course there was one easy way to solve this mystery. When I was clear of the administrative wing, I stepped into an alcove in the main building, a semicircle of stone with a short bench in the middle, and pulled my cell phone from my pocket. It would be late in Germany, but this was an issue that needed resolving.

"HOW IS RESEARCH?" I texted. I sent the message and waited; the reply took only seconds.

"THE ARCHIVES R RAD!" was my father's time-warped answer. I hadn't even had time to begin a response when a second message popped onto my screen, this one from my mother. "1ST PAGE IN GERMN JRNL OF PHILO!"

In dorky professor-speak, that meant my parents had secured the first article (a big deal) in some new German philosophy journal.

It *also* meant there would be a bound journal with my parents' names on it, the kind I'd seen in our house countless times before. You couldn't fake that kind of thing. Foley had to be wrong.

"Take that," I murmured with a slightly evil grin, then checked the time on my phone. European history class would be over in five minutes. I didn't think Peters would much care whether I came back for the final five minutes of class, so I walked back through the classroom building to the locker hall to switch out books for study hall later.

A note—a square of careful folds—was stuck to my locker door.

I dropped my books to the floor, pulled the note away, and opened it.

It read, in artsy letters:

I saw you and Scout, and I wasn't the only one.
Watch your back.

A knot of fear rose in my throat. I turned around and pressed my back against my locker, trying to slow my heart. Someone had seen me and Scout—someone, maybe, who'd followed us from the library through the main building to the door behind which the monster lay sleeping.

The bells rang, signaling the end of class.

I crumpled the note in my hand.

One crisis at a time, I thought. One crisis at a time.

7

I waited until Scout had returned to the suite after classes, during our chunk of free time before dinner, to tell her about the note. We headed to my room to avoid the brat pack, who'd already taken over the common room. Why they'd opted to hang out in our suite mystified me, given their animosity toward Scout, but as Scout had said, they seemed to have a thing for drama. I guessed they were looking for opportunities.

When my bedroom door was shut and the lock was flipped, I pulled the note from the pocket of my hoodie and passed it over.

Scout paled, then held it up. "Where did this come from?"

"My locker. I found it after I left Foley's office. And that's actually part two of the story."

Scout sat down on the floor, then rolled over onto her stomach, booted feet crossed in the air. I sat down on my bed, crossing my legs beneath me, and filled her in on my time in Foley's office and the things she'd said about my parents. The genetic stuff aside, Scout was surprised that Foley seemed interested in me at all. Foley wasn't known for being interested in her students; she was more focused on numbers—Ivy League acceptance rates and SAT scores. Individual students, to Foley, were just bits of data within the larger—and much more important—statistics.

"Maybe she feels sorry for me?" I asked. "Being abandoned by my parents for a European vacation?"

Okay, I can admit that sounded pretty pitiful, but Scout didn't buy it, anyway. "No way," she said. "This is a boarding school. No one's parents are around. Now, she said what? That your parents are doing research in genetics?"

I nodded. "That's exactly what she said. But my parents teach philosophy. I mean—they do research, sure. They write articles—that's why they're traveling right now. But not on genetics. Not on biology. They were into Heidegger and existentialism and stuff."

"Huh," Scout said with a frown, chin propped on her hand. "That's really strange. And you went to their offices, and stuff? I mean, they weren't just dumbing down their job to help you understand what they did?"

I shook my head. "I've been there. Seen their diplomas. Seen their books. I've watched them grade papers." Scout pursed her lips, eyebrows drawn down as she concentrated. "That's really weird. On the other hand, maybe Foley was just confused. It's not that hard to imagine that she'd mistake one student for another."

"That's what I thought at first," I said, "but she seemed pretty sure."

"Hmm." Scout rolled over onto her back and laced her hands behind her head. "While we're contemplating your parents' possibly secret identities, what are we going to do about this note thing?"

"What do you mean 'we'? The note thing is your deal, not mine. Someone must have seen you."

"It was on your locker, Parker. They probably saw you following me. Probably heard you clomping through the hall in those flip-flops like a Clydesdale."

"First of all, I took off the flip-flops so they wouldn't make noise. And second, I do not *clomp*." I threw my pillow at her to emphasize the point. "I am a very slender, spritely young woman."

"Doesn't mean you can't clomp."

"I am not above hitting a girl."

Scout barked out a laugh. "I'd like to see you try it."

"Dare me, Pinhead. Dare me."

That time, I got a glare. She pointed at her nose ring. "Do you have any idea how much it hurt to get this thing? How much I endured to achieve this look?"

"That's a 'look'?"

"I am the epitome of high fashion."

"Yeah, *Vogue* will surely be calling you tomorrow for the fall spread."

Scout snorted out a laugh. "What did someone tell me once? That they're not above hitting a girl? Well, neither am I, newbie."

"Whatever," I said. "Let's get back on track—the note."

"Right, the note." Scout crossed her legs, one booted foot swinging as she thought. "Well, clompy or not, someone saw us. Could have been one of our lovely suitemates; could have been someone else at St. Sophia's. The path to the basement door isn't exactly inconspicuous. I have to go through the Great Hall to get to the main building. That part's not so unusual—going into the main building, I mean. Girls sometimes study in the chapel, and there's a service in there on Wednesday nights." She sat up halfway and looked over at me. "Did you notice anyone noticing us?"

I shook my head. "I thought I was caught when you stopped in the Great Hall. I sat down at a table for a second, but I was up and out of there pretty fast afterward."

"Hmm," Scout said. "You're sure you didn't tell anyone?"

"Did I tell anyone I was running around St. Sophia's in the middle of the night, following my suitemate to figure out why she's sneaking around? No, I didn't tell anyone that, and I'm pretty sure that's the kind of thing I'd remember."

She grinned up at me. "Can you imagine what would

have happened if one of the"—she bobbed her head toward the closed door—"you-know-what pack found us down there?" She shook her head. "They would have gone completely postal."

"I nearly went completely postal," I pointed out.

"That is true. Although you did have your flip-flop weaponry."

"Hey, would you want to meet me in a dark alley with a flip-flop?"

"Depends on how long you'd been awake. You're an ogre in the morning."

We broke into laughter that was stifled by a sudden knock on my bedroom door. Scout and I exchanged a glance. I unknotted my legs and walked to the door, then flipped the lock and opened it.

Lesley stood there, this time in uniform—plaid skirt, oxford shirt, tie—wide blue eyes blinking back at me. "I'd like to come in."

"Okay," I said, and moved aside, then shut the door again when she was in the room.

"Hi, Barnaby," Scout said from the floor. "What's kicking?"

"Those girls are incredibly irritating. I can hardly hear myself think."

As if on cue, a peal of laughter echoed from the common room. We rolled our eyes simultaneously.

"I get that," Scout said. "What brings you to our door?"

"I need to be more social. You know, talk to people." Still standing near the door, she looked at us expectantly. The room was silent for nearly a minute.

"Okaaaay," Scout finally said. "Good start on that, coming in here. How was your summer?"

Barnaby shrugged, then crossed her ankles and lowered herself to the floor. "Went to cello camp."

Scout and I exchanged a glance that showed exactly how dull we thought that sounded. Nevertheless, Scout asked, "And how was cello camp?"

"Not nearly as exciting as you'd think."

"Huh," Scout said. "Bummer."

After blinking wide eyes at the floor, Lesley lifted her gaze to Scout, then to me. "Last year was dull, too. I want this year to be more interesting. You seem interesting."

Scout beamed, her eyes twinkling devilishly. "I knew I liked you, Barnaby."

"Especially when you disappear at night."

Scout's expression flattened. With a jolt, she sat up, legs crossed in front of her. "What do you mean, when we disappear at night?"

"You know," Lesley said, pointing at Scout, "when you head into the basement"—she pointed at me—"and you follow her."

"Uh-huh," Scout said, picking at a thread in her skirt, feigned nonchalance in her expression. "Did you by any chance leave a note for Lily? A warning?"

"Oh, on her locker? Yeah, that was me."

Scout and I exchanged a glance, then looked at Lesley. "And why did you leave it?" she asked.

Lesley looked back and forth between us. "Because I want in."

"In?"

Lesley nodded. "I want in. Whatever you're doing, I want in. I want to help. I have skills"

"I'm not admitting that we're doing anything," Scout carefully said, "but if we are doing something, do you know what it is?"

"Well, no."

"Then how do you know you have skills that would help us?" Scout asked.

Lesley grinned, and the look was a little diabolical. "Well, did you see me following you? Did you know I was there?"

"No," Scout said for both of us, appreciation in her eyes. "No, we did not." She looked at me. "She makes a good argument about her skills."

"Yes, she does," I agreed. "But why leave an anonymous note on my locker? If you wanted in, why not just talk to us here? We do live together, after all."

Lesley shrugged nonchalantly. "Like I said, things are dull around here. I thought I'd spice things up."

"Spice things up," Scout repeated, her voice dry as toast. "Yeah, we could probably help you out with that. We'll keep you posted."

"Sweet," Lesley said, and that was the end of that.

Scout didn't, of course, fill Lesley in about exactly how interesting she was. I, of course, didn't contribute much to that interestingness. I hadn't been more than an amusing sidekick, if that. It was probably more accurate to call me a nosy sidekick.

I was relieved we'd solved the note mystery, but I was quiet at dinner, quiet in study hall, and quiet as Scout and I sat in the common room afterward—which was thankfully empty of brat packers. I couldn't get Foley's comments out of my mind. Sure, I'd seen the articles and the offices and met the colleagues, but I'd also seen *Alias*. People had created much more elaborate fronts than collegiate careers. Had my parents concocted some kind of elaborate fairy tale about their jobs to keep their real lives hidden? If so, I highly doubted they'd tell me if I asked. I'd walked into St. Sophia's thinking I was beginning day one of my two-year separation from the people who meant more to me than anyone else in the world—two people who'd been honest with me, even if we hadn't always gotten along. (I was a teenager, after all.) But now I had to wonder. I had to look back over my life and decide whether everything I knew, everything I believed to be true about my mother and father, was a lie.

Or maybe Foley was wrong. Maybe she'd confused my parents for someone else's parents. Parker wasn't such an unusual name. Or maybe she'd known my parents before I was born, at a time when they'd had different careers.

The biggest question of all, though, didn't have anything to do with my parents. It was about *me*. Why did Foley's questions bother me so much? *Scare* me so much? Why did I put so much stock in what she had to say? Foley's words had struck a nerve, but why? Did I have my own doubts?

I kept replaying the memories, going over the details of my visits to the college, conversations with my parents, the conversation with Foley, to milk them of every detail.

I didn't reach any conclusions, but the thought process kept me quiet as Scout lay on the floor of the common room with her iPod and the *Vogue* from the coffee table, and I lay on the couch with an arm behind my head, staring at the plaster ceiling.

When her cell phone buzzed, Scout reached up and grabbed it, then mumbled something about exercise. I waved off the excuse.

"I know," I told her. "Just do what you need to do."

Without explanation, she packed her gear—or whatever was in her skull-and-crossbones messenger bag—and left the suite. Since I was going to do us both a favor by not spying, I decided I was in for the night. I went back to my room, and grabbed a sketch pad and a couple of pencils. I hadn't done much drawing since I'd gotten to Chicago, and it was time to get to work, especially if I was going to start studio classes soon.

Studio was going to be a change, though. I usually drew from my imagination, even if Foley hadn't been impressed. No fruit bowls. No flowerpots. No portraits of fusty men in suits. And as far as drawing from the imagination went, the Scout Green mystery made for pretty good subject matter. My pencil flew across the nubby paper as I sketched out the ogre I'd imagined behind the door.

The hallway door opened so quickly, and with such a cacophony of chirping that I nearly ripped a hole in the paper with the tip of my pencil. The brat pack rushed into the suite, a girly storm of motion and noise. Think-

ing there was no need to make things worse for me or
Scout, I flipped my sketchbook closed and stuffed it
under my pillow.

Veronica followed Amie, Mary Katherine behind
them, a glossy, white shoe box in her hands.

"Oh," M.K. said, her expression falling from devilish-
ness to irritation as she met my gaze through my bedroom doorway. "What are you doing here?"

Amie rolled her eyes. "She lives here?"

"So she does," Veronica said with a sly smile, perch-
ing herself in the threshold. "M.K. tells us you met with
Foley today."

M.K. was a talker, apparently. "Yep," I said. "I did."

Veronica crossed her arms over her untucked oxford
and tie as Mary Katherine and Amie moved to stand
behind her, knights guarding the queen. "The thing is,
Foley never talks to students."

"Is that so?"

"That is very much so," she said. "So we were all interested to hear that you'd been invited into the inner
sanctum."

"Did you learn anything interesting?" Mary Katherine asked with a snicker.

Out of some sarcastic instinct, I almost spilled, almost
threw out a summary of how five minutes in Foley's office had made me doubt nearly sixteen years of personal
experience and had made me question my parents, my
family, a lifetime of memories. But I kept it in. I wasn't
comfortable with these three having that kind of information about me or my fears. It was just the kind of
weakness they'd exploit.

I was surprised, though, to learn that Mary Katherine
hadn't simply listened at Foley's door. That also seemed
like the kind of situation she'd exploit.

"Not really," I finally answered. "Foley was just checking in. Since I'm new, I mean," I added at M.K.'s raised
brows. "She wanted to see if I was adjusting okay."

M.K.'s brows fell, her lips forming a pout. "Oh," she

said. "Whatever, then." Her hunt for drama unsuccessful, she uncrossed her arms and headed toward Amie's room. Amie followed, but Veronica stayed behind.

"Well," she said, "are you coming, or what? We haven't got all day."

It took me nearly a minute to figure out that she was talking to me.

"Am I coming?"

She rolled her eyes, then turned on her heel. "Come on," she said, then beckoned me forward. I blinked, but ever curious, uncrossed my legs, hopped down off the bed, and followed. She walked to the open door of Amie's room and stood there for a moment, apparently inviting me inside.

I had no clue *why* she was asking me inside, and I was just nosy enough to wonder what she was up to. That was an opportunity I couldn't pass up.

"Sure," I said, then joined Veronica at the threshold. When she bobbed her head toward the interior of the room, I ventured inside and got my first look ... at the room that pink threw up on.

Honestly—it looked like a Barbie factory exploded. There was pink everywhere, from the walls to the carpet to the bedspread and pillowcases. I practically had to squint against the glare.

On the other hand, the *stuff* in the room was choice: flat-screen TV; top-of-the-line laptop; fancy speaker system with an iPod port; thick, quilted duvet. I mean, sure it was all covered in kill-me-now pink, but I could appreciate quality.

"Nice room," I half lied, as Veronica shut the door behind me. Mary Katherine was already on Amie's bed, one leg crossed over the other and the glossy shoe box on her lap. Amie was in a sleek, clear plastic chair in front of a desk made of the same clear plastic. "Why, exactly, is she here?" Mary Katherine asked.

Veronica gave me an appraising look. "We're going to see how cool she is."

When Mary Katherine stroked the sides of the shoe box, I assumed my field trip into the Kingdom of Pink and the coolness test were related to whatever was in the shoe box in Mary Katherine's lap ... or my reaction to it.

"How do we know she's not a Little Mary Tattletale?" Mary Katherine asked.

"Oh, come on, M.K. Lily's from New York. She's hip." Veronica arched a challenging eyebrow. "Aren't you?"

I was from Sagamore, *not* New York, but I was too busy contemplating the first-degree peer pressure to bother correcting her. But since the surprise invitation was a mystery that would be solved when M.K. flipped the lid off the shoe box, I figured I'd go for it. I wasn't getting a whole lot of closure on mysteries these days.

"I'm wicked hip," I agreed, my voice wicked dry.

"Are you ready?" Veronica asked, as Mary Katherine slipped her fingers beneath the lip of the shoe box.

"Sure," I said.

I'm not sure what I expected for all the buildup. Mind-altering substances? Diamonds? Stolen electronics? Weapons-grade plutonium? Or, if they'd been teenage boys, fireworks and nudie magazines?

It wasn't quite that dramatic.

With her girls—and me—around her, Mary Katherine lifted the lid. It was filled with candy, diet soda, back issues of *Cosmo*, energy drinks and clove cigarettes. It was like a supermodel's necessities kit.

"Well?" M.K. prompted. "Pretty sweet, huh?"

I opened my mouth, then closed it again with a snap. Surely they weren't so sheltered that issues of *Cosmo*— which were probably available at every drugstore, bodega, and grocery store in the United States—were contraband. Still, I was a guest in enemy territory. Now was not the time for insults. "There's definitely . . . all sorts of stuff in there."

Veronica reached in and grabbed a box of candy cigarettes, then pulled out a stick of white candy. "We have friends who bring it in," she said, nipping a bit off the end.

"And Mary Katherine's parents practically make shipments," Amie added, disapproval ringing in her voice.

M.K. rolled her eyes. "We *need* it," she said. "St. Sophia's is all about health and vigor, organic and free-range and vitamin-enhanced. Weaknesses like these don't figure into that. And if Foley ever found this stuff in our room, we'd be toast." She gave me an appraising glance. "So—can you keep your mouth shut?"

My gaze on a small bag of black licorice—my greatest weakness—I nodded. "That shouldn't be a problem."

Mary Katherine snorted and, seeing the direction of my gaze, reached over, grabbed the packet of licorice Scotties, and tossed it to me. I pulled it open—not even pausing to question why she was offering me candy—and began to nibble the head off a tiny, chewy dog.

Veronica looked at her BFFs, then slid a glance my way, her eyes bright with promise. "You know, Parker, we don't keep all of Mary Katherine's stash up here, just in case Foley decides to start doing room checks again. The rest of it is in our little hidey-hole. We call it our treasure chest. We were going there, you know, to replenish our stack." She glanced back at Mary Katherine. "M.K.'s almost out of Tab."

When Veronica looked at me again, her gaze was cool . . . and calculating. "You can go with us if you want. Share in the bounty."

I'd have been stupid not to be suspicious. The stash these trendy big-city girls played at being so excited about wasn't really that exciting. More important, they were being unusually nice. While I guessed it was possible they were still making some kind of misguided attempt to steer me toward "better" pals, it seemed more likely that something more nefarious was on their agenda.

But they weren't the only ones with secret plans.

Foley had nearly ripped the rug out from under me earlier today; this was my chance to retake control, to take
charge, to *act*.

"Where, exactly, is this stash?" I looked at Amie,
thinking she offered the best chance to get an honest
answer.

"Downstairs," she said. "Basement."

And we have a winner, I thought. A trip downstairs
would get me one step closer to figuring out what Scout
was involved in—and what else was going on at St. Sophia's School for Girls.

I nodded at the group. "I'm in. Let's go treasure
hunting."

8

We were armed with pink flashlights, Amie having produced the set of them from a bottom-drawer stash. I also saw a set of pink tools, a pink first aid kit, and some pink batteries in there. Amie was apparently the prepared (and single-minded) type.

I was also armed with a pretty good dose of skepticism at their motives. I assumed the brat pack was leading me into trouble, that the "treasure" at the end of our hunt was a prank with my name on it. Given the strong possibility that I'd have to make a run for it, I was glad I'd worn boots. I figured they offered at least a little more traction than the flip-flops, and they'd probably pack a bigger wallop, if it came to that.

Scout was still gone when we left the suite, three brat packers and one hanger-on, Veronica in the lead. It was nearly ten p.m., and the hallways were silent and empty as we followed the same route I'd taken behind Scout two days ago—down the stairs to the first floor, back through the long, main corridor to the Great Hall, then through the Great Hall and into the main building. But instead of stopping at the door Scout had taken, we took a left into the administrative corridor I'd taken with M.K. earlier in the day.

We hadn't yet turned on our flashlights, so I'm not entirely sure why we had them. But when footsteps suddenly echoed through the hall, I was glad we hadn't turned them on. Veronica held out a hand, and we all stopped behind her. She turned, excitement in her eyes, and motioned us back with a hand. We tiptoed back a few steps, then crowded into one of the semicircular alcoves in the hallway. I gnawed my lip as I tried to control my breathing, sure that the thundering beat of my heart was echoing through the hallway for all to hear.

After what felt like an hour, the sound of footfalls faded as the person—probably one of the clipboard-bearing dragon ladies—moved off in the other direction.

Veronica peeked out of the nook, one hand behind her to hold us back while she surveyed the path.

"Okay," she finally whispered, and we set off again— Veronica, then Mary Katherine, Amie, and I. I couldn't help but glance behind us as we moved, but the hall was empty except for the cavernous silence we left in our wake, and the moonlight-dappled limestone floor.

We continued down the administrative hallway, but before we got as far as Foley's office, we turned down a side corridor that dead-ended in a set of limestone stairs. The air got colder as we descended to the basement, which didn't help the feeling that we were heading toward something unpleasant. We probably *were* headed toward the nasty that had been chasing Scout, but I couldn't imagine the brat pack had any clue what lurked in the corridors beneath their fancy school. If they had known, they surely would have tortured Scout about it. They seemed like the type.

"Almost there," Veronica whispered as we reached the bottom of the staircase. True to St. Sophia's form, we entered another limestone hallway. I'd heard about buildings that contained secret catacombs, but I wondered why the nuns had bothered building out the labyrinthine basement of the convent—a task they'd taken on without trucks, cranes, or forklifts.

"Here we are," Veronica finally said as we stopped before a simple, wooden door. The word CUSTODIAN was written in gold capitals across it, just like the letters on Foley's office.

I arched an eyebrow at the door. "We're going into the janitorial closet?"

Without bothering to answer, Mary Katherine and Veronica fiddled with the brass doorknob, then opened the door with a click.

"Check it," Veronica said, grinning as she held the door open.

I walked inside, and my jaw dropped at the scene before me.

The room was a giant limestone vault, completely empty but for one thing—it held an entire, little Chicago, a scale model of the city. From a two-foot-high Sears Tower and its two gleaming points (which even I could recognize), to the Chicago River, to the Ferris wheel at Navy Pier. All in miniature, all exactingly detailed, laid out across the floor of the giant room by someone who clearly loved Chicago—someone who *knew* Chicago.

"Who did this?" I asked.

"No clue," Veronica said. "It's been here as long as we've been here. Pretty sweet, huh?"

"Very," I muttered, eyes wide as I walked the empty perimeter of the limestone room, just taking it all in.

The model was almost totally devoid of color—the buildings and landscape rendered in various shades of thin, gray cardboard—but for symbols that were stamped on a few points across the city. In navy blue was a symbol that looked like four circles stuck together, or a really curvy plus sign. In apple green was a circle enclosing a capital *Y*.

Markers, I thought, pointing out the locations of two kinds of *something* across the city.

I moved into the middle of Lake Michigan—an empty space across the floor—and peered between the buildings, looking for St. Sophia's. When I found East Erie, I realized there were two symbols nearby: the four-circle thing on Michigan Avenue and, more interesting, the enclosed *Y* only a couple of blocks from St. Sophia's. "What do the symbols mean?" I asked.

I got only silence in response.

I glanced up and looked behind me just in time to watch them shut the door, and just in time to hear the lock tumblers click into place. I hurdled Navy Pier, ran to the door, gripped the doorknob in both hands, and pulled.

Nothing.

I shook it, tried to turn it, pulled again.

Still nothing, not even a knob to unlock the door from the inside. Just a brass keyhole.

"Hello?" I yelled, then beat my fist against the door. "Veronica? Amie? Mary Katherine? I'm still in here!"

I added that last part in the off chance they were somehow unaware that they'd locked me into a room in the basement of the school; in case they'd forgotten that the four of us had traveled the halls of St. Sophia's to get to this underground room, but only three were headed back up.

But it wasn't an accident, of course, and the only answer I got back was giggling, which I could hear echoing down the hallway.

"Way mature!" I yelled out, then muttered a curse, mostly at my own stupidity.

Of course there was no candy, no Tab, no hidden cigarettes, or black-market energy drinks down here. There was a treasure—the brat pack had stumbled upon something, a hidden room that contained an intricate scale model of the city. But they'd probably missed the point, being only interested in how to use the room to prank me—how to punk me.

I kicked a foot against the door, which did nothing but vibrate pain up through my foot. Turned out, even my favorite boots didn't provide much more insulation than flip-flops. I braced one arm against the door and rubbed my foot with my free hand, berating myself for following them into the room.

Traipsing around the school was one thing; I'd done that already. But being locked in a custodial closet in the all-but-abandoned basement of a private school was something else. My love of exploration notwithstanding, I knew better.

When my foot finally stopped throbbing, I stood up again. For better or worse, I was stuck down here, in a hidden room that was probably a little too close to whatever lurked behind the metal door. It was time for action.

One hand around my pink flashlight, the other on my hip, I took a look around. Unfortunately, the obvious exit wasn't an option. The door was locked from the outside, and I didn't have a key.

"Hold that thought," I muttered, put my flashlight on the floor. This was an old building, and I had a skeleton key. I pulled the ribboned room key off my head.

"Come on, Irene," I said. Two fingers crossed for good luck, I slipped the key into the lock.

The tumblers didn't budge.

I muttered out another curse, then pulled back the key and slipped the ribbon over my head again. I slid my gaze to the flashlight on the floor and considered, for a minute, pummeling the lock with it, but God only knew how long I'd be down here. Sacrificing the flashlight probably wasn't the brightest idea (ha!).

I stepped back and surveyed the door. Like the doors in the main building, this one was an old-fashioned panel of thin wood, attached to the jamb by two brass hinges. The pins in the hinges were pretty big, so I figured I could try to pull them out, unhinge the door, and squeeze through the crack, but I really didn't like the thought of ending up in Foley's office again, this time for destruction of St. Sophia's property. There was no doubt the brat pack would tell her who was responsible, and I guessed that was the kind of thing she'd put in my permanent record.

All that in mind, I put "taking the door apart" at the

bottom of my mental list and glanced back at the rest of the room, looking for another way. What about a secret door? Since Foley had one, it didn't seem far-fetched that I'd find one in a secret, locked basement room. I walked the perimeter of the room, pressing my palms against the limestone tiles as I walked, hoping to find some kind of trigger mechanism.

I made two passes.

I found nothing.

Just as I was about to give up on an escape route that didn't involve dismantling the door, something occurred to me. The model had obviously taken a lot of work, a lot of craftsmanship, with all those tiny buildings, all that architecture. And that meant someone spent a lot of time in here. A lot of *hours* in here.

But the door was locked from the outside, so what if the architects got locked in while they were whiling away the hours on their obsessively detailed project? Wouldn't they need another way out? Surely they—or he or she or whoever—had their own escape route. I must have missed something.

I was on the far side of the room when I saw it—when I noticed the glint of light, the reflection, on the eastern edge of the city. I cocked my head at it, realizing the glint was coming from the two spires on the Sears Tower.

I moved closer.

The spires were metal, which was weird because they were the only metal in the tiny city. Everything else was rendered in that same, gray paperboard.

"Interesting," I mumbled, and kneeled down in what I assumed was a branch of the Chicago River. I reached out and carefully, oh so carefully, tugged at a spire.

It didn't budge.

"Come on," I said, and reached for the second. I grasped the end, wiggled, and felt it begin to slide free of the cardboard. One tug, then another, just enough to pull the metal through, but not hard enough to tear the roof from the building.

It finally slid free. I held it up to the light.

It was a key.

"Oh, *rock on*," I said with a grin, then rose from the lake. It may not have been a huge victory—and I wasn't even sure the key would work in the lock—but it sure felt like one. A victory for the architect who'd been locked in, and a victory for me. And more important, a loss for the brat pack.

I walked along the river until I reached the lake, then turned for the door, where I slipped the key into the lock and turned.

The lock flipped open.

I'm not embarrassed to say that I did a little dance of happiness, yellow boots and all.

Thinking the next person who was locked into the room might need the key, I pulled it from the lock and returned it to its home in the Sears Tower. I glanced across the city, making a mental note to tell Scout about the model in case she hadn't already seen it. I had a suspicion the symbols on the buildings were related to whatever she was doing, and whatever "litter" she and her friends were battling against.

And speaking of battling, it was time to consider my next step.

Option one involved my returning to the suite to face down Veronica et al. They'd gloat about locking me in; I'd gloat about getting out. Not exactly my idea of a thrilling Thursday night.

Option two was a little riskier. I'd joined the brat pack in their trip to the basement on the off chance they might lead me somewhere interesting. Success on that one, I think.

Now that they'd returned to the Kingdom of Pink, I had the chance to do a little exploring of my own. So, for the second time in a single night, I opted for danger. I'd managed to finagle my way out of a locked room, so I figured luck was on my side.

I took a final look at the city and pulled the door closed behind me.

"Good night, Chicago," I whispered.

Maybe not surprising, the hallway was empty when I emerged from the custodian's closet, the brat pack nowhere to be seen. They were probably celebrating their victory somewhere. Little did they know. . . .

The corridor split into two branches—one that led back to the stairs and the first floor, and one that probably led deeper into the basement. My decision to play Nancy Drew already made, I took the road not yet traveled.

I moved slowly, one shoulder nearly against the wall, trying to make myself as invisible as possible. The hallway dead-ended in a T-shaped corridor; I headed for it. This part of the basement was well lit, so I kept the flashlight off, but gripped it with such force, my palm was actually sweating. I was still in the basement, still close to whatever nasties Scout had locked behind the big metal door. That meant I needed to be on my guard.

I made it to the dead end without incident, then glanced down the left- and right-hand corridors. Both were empty, and I had no clue where I was relative to the rest of the building. Worse, both hallways were long and dark. There were no overhead lights and no wall sconces—just darkness.

Not the best of choices. I didn't have a coin to flip or a Magic 8-Ball to ask, so I went with the only other respectable method of making a decision as important at this one.

Unfortunately, I'd only made it through "eeny meeny miney mo" when the ground began to rumble beneath my feet. I was thrown forward into the crux of the hallway, and had to brace myself against the limestone wall to stay upright as the floor vibrated beneath me.

But just as suddenly as it had begun, the rumbling stopped. My palm still flat against the limestone bricks, heart pounding in my chest, I looked up at the ceiling above me as I waited for screaming and footfalls and other telltale signs of the aftermath of the Earthquake That Ate Chicago.

There was only silence.

I snapped my gaze to the left as hurried footsteps echoed toward me from that end of the hallway and tried to swallow down the panic.

I flicked on my flashlight and swung the beam into the dark, the arc of light barely penetrating the blackness, even as I squinted to get a better look.

And then I saw them—Scout and Jason behind her, both in uniform, both running toward me as if they were running for their lives. I dropped the beam of the flashlight to the floor to keep from blinding them, afraid that's exactly what was happening.

"Scout?" I called out, but fear had frozen my throat. I tried again, and this time managed some sound. "Scout!"

They were still far away—the corridor was a deep one—but they were running at sprinter speed . . . and there was something behind them.

It almost didn't surprise me to see that they were being chased. After all, I'd already helped Scout try to escape from *something*. But I'm not sure what I expected to see chasing her.

As they drew closer, I realized that behind them was the blonde we'd seen outside the pillar garden on Monday—the girl with the hoodie who had watched us from the street. She ran full-bore behind Scout and Jason. But even as she sprinted through the corridor, her expression was somehow vacant, a strange gleam in her eyes the only real sign of life. Her hair was long and wavy, and it flew out behind her as she ran, arms pumping, toward us.

Suddenly she pulled back her hand, then shot if forward, as if to throw something at the two of them. The air and ground rumbled, and this time, the rumble was strong enough to knock me off my feet. I hit the ground on my knees, palms extended.

By the time I glanced up again, Scout and Jason were only feet in front of me. That meant the blond girl was only a few yards behind. I saw the look of horror on Scout's face. "Get up, Lily!" she implored. *"Run!"*

I muttered a curse that would have made a string of sailors blush, and ignoring the bruises blossoming on my knees, jumped to my feet and did as I was ordered. The three of us took off down the hallway, presumably for a safer place.

We ran through one corridor, then another, then another, heading in the opposite direction of the path I'd taken with the brat pack—probably a good thing, since there was no giant metal door in that part of the convent to keep them out.

To keep *her* out.

Whatever juju the blonde used before, she used again, the ground rumbling beneath our feet. I don't know how she managed it, how she managed to make the earth—and all the limestone above it—move, but she did it sure enough. We all stumbled, but Scout reached out a hand and grabbed at the wall to keep her balance, and Jason caught Scout's elbow. I caught limestone, the stones rushing toward my face as she knocked me off my feet again. I braced myself on my hands, the pads of my hands burning as I hit the floor.

They were on their feet again and yards ahead before they realized I wasn't with them.

"Lily!" Scout screamed, but I was already looking behind me, watching the blonde. The earthquake-maker just stood there, and I figured if I was already on the floor, there wasn't much else she could do to me.

Of course, that didn't mean the guy who stepped out from behind her couldn't do damage. He was older than she was—college, maybe. Curly dark hair, broad shoulders, and blue eyes that gleamed with a creepy intensity.

With a hunger. And all that hunger and intensity was directed at me.

I swallowed down fear and panic and tried to make my brain work, tried to make my arms and legs push me up from the floor, but I was suddenly puppy-clumsy, unable to order my limbs to function.

The boy stepped beside the blonde, muttered something, and just as she had done, whipped his hand in my direction.

The air pressure in the room changed, and something flew my way, some *thing* he'd created with that flick of his hand. It looked like a contact lens of hazy, green smoke, but it wasn't really smoke. It wasn't really a *thing*. It was more like the very air in the room had warped.

Still on the floor—only a second or two having passed since I fell to the ground, time slowing in the midst of my panic—I stared, eyes wide, mouth open in shock as it moved toward me. Nothing in my life in Sagamore, or my week in Chicago, had prepared me for . . . whatever it was. And whatever it was, it was about to make contact.

They say there are moments in your life when time slows down, when you can see your fate rushing toward you. This was one of those times. I had a second to react, which wasn't enough time to move out of the way, so I turned my back on it. That warp of air slammed into me with the force of a freight train, pushing the air from my lungs. It arced across my body like alien fire, like a living thing that tunneled into my spine, through my torso, across my limbs.

"Lily!" Scout screamed.

The floor rumbled beneath me again, and I heard a growl, a roar, like the scream of an angry animal. I heard shuffling, the sounds of fighting, but I could do nothing but lie there, my body spasming as pain and fire and heat raced through my limbs. I blinked at the colors that danced before my eyes, the world—or the portions of the floor and room that I could see from my sprawled-out position on the floor—covered by a green haze.

I must have passed out, because when I lifted my eyelids again, I was in the air, cradled by strong arms. I looked up and found bright eyes, eyes the same blue as a spring prairie sky, staring back at me.

"Jason?" I asked, my voice sounding hollow and distant.

"Hold on, Lily," he said. "We're going to get you out of here."

The world went black.

9

I woke blinking, my eyes squinted against the sunlight that streamed through the wall of windows on my left, and bounced off white walls on the other three sides of the room I was in. I looked down. I was on a high bed, my legs covered by a white sheet and thin blanket, the rest of me wrapped in one of those nubby, printed hospital gowns.

"You're awake."

I lifted my gaze. Scout sat in a plastic chair across from my bed, a thick leather book in her hands. She was in uniform, but she'd covered her button-up oxford shirt with a cardigan.

"Where am I?" I asked her, shading my eyes with a hand.

"LaSalle Street Clinic," she said. "A few blocks from the school. You've been sleeping for twelve hours. The doctor was in a few minutes ago. She said you didn't have a concussion or anything; they just brought you in since you passed out."

I nodded and motioned toward the windows. "Can you do something about the light?"

"Sure." She put aside the book and stood up, then walked to the wall of windows and fidgeted with the cord until the blinds came together, and the room darkened. When she was done, she turned and looked at me, arms crossed over her chest. "How are you feeling?"

I did a quick assessment. Nothing felt broken, but I had a killer headache and I was pretty sore—as if I'd taken a couple of good falls onto unforgiving limestone. "Groggy, mostly. My head hurts. And my back."

Scout nodded. "You were hit pretty hard." She walked to the bed and hitched one hip onto it. "I'd say that I'm sorry you got dragged into this but, first things first, why, exactly, were you in the basement?"

There was an unspoken question in her tone: *Were you following me again?*

"The brat pack went down there. I was invited along."

Scout went pale. "The brat pack? They were in the basement?"

I nodded. "They fed me a story about a stash of contraband stuff, but it was just a prank. They locked me in the model room."

"The model room?"

I drew a square with my fingers. "The secret custodian's closet that contains a perfect-scale model of the city? I'm guessing you know what I'm talking about here."

"Oh. That."

"Yeah. Look, I was patient about the midnight disappearances, the secret basement stuff, but"—I twirled a finger at the hospital room around us—"the time has come to start talking."

After a minute of consideration, she nodded. "You're right. You were hit with firespell."

For a few seconds, I just looked at her. It took me that long to realize that she'd actually given me a straight answer, even if I had no idea what she'd meant. "A what?"

"Firespell. The name, I know, totally medieval. Actually, so is firespell itself, we think. But that's really a magical archaeology issue, and we don't need to get into that now. Firespell," she repeated. "That's what hit you. That green contact-lens-looking deal. It was a spell, thrown by Sebastian Born. Pretty face, evil disposition."

I just stared blankly back at her. "Firespell."

"It's going to take time to explain everything."

I hitched a thumb at the monitor and IV rack that stood next to my bed. "I think my calendar is pretty free at the moment."

Scout's expression fell, her usual sarcasm replaced by something sadder and more fearful. There was worry in her eyes. "I'm so sorry, Lil. I was so scared—I thought you were gone for a minute."

I nodded, not quite ready to forgive her yet. "I'm okay," I said, although I wasn't sure I meant it.

Scout nodded, but blinked back tears, then bobbed her head toward the table beside my bed. "Your parents called. I guess Foley told them you were here? I told them you were okay—that you fell down the stairs. I couldn't—I wasn't sure what to tell them."

"Me, either," I muttered, and plucked the phone from the nightstand. They'd left me a voice mail, which I'd check later, and a couple of text messages. I opened the phone and dialed my mom's number. She answered almost immediately through a crackling, staticky connection.

"Lily? Lily?" she asked, her voice a little too loud. There was fear in her tone. Worry.

"Hi, Mom. I'm okay. I just wanted to call."

"Oh, my God," she said, relief in her voice. "She's okay, Mark," she said, her voice softer now as she reassured my father, who was apparently beside her. "She's fine. Lily, what happened? God, we were so worried—Marceline called and said you'd taken a fall?"

I opened and closed my mouth, completely at a loss about how I was supposed to deal with the fact that I now had proof my Mom was on a first name basis with Foley—not to mention Foley's perspective on my parents' careers—so I asked the most basic question I could think of. "You know Foley? Ms. Foley, I mean?"

There was a weird pause, just before a crackle of static rumbled through the phone. I pressed my palm against my other ear. "Mom? You're cutting out. I can't hear you."

"Sorry—we're on the road. Yes, we're—*yes*. We know Marceline." *Crackle*. "—you all right?"

"I'm fine," I said again. "I'm awake and I feel fine. I just—slipped. Why don't you call me later?"

That time, I only heard "traveling" and "hotel" before the connection went dead. I stared at the phone for a few seconds before flipping it shut again.

"I just lied to my parents," I snottily said when I'd returned the phone to the table. I heard the petulance in my voice, but given my surroundings, I thought I deserved it.

Scout opened her mouth to respond but before she could get words out, a knock sounded at the door. Scout met my gaze, but shrugged.

"Come in?" I said.

The door opened a crack, and Jason peeked through.

"My, my," Scout murmured, winging up eyebrows at me. I sent her a withering look before Jason opened the door fully and stepped inside. He was out of his Montclare Academy duds today, and was dressed casually in jeans and a navy zip-up sweater. I knew this was neither the time nor the place, but the navy did amazing things for his eyes. On one shoulder was the strap of a backpack, and in his hand was a slim vase that held a single, puffy flower—a peony, maybe.

The flower and backpack weren't Jason's only accessories. When Michael appeared behind him, I gave Scout the same winged-up eyebrows she'd given me. A blush began to fan across her cheeks.

"Just wanted to see how you were feeling," Jason said, closing the door once he and Michael were in the room. He dropped his backpack on a second plastic chair, then extended his arm, a smile on his face. "And we brought you a flower."

"Thanks," I said, self-consciously touching a hand to my hair. I couldn't imagine that anything up there looked pretty after twelve hours of unconsciousness. Scout reached out to take the vase, then placed it atop a bureau next to a glass container of white tulips.

I pointed at the arrangement. "Where'd those come from?"

"Huh?" Scout asked, then seemed to realize the tulips were there. "Oh. Right. Let's see." She pulled out the card, frowned, then glanced back at me. "It just says, 'Board of Trustees.'"

"That was surprisingly thoughtful," I mumbled, thinking Foley must have given them a call.

"Garcia didn't want to study," Jason said, "so we thought we'd amble over."

Scout arched a brow at Michael. "Does Garcia ever want to study?"

"I have my moments, Green," he said, then moved toward the bed. When he reached me, he picked up my hand and squeezed it. "How are you feeling?"

"Like I was hit by a freight train."

"Understandable," Jason said behind him, and Michael nodded in agreement.

"Scout was just about to explain to me exactly what's going on beneath Chicago." Jason and Michael both snapped their gaze to Scout. I guessed they had mixed feelings about her confession. She waved cheekily.

"But now that the full club has convened," I continued, linking my hands in my lap, "you can decide amongst yourselves who wants to do the explaining. Blue eyes? Brown eyes?" I glanced over at Scout. "Instigator?"

"I am so *not* an instigator," Scout said. "I was the one being chased, if you'll recall, not doing the chasing."

"Instigator," Michael said with a grin. "I like that."

When Scout stuck her tongue out at him, he winked back at her. Her blush flared up again. I bit back a smile.

"All right," Jason said. "You got dragged into the conflict, so you deserve some answers. What do you want to know?"

"Scout already said I was hit by firespell," I said, "and

I've figured out some of the rest of it. You three are in cahoots and you roam around under the convent and battle bad guys who make earthquakes and shoot fire from their hands."

Silence.

"That's not bad, actually," Scout finally said.

Michael cocked his head at me. "How are you feeling about the earthquakes-and-shooting-fire part of that?"

I frowned down at the thin hospital sheet, then picked at a pill in the fabric. It was probably time for me to give some thought to whatever it was I'd been dragged into—or, maybe more accurately, that I'd *fallen* into.

"I'm not sure," I said after a minute. "I mean, I'm not really in a position to doubt the earthquakes-and-shooting-fire part. I've felt the earthquakes, felt the fire. It hurt," I emphasized. The memory of that burning heat made my shoulders tense, and I rolled them out to relieve the tension.

"I'm alive," I said, glancing up at them, "which I guess isn't something I can really take for granted right now. But beyond that, I haven't really had time to think much about it. To process it, if that makes sense."

I glanced up at Scout. Her expression had fallen, and she nibbled the edge of her lip. There was fear in her face, maybe apology, as well. It was the insecurity that comes from knowing that someone you'd brought into your life could disappear again, leaving you alone.

"It makes sense," she quietly said. Her words were a statement, but there was a question in her tone: *Is this it for us? For our friendship?*

Scout and I looked at each other for a few seconds, and in the time that elapsed during that glance, something happened—I realized I'd been given an opportunity to become part of a new kind of family; an opportunity to trust someone, to take a chance on someone. My parents may have been four thousand miles away, but I'd gained a new best friend. And that was something. That was the kind of thing you held on to.

"Well then," I said, my gaze on hers, "I suppose you'd better fill me in."

It took her a moment to react, to realize what I'd said, to realize that I was committing to being a part of whatever it was they were really, truly involved in. And when she realized it, her face lit up.

But before we could get too cozy, Jason spoke up.

"Before you tell her more than she already knows," he said, "you need to think about what you're doing. She was underground for only a little while. That means there's a chance they won't recognize her. We can all go about our business, and there's no need for them to know she exists."

He crossed his arms and frowned. "But if you bring her into it, she becomes part of the conflict. Not a JV member, sure, but part of the community. You'll put her on the radar, and they'll mark her as a supporter of the enclave. She may become a target. If you tell her more, she's in this. For better or worse, she's in it."

I was okay with "for better or worse." It was "till death do us part" that I wasn't really excited about.

"Look around," Scout quietly said, her gaze on me. "She's in the hospital wearing a paper nightgown. She has a tube in her arm." She shifted her gaze to Jason, and there was impatience there. "She's already in this."

As if she'd made the decision, Scout half jumped onto the bed and arranged herself to sit on the edge. As she moved around, Michael and Jason took a step backward to get out of her way, exchanging a quiet glance as they waited for her to begin.

"Unicorns," she said.

There was silence in the room for a few seconds. "Unicorns," I repeated.

She bobbed her head. "Unicorns."

I just blinked. "I have no idea what I'm supposed to do with that."

"Aha," she said, a finger in the air. "You didn't expect me to start with that, did you? But, seriously, unicorns.

Imagine yourself in medieval Europe. You've got horses, oxen, assorted beasts of burden. Times are dark, dirty, generally impoverished."

Jason leaned toward Michael. "Is this going somewhere?"

"Not a clue," Michael said. "This is the first time I've heard this speech."

"Zip it, Garcia. Okay, so dark, dirty, lots of peasants, things are dreary. All of a sudden, a maiden walks into a field or some such thing, and she expects to see a horse there. But instead, there's a unicorn. Horn, white mane, magical glow, the whole bit."

She stopped talking, then looked at me expectantly.

"I'm sorry, Scout, but if that was supposed to be a metaphor or something, I got nothin'."

"Seconded," Michael added.

Scout leaned forward a little, and when she continued, her voice was quieter, more solemn. "Think about what I said. What if, all of a sudden, every once in a while, it wasn't just another horse in the field? What if it really was a unicorn?"

"*Ohhh*," Jason said. "Got it."

"Yep," Michael agreed.

"There are people in the world," Scout said, "like those unicorns in the field. They're unique. They're rare." She paused and glanced up at me, her expression solemn. "And they're gifted. With magic."

Okay, I guess with all the unicorn talk, I probably should have seen that coming. Still, I had to blink a few times after she laid that little egg.

"Magic," I finally repeated.

"Magical powers of every shape and size," she said. "I can see the doubt in your eyes, but you've seen it. You've felt it." She bobbed her head toward my IV. "You have firsthand experience it exists, even if you don't know the what or the why."

I frowned. "Okay, earthquakes and fire and whatnot, but magic?"

Jason leaned forward a little. "You can have a little time to get used to the idea," he said. "But in the meantime, you might want to have her move along with the explanation. She's got quite a bit to get through yet." He smiled warmly, and my heart fluttered, circumstances notwithstanding.

"You must be a real hit with the ladies, Shepherd, with all that charm." Scout's tone was dry as toast. I bit back a grin, at least until she looked back at me again. She gave me a withering expression, the kind of raised-eyebrow look you might see on a teacher who'd caught you passing notes in class.

"Please," I said, waving an invitational hand. "Continue."

"Okay," she said, holding up her hands for emphasis, "so there's a wee percentage of the population that has magic."

"What kind of magic? Is it all earthquakes and air-pressure-contact-lenses and whatnot?"

"There's a little bit of everything. There are classes of powers, different kinds of skills. Elemental powers—that's fire and water and wind. Spells and incantations—"

One of the puzzle pieces fell into place.

"That's you," I exclaimed, thinking of the books in Scout's room. Recipe books. *Spell* books. "You can do spells?"

"Of a sort," she blandly said, as if I'd only asked if she had a nose ring. "They call me a spellbinder."

I glanced over at Jason and Michael, but they just shook their heads. "This is your field trip. You can get to us later," Michael said, then glanced at Scout. "Keep going."

"Anyway," Scout said, "the power usually appears around puberty. At the beginning of the transition to adulthood."

"Boobs *and* earthquakes?" I asked. "That's quite a change."

"Seriously," she agreed with a nod. "It's pretty freaky. You wake up one morning and *boom*—you're sporting B cups and the mystical ability to manipulate matter or cast spells or battle Reapers for dominion over Chicago. *Gossip Girl* has nothing on us."

I just stared at her for a minute, trying to imagine exactly what that life would have been like. Not just the part about waking up with B cups—although that would be a pretty big adjustment. I glanced down at my chest. Not a horrible adjustment, I guessed, but nonetheless . . .

"You still with us?" Scout asked.

I glanced up quickly, a flush rising on my cheeks. She grinned cheekily. "I've thought the same thing," she said with a wink.

"Before you two get too friendly," Michael said, "tell her the catch."

"There's a catch?" I asked.

"Isn't there always?" she asked dryly. "The thing is, the magic isn't eternal. It doesn't last forever, at least, not without a price. When we're young—teens, twenties—the magic makes us stronger. It works in conjunction with our bodies, our minds, our souls. When we're young, it's like an extra sense or an extra way to understand the world, an extra way to manipulate it. We have access to something humans forgot about after the witch trials scared it out of everyone, after fear made everyone forget about the gift."

"And when you get older?"

"The power comes at a cost," Jason said. "And our position is, the cost is pretty nasty."

"Too high," Michael added with a nod.

I arched an eyebrow. "A cost? Like mentally? Does it make you crazy or something?"

"It could," Scout said. "It rots the body, the soul, from the inside out."

I raised my eyebrows. "What do you mean, it rots the body? Like, it kills people?"

She nodded. "The older you get, the more the magic

begins to feed from you. It drains you, transforms you. The magic shifts, from something symbiotic to a parasite. And in order to stay alive, to keep up with the power's constant craving, you have to feed it."

"With what?" My voice was quiet. So was Scout's when she answered.

"With the energy of others. Those who keep their power must learn to drink the essence of others—like vampires of the soul. We call them Reapers."

"Takers of life," I thought aloud.

"Bringers of death," she said. "You want a shorter life span, they're the folks you call."

"You said they take the energy of others," I repeated. "What does that mean?"

Jason took a step forward. "Have you ever seen people who you thought seemed drained of energy? Depressed? Like, kids who are sleeping in class all the time, dragging around, that kind of thing?"

"I'm a teenager," I flatly said. "That's pretty much how we live."

"Puberty takes its toll," Scout agreed, "but hormones aren't the only problem. Reapers target people with self-confidence issues—people who don't fit in. And slowly, so they don't gain too much attention, the Reapers consume their energy. Call it their aura, their soul, their will to live. That spark that makes us who we are, that makes us more than walking robots."

"The earthquake and fire kids," I said, "The ones chasing you—chasing *us*—under the convent. Those were the Reapers?"

Scout nodded. "It's a belated introduction, but meet Alex and Sebastian. She's a senior in the publics; he's a sophomore at Northwestern. They don't actually need to do any reaping right now—they're too young—but they help find victims for the older ones. That's the Reaper way. Do whatever you have to do to keep your grip on the magic, regardless of how many people you hurt—or kill—to do it."

"Okay," I said. "So these bad guys, these Reapers, suck the souls out of people so they won't become walking zombies. But what about the rest of you?" I looked at each of them in turn. "I assume you don't plan on doing any soul sucking in the future?"

Before they could answer, there was another knock on the door. Before I could answer, a scrubs-clad nurse walked in, tray in hand.

"Good afternoon," she said. "How are you feeling?" She shooed Scout off the bed, then put the tray—which held a small plastic tumbler of water, a small plastic pitcher, and a chocolate pudding cup.

"Okay. Considering."

"Mmm-hmm," she said, then came to my bedside and measured my pulse. She pulled the end of a tube from a machine connected to the wall, then held it toward me.

"Stick out your tongue," she said. When I did, she stuck the chunk of cold plastic beneath my tongue, then watched a read-out behind me. "Shouldn't you all be in school right now?" she asked without glancing up.

"We have passes," Scout said.

"Mmm-hmm," she said again. When the machine beeped, she pulled out the thermometer, put it away, and then moved to the end of my bed, where she scribbled something on my chart. When she'd returned it to its slot, she looked at me. "Visiting hours are over in an hour."

"Sure," I said. After a final warning glance at Scout, Michael, and Jason, she disappeared out the door again.

Suddenly starving, I pointed at the tray at the end of the bed. "Hand me the pudding cup and get on with the story," I told Scout. She peeled off the foil top, then handed me the cup and spoon as she licked the remnant of chocolate pudding from the foil. I dug in.

"No soul sucking," Michael continued. "From our perspective, keeping the power isn't worth it—not to feed off others. We aren't willing to pay that cost, to take lives so we can wax poetic about how great it is to be an Adept."

I swallowed a giant spoonful of chocolate pudding—magical near misses really built up the appetite—then lifted my brows at him. "Adept?"

"Those of us with magic," he said, "but who are willing to give it up. It's what we call ourselves. Our philosophy is, we hit twenty-five, and we return our power to the universe. We stop using it. We make a promise, take a vow."

"It's an even trade," Scout said, with a small smile. "No more power, but no more upsetting the balance of the universe."

"No more being Adepts," Jason said, his voice quieter and, I thought, a little wistful, as if he'd considered the blow that giving up his magic would be, and he wasn't thrilled about it.

"Okay," I said. "So, to review, you've got kids with magical powers running around Chicago. Some of them are willing to give it up when the magic gets predatory—that would be you guys."

Scout bobbed her head.

"And some of them aren't willing to give it up, so they have a future of soul sucking to look forward to."

"That's a fair summary," Michael said with a nod.

"But that doesn't explain why you guys are running around under the convent throwing, what, firespell, at one another."

Scout looked up at Michael, who nodded, as if giving her permission to answer the question. "We found a list," she said. "A list of, well, I guess you'd call them leads. Kids who've been scoped out by Reapers. Kids they're targeting for a power lunch, no pun intended."

I nodded my understanding.

"I've been working out a spell of protection, a little half charm, half curse, to keep the Reapers from being able to zero in on their targets."

"How do you do that?"

"Have you ever tried to look at a faraway star," Scout asked, "but the closer you look at it, the fuzzier it gets?"

"Sure. Why?"

"That's what Scout's trying to do here," Michael said, crossing his arms and bobbing his head in her direction. "Making the targets invisible to the Reapers. She's been working on a kid who lives in a condo on Michigan, goes to a high school in South Loop. They haven't been real thrilled with that."

"And that's why they've been chasing you?" I asked, sliding my gaze to Scout.

"As you might imagine," she said, "we aren't exactly popular. Our ideas about giving up our power don't exactly put us in the majority."

"The gifted are proud to have magic," Jason said, "as well they should be. But most of them don't want to give it up."

"That puts us in the minority," Michael added. "Rebels, of a sort."

"A magic splinter cell?"

"Kinda," Scout said with a rueful smile. "So the Reapers identify targets—folks who make a good psychic lunch—and kids who are coming into their own, coming into their own gifts. Spotters," she added, anticipating my question. "Their particular gift is the ability to find magic. To detect it."

"Once a kid is identified," Michael said, "the Reapers circle like lions around prey. They'll talk to the kid, sometimes their parents, about the gift, figure out the parameters, exactly what the kid can do. And they'll teach the kid that the gift is nothing to be embarrassed about, and that any souls they take are worth it."

"The Reapers try to teach the kids that the idea of giving up your power willingly is a conspiracy," Jason said, "that feeding on someone else's energy, their essence, is a kind of magical natural selection—the strong feeding on the weak or something. We disagree. We work our protective spells on the targets, or we try to intercede more directly with the gifted, to get the kids to think for themselves, to think about the consequences of their magic."

"For better or worse," Scout added.

"So you try to steal their pledges," I concluded.

"You got it," Scout said. "We try to teach kids with powers that giving up their powers is the best thing for humanity. You know, because of the soul sucking."

I smiled lightly. "Right."

"That makes us pretty unpopular with them, and it makes the Reapers none too popular with us," she added. "We didn't need the original Reapers. And we certainly don't need Reapers spawning out there."

"Seriously," Jason muttered. "There're already enough Cubs fans in Chicago."

Michael coughed, but the cough sounded a lot like, "Northside."

I arched an eyebrow, and returned my glance to Scout. "Northside?"

"Where the Cubs are," she said. "They're territorial."

"I see. So, what do you do about the evangelizing? About the Reaper spawn, I mean?"

"Well, we *are* the good guys," Michael said. "They're bullies, and we're a nuisance. We make it harder for them to do their jobs—to recruit, to brainwash, to convince kids with magic that they can keep their powers and live long, fulfilling lives as soul-sucking zombies."

"We thwart with extreme prejudice," Scout said with a grin. "Right now, we're doing a lot of protecting targets, and a lot of befriending the gifted who haven't yet been turned toward the dark side."

"A lot of things that get you chased," I pointed out, giving Scout a pointed look.

"That is true," she said with a nod. "Reapers are tenacious little suckers. We spend a lot of time keeping ourselves alive."

I crossed my legs beneath the thin blanket. "Then maybe you shouldn't have let them into St. Sophia's."

Scout snorted. "We didn't *let* them in. The tunnels beneath the convent connect it to half the buildings in the Loop. Welcome to the Pedway."

"How many of them are there?" I asked.

"We think about two hundred," Scout said. "Sounds like a lot, but Chicago is the third-biggest city in the country. Two hundred out of nearly three million isn't a lot. And we don't really have an 'in' with them, obviously, so two hundred's only a best guess."

"And you guys?"

"This month, we're holding steady at twenty-seven identified Adepts in and around Chicago," Michael said. "That includes Junior Varsity—high schoolers—and Varsity. V-squad is for the college Adepts, their last chance to play wizard and warlock before it's time to return to a life of mundane living. We're organized into enclaves in and around the city. Headquarters, kind of."

Another puzzle piece fell into place. "That's what the symbols on the buildings in the model room mean." My voice rose a little in excitement. "There was a *Y* in a circle, and these kind of combined circles, sort of like a cross. Those are enclave locations?"

"Those circle things are called 'quatrefoils,'" Michael said. "The *Y* symbol indicates enclave and sanctuary locations—that's where the Reapers plan their minion baiting—around the city. There are six enclaves in Chicago. St. Sophia's is Enclave Three."

"Or ET, as the idiots like to call it," Scout added with a grin, bobbing her head toward the boys.

Jason lifted his gaze to mine, and there was concern there. "Did you say you've been to the city room?" He looked over at Scout, and this time his gaze was accusatory. "You let her into the city room?"

"I didn't let her in," Scout defended. "I wasn't even there. The preps found the room and led her down there, locked her in."

Jason put his hands on his hips. He was definitely not happy. "Regulars know about the city room?"

"I told you people would get through," Scout said.

"Not all the tunnels are blocked off. I told you this was going to happen eventually."

"Not now," Michael interjected. "We don't need to talk about this right now."

A little tension there, I guessed. "Why the tunnels in the first place?" I wondered. "If Reapers are out to suck the souls from humans and keep you guys from getting in their way, why don't they just bust through the front door of St. Sophia's and take out the school?"

"We may be a splinter cell," Jason said, "but we've got one thing in common with the Reapers—no one wants to be outed to the public. We don't want to deal with the chaos, and Reapers like being able to steal a soul here and there without a lot of public attention."

"People probably wouldn't take that very well," I said.

"Exactly," Scout agreed with a nod. "Reapers don't want to be locked up in the crazy house—or experimented on—any more than we do. So we keep our fights out of the public eye. We keep them underground, or at least off the streets. We usually make it out and back without problems, but they've been aggressive lately. More aggressive than usual," she muttered.

I remembered what Scout had told me about their long, exhausting summer. I guessed ornery, magic-wielding teenagers could do that to a girl.

"They have given chase a lot lately," Jason said. "We're all thinking they must be up to something."

The room got quiet, the three of them, maybe contemplating just what the Reapers might be up to. Then they looked at me expectantly, maybe waiting for a reaction—tears or disbelief or enthusiasm. But I still had questions.

"Do you look forward to it?" I asked.

Scout tilted her head. "To what?"

"To giving up your powers?" I uncrossed my legs and buried my toes in the blanket—this place was as frosty as St. Sophia's. "I mean, you've got costs and benefits either way, right? Right now, you all have some kind of power. You hit puberty, and you get used to being all magically inclined, but then you have to give it up. Doesn't that bother you?"

They exchanged glances. "It's the way it is," Scout quietly said. "Magic is part of who we are now, but it won't be part of us forever."

"But neither will midnight meetings and obnoxious Reapers and power-happy Varsity Adepts."

Scout lifted her eyebrows at Jason's mini-tirade.

"I know," Jason said. "Not the time."

I guessed things weren't entirely hunky-dory in Enclave Three. "So the guy that blasted me, or whatever. You said his name was Sebastian. And he's a Reaper."

Scout nodded. "That's him."

"He said something before he blasted me. What was that?"

"*Ad meloria*," Michael said. "It's Latin. Means 'toward better things.'"

I raised my eyebrows. "I'm guessing that's their motto."

"You'd be right," Scout said. "They think the world would be a better place if they kept their magic. They think they're the elite, and everyone should give them their due. A survival of the fittest kind of thing."

"Survival of the craziest, more like," Jason muttered. He glanced down at his watch, then looked up at Michael. "We probably need to head," he said, then glanced at me. "Sorry to leave you in here. We've got some stuff at MA this afternoon."

"No problem. Thanks for coming by. And thanks for the flower."

He stuck his hands into his pockets and grinned back at me. "No problem, Parker. Glad you've rejoined the land of the living."

I grinned back at him, at least until Scout's throat clearing pulled my attention away.

"I should also head back," she said, pulling a mas-

sive, baffled down jacket off the back of her chair. She
squeezed into it, then fastened the clips that held it together. The white jacket went past her knees, which made
it look like she had on nothing but tights and thick-soled
Dr. Martens Mary Janes beneath it.

"You look like the Pillsbury Snow Boy."

She rolled her eyes. "It's breezy out there today. Not
all of us have these warm, lush accommodations to look
forward to."

I snuggled into the bed, thinking I'd better gather
what warmth I could, given the possibility that I'd be
returning to my meat locker of a room tomorrow.

"Take care," Michael said, rapping his knuckles on
the tray at the end of the bed. I assumed that was the
macho-guy equivalent of giving me a hug. Either way, I
appreciated the gesture.

I smiled back at him. "I'm sure I'll see you soon."

"And hopefully under better circumstances." He cast
Scout a sideways glance. "Green."

She rolled her eyes. "Garcia." When she looked at me
again, she was smiling. "I'll give you a call later."

I nodded.

The trio gathered up their things, and I clenched my
fingers, itching to ask one final question. Well, scared to
ask it, anyway. My palms were actually sweating, but I
made myself get it out.

"Jason."

They all turned back at the sound of his name.

He arched his eyebrows. "Yeah?"

"Could I talk to you for a sec?"

"Um, sure." He shouldered his backpack, then exchanged a glance with Scout and Michael. She winged
up her brows, but let Garcia push her toward and out
the door.

When the door shut behind them, Jason glanced back
at me. "Everything okay?"

"Oh, yeah." I frowned down at the blanket for a minute before finally raising my gaze to his crystal blue eyes.

"Listen, I just wanted to say thanks. For getting me out of the basement, I mean. If it hadn't been for you and Scout—"

"You wouldn't have gotten hit in the first place," he finished.

I opened my mouth, then closed it again, not really able to argue that point.

"I'm glad you're okay," he softly said. "And for what it's worth, you're welcome, Lily."

I liked the way he said my name, as if it weren't just a series of letters, but a word thick with meaning. *Lily.*

"I mean, I'm not glad you got wrapped up in this—especially since you don't have magic to defend yourself with." He tipped his head to the side. "Although, I think I heard something about a flip-flop?"

"I guess Scout's been giving up all my offensive moves?"

He crossed his arms over his chest. "And impressive moves they are. I mean, who'd have thought that a few square inches of foam were really a technologically advanced—"

"All right, Shepherd. You've made your point."

"Have I?" he asked, with a half smile.

Turned out, Jason's half smile was even more deadly than the full, dimpled grin. The half smile was drowsier—almost ridiculously handsome.

"You did," I finally said.

We stared silently at each other for a moment before he bobbed his head toward the door. "I guess I should join Scout and Michael?"

He made it a question, as if he didn't want to leave, but could sense my nerves. Heart pounding fiercely in my chest, I stopped him. "Actually, one more thing."

He raised questioning brows.

"When we were down there in the basement. When I got hit. I thought—I thought I heard a growl. Like an animal."

His eyes widened, lips parting in surprise. He hadn't

expected me to bring it up, but I couldn't get the sound out of my mind.

Jason hadn't yet given me an answer, so I pressed on. I knew the growling hadn't come from Scout—she'd admitted to being a spellbinder. And I didn't think it had come from earthquake girl or firespell boy. Jason was the only other person there.

"That sound," I said. "Was it you?"

He gazed at me, a chill in his blue eyes, shards of icy sapphire.

"Scout gave you the simple answer about Adepts," he finally said. "She told you that we each have magic, a gift of our own. That's a short answer, but it's not entirely accurate." He paused, then wet his lips. "I'm not like the others."

My heart thudded so fiercely, I wouldn't have been surprised if he could hear it. It took me a moment to ask him. "How much not like them?"

When Jason looked up at me again, the color of his eyes had shifted to green and then to a silvered yellow, like those of a cat caught in the light. And there was something wolfish in his expression.

"Enough," he said, and I'd swear his voice was thicker, deeper. "Different enough."

He turned to go.

My heart didn't stop pounding until the door closed behind him.

10

The room was quiet after the triplets left, at least for a few minutes. The doctor finally visited and looked me over, and reached the same conclusion that had been passed along earlier—I was fine. Notably, he didn't ask me what threat sent me from an all-girls' private school to a hospital.

Whatever he knew, I had hours yet to kill in the hospital. For the first ten minutes, I flipped my cell phone over and over in my hand, trying to gather up the nerve to call Ashley. But she was probably still in class and, besides, what was I going to tell her? That I'd met some magical weirdos who'd managed to rope me into their shenanigans? I wasn't crazy about the idea of that conversation, or how I was going to explain it without sounding completely loopy—so I put the phone down again and glanced around the room. Since no one had brought me homework—and I wasn't about to ask for any—I turned on the television bolted to the wall, settled back into the bed, and had just started watching a reality show about bored, rich housewives when there was a knock at the door.

I had no idea who else would visit—other than brat packers hoping to gloat about their victory—but I pointed the remote at the television and turned it off.

"Come in," I said.

The door opened and closed, followed by the sound

of heels clacking on the tile floor. Foley appeared from around the corner, hands clasped before her, a tidy, pale suit on her slender frame, ash-blond hair tidy at her shoulders. Her expression was all business.

"Ms. Parker." Foley walked to the window, pushed aside a couple of the slats in the blinds, and glanced out at the city. "How are you feeling?"

"Good, considering."

"You lost consciousness," she said. Said, not asked.

"That's what I hear."

"Yes, well. I trust, Ms. Parker, that you understand the importance of our institution's reputation, and of the value of discretion. We, of course, do not wish to elicit untoward attention regarding the hijinks of our students. It would not serve St. Sophia's, nor its students or alumnae, for the community or the press to believe that our institution is not a safe place for its students."

I don't know what she knew about what went on—or what she thought went on—but she was certainly keen on keeping it quiet.

"I also trust that you understand well enough the importance of caring for your physical well-being, and that you will take sufficient care to ensure that you do not lose consciousness again."

That made me sit up a little straighter. What did she think—that I was starving myself and I'd passed out for lack of food? If only she'd seen the private moment I shared with the pudding cup earlier.

"I take care of myself," I assured her.

"All evidence to the contrary."

Okay, honestly, there was a tiny part of me that wanted to rat on Scout, Jason, Michael, and the rest of the Adepts, or at least on the brat packers who threw me into harm's way. It would have been satisfying to wipe that smug expression from Foley's face, and replace it with something a bit more sympathetic.

There were two problems with that theory.

First, I wasn't entirely sure Foley was capable of sympathy.

Second, I had to be honest. I hadn't gone downstairs because Veronica and the rest of her cronies had forced me. And I'd made my way down the other hallway—and into the Reapers' path—because I'd decided to play junior explorer. I'd been curious, and I'd walked that plank willingly.

Besides, I could have walked away from all of it earlier. I could have stepped aside, told Jason, Michael, and Scout that I didn't want to be included in their magical mystery tour, and let them handle their Reaper problems on their own. But I'd invited their trust by asking them to fill me in, and I wasn't about to betray it.

So this time, I'd take one for the team. But Scout *so* owed me.

"You're right," I told her. Her eyes instantaneously widened, as if she were surprised a teenager would agree with her orders. "It's been a stressful week." Total truth. "I should take better care of myself."

She lifted her eyebrows. "That's a surprisingly mature attitude."

"I'm surprisingly mature." It wasn't that I wanted to snark back to the principal of my high school, the head honcho (honchess?) of the place I lived, slept, ate, and learned. But her attitude, her assumption that I was here because I lacked some fundamental ability to keep myself safe, practically begged for snark.

On the other hand, since I'd made the decision to move deeper into the convent instead of heading back to my room, maybe I did.

Foley lifted her brows, and her expression made her thoughts on my snark pretty clear. "Ms. Parker, we take the well-being of our students and the reputation of our institution very seriously."

Given what was going on beneath her institution, I wondered about that. But I managed to keep my mouth shut.

"I expect you'll return to St. Sophia's tomorrow?"

"That's what they say."

Foley nodded. "Very well. I've asked Ms. Green to gather your assignments. Given that tomorrow's Saturday, you'll have some time to complete them before classes resume. I'll arrange for a car to transport you back to St. Sophia's. If you require anything before your return, you may contact our staff."

I nodded. Her work apparently done, she walked toward the door. But then she glanced back.

"About our conversation," she said, "perhaps I was . . . ill informed about your parents' professions."

I stared at her for a few seconds, trying to make sense of the about-face. "Ill informed?"

"I recognize that you, of course, would know better than I the nature of your parents' work." She glanced down at her watch. "I need to return to the school. Enjoy your evening."

My mind began to race, but I managed to bob my head as she disappeared around the corner, then opened and closed the door again.

I stared down at the remote control in my hand for a minute after she'd left, flipping it through my fingers as I ruminated.

It was weird enough that she'd dropped by in the first place—I mean, how many high school principals visited their students in the hospital? She clearly had her own theories about what had happened to me—namely, that it was my fault. I guess she wanted to cover her bases, make sure I wasn't going to spill to the media or call a lawyer about my "accident."

But then, out of the blue, she brought up my parents and changed her story? And even weirder, she actually seemed sincere. Contrite, even, and Foley didn't exactly seem like the nurturing type, much less the type to admit when she was wrong.

I gnawed the edge of my lip and gave the remote a final flip. Call it what you want—Reapers, Adepts,

magic, firespell, whatever. Things were seriously weird
at St. Sophia's.

True to the doc's word, I was released the next morning.
True to Foley's word, one of the glasses-clad matrons who
usually patrolled the study hall brought casual clothes for
me to change into—jeans and a T-shirt, probably selected
by Scout—and signed me out. A nurse wheeled me, invalid
style, to the front door of the clinic and the St. Sophia's-
branded minivan that sat at the curb. The matron was silent
on the way back to the convent, but it was a pretty short
ride—only a few blocks back to my new home on Erie.
They dropped me off at the front door without a word,
and I headed up the stairs and into the building. Although
I'd been gone only a couple of days, the convent seemed
almost . . . foreign. It hadn't yet begun to feel like home,
but now, it felt farther from Sagamore than ever.

It was a Saturday afternoon, and the main building
was all but empty. A handful of students peppered the
study hall, maybe catching up on weekend homework or
trying to get ahead to pad their academic resumes. The
halls that held the suites were louder, music and television spilling into the hallway as St. Sophia's girls relaxed
and enjoyed the weekend.

I unlocked the door to our suite. Scout jumped up
from the couch, decked out in jeans and layered T-shirts,
her hair pulled into a short ponytail, and practically
knocked me over to get in a hug.

"Thank God," she said. "The brat packers were getting almost unbearable." She let me go, then gave me an
up-and-down appraisal. "Is everything where I left it?"

"Last time I checked," I said with a smile, then waved
at Barnaby, who sat on the couch behind us. She wore a
fitted pale blue T-shirt with a rainbow across the front,
and her hair was up in some kind of complicated knot. It
was very *Sound of Music*.

"Hello, Lily," she said.

"Hi, Lesley."

The door to Amie's suite opened. Amie, M.K., and Veronica piled out of the room, their smiles fading as they realized I'd come home. They were all dressed in athletic shorts, snug tank tops, and sneakers. I assumed it was workout time.

Amie's smile faded to an expression that was a lot heavier on the contrition and apology. M.K.'s smile was haughty. Veronica was using both hands to pull her hair into a ponytail. I wasn't even on her radar.

"You were in the hospital," M.K. said. There was no apology behind her words, no indication that she thought they might have been responsible for anything that happened to me. They weren't, of course, responsible, but they didn't know that. I'd hoped for something a little more contrite, honestly—maybe something in a nice "sheepish embarrassment."

"Yep," I said.

"What happened to you?" M.K. had apparently skipped embarrassment and gone right to being accusatory.

"I'm not at liberty to say," I told them.

"Why? Is it catching?" M.K. snickered at her joke. "Something contagious?"

"There are certain . . . liability issues," I said, then looked over at Amie. She was the worrywart of the group, so I figured she was my most effective target. "Insurance issues. Parental liability issues. Probably best not to talk about it. We don't want to have to get the lawyers involved. Not yet, anyway."

Scout, half turning so that only I could see her, winked at me.

Veronica and Amie exchanged a nervous glance.

"But thanks for the tour," I added as I headed for my bedroom. I unlocked the door, then stood there as Scout and Barnaby skipped inside.

"It was very educational," I said, then winked at the brat pack, walked inside, and closed the door behind us.

As dramatic exits went, it wasn't bad.

I gave Scout and Lesley a mini-update, at least the parts I could talk about in Lesley's company. Lesley wasn't an Adept, at least as far as I was aware, so I kept my replay of Foley's visit and my chat with Jason purely PG. But I shooed them out of my room pretty quickly.

I needed a shower.

A superhot, superlong, environmentally irresponsible shower. As soon as they were out the door, I changed into my reversible robe (stripes for perky days, deep blue for serious ones), grabbed my bucket o' toiletries, and headed for the bathroom.

I spent the first few minutes with my hands against the wall, my head dunked under the spray. The heat probably didn't do much good for my hair, but I needed it. I had basement and hospital grime to wash off, not to mention the emotional grime of (1) more of Foley's questioning of my parents' honesty; (2) having been unconscious and apparently near death for twelve hours; (3) having been the victim of a prank that led to point number two; and (4) having been carried out of a dangerous situation by a ridiculously pretty boy and having almost *no* memory of it whatsoever. That last one was just a crime against nature.

And, of course, there was the other thing.

The magic thing.

Varsity, Junior Varsity, Adepts, firespell, Reapers, enclaves. These people had their own vocabulary and apparently a pretty strong belief that they had magical powers.

Sure, I'd seen *something*. And whatever was going on beneath St. Sophia's, beneath the city, I wasn't about to rat them out. But still—what had I seen? Was it really magic? I mean—*magic*, as in unicorns and spells and wizards and witchcraft magic?

That, I wasn't so sure about.

I gave it some thought as I repacked my gear and padded back to the room in my shower shoes, then waved at Scout and Lesley, who were playing cards in the common room. I gave it some thought as I scrubbed my hair dry, pulled flannel pajama bottoms from the drawer of my bureau, and got dressed again.

There was a single, quick rap at the door. I turned around to face it, but the knocking stopped, replaced by a pink packet that appeared beneath my door. I hung the damp towel on the closet doorknob, then plucked the packet from the floor. Out of an abundance of caution—I couldn't be too sure these days—I held it up to my ear. When I was pretty sure it wasn't ticking, I slipped a finger beneath the tab of tape that held the sides together.

And smiled.

Wrapped in the pink paper—that could only have come from Amie's room—was the rest of the bag of licorice Scotties I'd started on before my trip to the basement. I wasn't sure if the gift was supposed to be an apology or a bribe.

Either way, I thought, as I nipped the head from another unfortunate Scottie, I liked it.

Unfortunately, as I had realized on my way to pick up the Scotties, my knees still ached from the double falls on the limestone floor. I put my prize on the bureau, rolled up my pants legs, and moved in front of the mirror to check them out. Purple bruises bloomed on my kneecaps, evidence of my run-in with . . . well, whatever they were.

My back had cramped as I rolled the hems of my pants down. I twisted halfway around in the mirror, then tugged up the back of the Ramones T-shirt I'd paired with my flannel pajama bottoms to check out the place where the firespell had hit me. I expected to see another bruise, some indication of the force that had pushed me to the floor and knocked the breath from my lungs.

There was no bruise, at least that I could see from my position—half-turned as I was to face the mirror, one hip cocked out, neck twisted. I almost dropped the bottom of my shirt and went on my merry way—straight into bed with the coffee table's *Vogue*.

But then I saw it.

My heart skipped a beat, something tightening in my chest.

At the small of my back was a mark. It wasn't a bruise—the color wasn't right. It wasn't the purple or blue or even that funny yellow that bruises take on.

It was green. Candy apple green—the same color as the firespell that had bitten into my skin.

More important, there was a defined shape. It was a symbol—a glyph on the small on my back, like a tattoo I hadn't asked for.

It was a circle with some complicated set of symbols inside it.

I'd been marked.

11

I stood in front of the mirror for fifteen minutes, worrying about the mark on my back. I turned this way and that, my hem rolled up in my hands, neck aching as I stretched until I thought to grab a compact from my makeup bag. I flipped it open, turned around, and aimed it at the mirror.

It wasn't just a mark, or a freckle, or a weird wrinkle caused by lounging in a hospital bed for twenty-four hours.

It was a circle—a perfect circle. A circle too perfect to be an accident. Too perfect to be anything but purposeful. And inside the circle were symbols—squiggles and lines, all distinct, but not organized in any pattern that looked familiar to me.

But still, even though I didn't know what they meant, I could tell what they *weren't*. The lines were clear, the shapes distinct. They were much too perfect to be a biological accident.

I frowned and dropped my arm, staring in confusion at the floor. Where had it come from? Had something happened to me when I was unconscious? Had I been tattooed by an overeager ER doctor?

Or was the answer even simpler . . . and more complex?

The mark was in the same place I'd been hit with the

firespell, where that rush of heat and fire (and magic) thrown by Sebastian had roared up my spine.

I had no idea *how* firespell could have had anything to do with the symbol, but what else could it have been? What else would have put it there?

Without warning, there was a knock at the door. Instinctively, I flipped the compact shut and pulled down my T-shirt. "Yeah?"

"Hey," Scout said from the other side of the closed door. "We're going to grab a Rainbow Cone at a place down the street. You wanna come with? It's only three or four blocks. Might be nice to get some fresh air?"

Something in my stomach turned over, maybe at the realization that, at some point, I'd have to tell Scout about the mark and enlist her help to figure out what it was. That didn't sit well. Her telling me about her adventures was one thing. My being part of those adventures and part of this whole magic thing—being permanently marked by it—was something else.

"No, thanks," I said, giving the closed door the guilty look I couldn't stand to give Scout. "I'm not feeling so great, so I think I'm just going to rest for a little while."

"Oh, okay. Do you want us to bring some back?"

"Uh, no thanks. I'm not really hungry." That was the absolute truth.

She was quiet for a minute. "Are you okay in there?" she finally asked.

"Yeah. Just, you know, tired. I didn't get much sleep in the hospital." Also the truth, but I felt bad enough that I crossed my fingers, anyway.

"Okay. Well, take a nap, maybe," she suggested. "We'll check in later."

"Thanks, Scout," I said. When footsteps echoed across the suite, I turned and pressed my back against the door and blew out a breath.

What had I gotten myself into?

True to my word, I climbed into bed, pulling the twin-spired symbols of St. Sophia's over my head as I tried, unsuccessfully, to nap. I'd been supportive of Scout and the Adept story in the hospital. I'd made a commitment to believe them, to believe in them, even when Foley showed up. I'd also made a commitment not to let the basement drama—whatever it was about—affect my friendship with Scout.

And now I was in my room, head buried in cotton and flannel, hiding out.

Some friend I was.

Every five minutes, I'd touch the tips of my fingers gingerly to the bottom of my spine, thinking I'd be able to feel some change when, and if, the mark disappeared. Every fifteen minutes, I'd climb out of bed and twist around in front of the mirror, making sure the mark hadn't decided to fade.

There was no change.

At least, not physically. Emotionally, I was freaking out. And not the kind of freaking out that lent itself to finding a friend and venting. This was the kind of freaking out that was almost . . . *paralyzing*. The kind of fear that made you hunker down, avoid others, avoid the issue.

And so I lay in bed, sunlight shifting across the room as the day slipped away. The suite being relatively small, I heard Scout and Lesley return, mill about in the common room, and then head into their respective bedrooms. They eventually left for dinner, after a prospective knock on the door to see if I wanted anything. For the second time, I declined. I could hear Scout's disappointment—and fear—when she double-checked, but I wasn't up for company. I wasn't up for providing consolation.

I needed to be consoled.

Eventually, I fell asleep. Scout didn't bother knocking for breakfast on Sunday morning. Not that I could blame her, I supposed, since I'd ignored her for the last twenty-four hours, but her absence was still noticeable. She'd become a fixture during my first week at St. Sophia's.

I snuck down to breakfast in jeans and my Ramones T-shirt, my hair in a messy knot, the ribboned key around my neck. I wasn't dressed for brunch or socializing, so I grabbed a carrot raisin muffin and a box of orange juice before heading back to my room, bounty in hand.

What a difference a day makes.

It was around noon when they knocked on the door.

When I didn't answer, Amie's voice rang out. "Lily? Are you in there? Are you . . . okay?"

I closed the art history book I'd been perusing in bed, went to the door, opened it, and found Amie and Veronica, both in jeans, brown leather boots, snug tops, and dangly earrings, standing there. Not bad outfits, actually, if you ignored the prissiness.

The last time they'd sought me out, they offered a chance to go treasure hunting. The offer this time wasn't much different.

"We're really sorry about what happened," Amie said. "We're heading to Michigan Avenue for a little shopping. Are you up for a field trip?"

I was an intelligent person, so my first instinct was, of course, to slam the door in their faces. But as they stood there in my doorway, hair perfect, makeup just so, they offered me something else.

Oblivion.

The opportunity to pretend to be an It Girl for a little while, in a world with much simpler rules, where what you wore meant more than how many Reapers you'd thwarted, how much firespell had taken you down.

Call it a weak moment, a moment of denial. Either way, I said yes.

Twenty minutes later, I was in boots and leggings, black skirt, black fitted shirt, jacket and drapey scarf, and I was following Amie and Veronica out the door and toward Michigan Avenue. We strode side by side down the sidewalk—Amie, then me, then Veronica—as though we were acting out the opening credits of a new teen drama.

Even on a Sunday, Michigan Avenue was full of tourists and locals, young and old, shoppers and picture-snappers, all out to enjoy the weather before the cold began to roll in. It was understandable that they were out—the sky was ridiculously blue, the temperature perfect. Windy City or not, there was just enough breeze to keep the sun from being oppressive.

This was my first time on Michigan Avenue, my first opportunity to explore Chicago beyond the walls of St. Sophia's (apart from my quick jaunt around the block with Scout). I was surprised at how open Chicago felt—less constricting, less overwhelming, than walking through the Village or midtown Manhattan. There was more glass, less concrete; more steel, less brick. With the shine of new condos and the reflection of Lake Michigan off mirrored glass, the Second City looked like Manhattan's younger, prettier sister.

We passed boutique after boutique, the chichi stores nestled between architectural masterpieces—the ribbon-wrapped Hancock Building, the castlelike form of the Water Tower and, of course, lots of construction.

"So," Amie said, "are you going to tell us exactly what went on in the basement?"

"What basement?" I asked, my gaze on the high-rises above us.

"Coyness is not becoming," Veronica said. "You were in the basement, and then you were in the hospital. We know those things happened." She slid me a sideways glance. "Now we want to know how they connect."

Sure, I was taking a breather from Scout and the rest of the Adepts, but I wasn't about to rat them out, especially to brat packers. Trying to be normal for a few minutes was one thing; becoming a fink was something else entirely.

"I fell," I told her, stating the absolute truth. "I was on my way back upstairs, and I slipped. The edges of those limestone stairs to the first floor, you know how they're warped?"

"You'd think they could fix those," Amie said.

"You'd think," I agreed.

"Uh-huh," Veronica said, doubt in her voice. "They sent you to the hospital because you fell down the stairs?"

"Because I was knocked unconscious," I reminded them with a bright smile. "And had I not been down in the basement in the first place . . ."

I didn't finish the sentence, letting the blame remain unspoken. Apparently, that was a good strategy. When I glanced over at Veronica, she was smiling appreciatively, as if my reminder of their culpability was just the kind of strategy she'd have used.

Suddenly, as if we were the best of friends, Veronica linked her arm in mine, then steered me in and through the pedestrian traffic.

"In here," she said, bobbing her head toward a shopping center on the west side of the street. It was three stories high, the front wall a giant window of mannequins and clothing displays. A coffee bar filled most of the first floor, while giant hanging sculptures—brightly colored teardrops of glass—rained down from the three-story atrium.

"Nice place," I said, my gaze rising as I surveyed the glass.

"It's not bad," Veronica said. "And the shopping's pretty good, too."

"Pretty good" might have been an understatement. The stores that spanned the corridors weren't the kind of places where you dropped in to pick up socks. These were *investment* stores. Once-in-a-lifetime stores. Stores with clothes and bags that most shoppers saved months or years for.

Amie and Veronica were not your average shoppers. We spent three hours working our way down from the third floor to the first, checking out stores, trying on clothes, posing in front of mirrors in clunky shoes, tiny jeans, and Ikat prints. I bought nothing; I had the emergency credit card, but buying off the rack didn't have much appeal. There was no *hunt* in buying off the rack, no thrill of finding a kick-ass bag or pair of shoes for an incredible discount. With occasional exceptions, I was a vintage and thrift store kind of girl—a handbag huntress.

Amie and Veronica, on the other hand, bought *everything*. They found must-haves in almost every store we stopped in: monogram-print leather bags, wedge-heeled boots with elflike slits in the top, leggings galore, stilettos with heels so skinny they'd have made excellent weaponry . . . or better weaponry than flip-flops, anyway. The amount of money they spent was breathtaking, and neither of them so much as looked at the receipts. Cost was not a factor. They picked out what they wanted and, without hesitation, handed it over to eager store clerks.

Although I put a little more thought into the financial part of shopping, I couldn't fault their design sensibilities. They may have been dressed like traditional brat packers for their excursion to Magnificent Mile, but these girls knew fashion—what was hot, and what was on its way up.

Even better, maybe because they were missing out on Mary Katherine's obnoxiously sarcastic influence, Amie and Veronica were actually pleasant. Sure, we didn't have a discussion in our three-hour, floor-to-floor mall survey that didn't involve clothes or money or who's-seeing-whom gossip, but I had wanted oblivion. Turned out, trying to keep straight the intermingled dating lives of St. Sophia's girls and the Montclare boys they hooked up with was a fast road to oblivion. I barely thought about the little green circle on my back, but even self-induced oblivion couldn't last forever.

We were on the stairs, heading toward the first floor with glossy, tissue-stuffed shopping bags in hand, when I saw him.

Jason Shepherd.

My heart nearly stopped.

Not just because it was Jason, but because it was Jason in jeans that pooled over chunky boots, and a snug, faded denim work shirt. Do you have any idea what wearing blue did for a boy with already ridiculously blue eyes? It was like his irises glowed, like they were lit by blue fire from within. Add that to a face already too pretty for anyone's good, and you had a dangerous combination. The boy was completely *en fuego*.

Jason was accompanied by a guy who was cute in a totally different kind of way. This one had thick, dark hair, heavy eyebrows, deep-set brown eyes, a very intense look. He wore glasses with thick, black frames and hipster-chic clothes: jacket over T-shirt; dark jeans; black Chuck Taylors.

I blew out a breath, remembered the symbol on the small of my back, and decided I wasn't up for handsome Adepts or their buddies any more than I had been for funky, nose-ringed spellbinders. Mild panic setting in, I planned my exit.

"Hey," I told Amie, as we reached the first floor, "I'm going to run in there." I hitched a thumb over my shoulder.

Amie glanced behind me, then lifted her eyebrows. "You're going to the orthopedic shoe store?"

Okay, so I really should have looked before I pointed. "I like to be prepared."

"For your future orthopedic shoe needs?"

"Podiatric health is very important."

"Veronica!"

Frick. Too late. I muttered a curse and looked over. Jason's friend saluted.

I risked a glance Jason's way and found blue eyes on me, but I couldn't stand the intimacy of his gaze. It seemed wrong to share a secret in front of people who knew nothing about it, nothing about the world that existed beneath our feet. And then there was the guilt about having abandoned Scout for Louis Vuitton and BCBG that was beginning to weigh on my shoulders. I looked away.

"That's John Creed," Veronica whispered as they walked over. "He's president of the junior class at Montclare. But I don't know the other guy."

I didn't tell her that I knew him well enough, that he'd carried me from danger, and that he was maybe, *possibly*, a werewolf.

"Veronica Lively," said the hipster. His voice was slow, deep, methodical. "I haven't seen you in forever. Where have you been hiding?"

"St. Sophia's," she said. "It's where I live and play."

"John Creed," said the boy, giving me a nod in greeting, "and this is Jason Shepherd. But I don't know you." He gave me a smile that was a little too coy, a little too self-assured.

"How unfortunate for you," I responded with a flat smile, and watched his eyebrows lift in appreciation.

"Lily Parker," Veronica said, bobbing her head toward me, then whipping away the cup John held in his hand. She took a sip.

"John Creed, who is currently down one smoothie," he said, crossing his arms over his chest. "Lively, I believe you owe me a drink."

A sly grin on her face, Veronica took another sip before handing it back to him. "Don't worry," she said. "There's plenty left."

John made a sarcastic sound, then began quizzing her about friends they had in common. I took the opportunity to steal a glance at Jason, and found him staring back at me, head tilted. He was clearly wondering why I was acting as if I didn't know him, and where I'd left Scout.

I looked away, guilt flooding my chest.

"So, new girl," John suddenly said, and I looked his way. "What brings you to St. Sophia's?"

"My parents are in Germany."

"Intriguing. Vacation? Second home?"

"Sabbatical."

John raised his eyebrows. "Sabbatical," he repeated. "As in, a little plastic surgery?"

"As in, a little academic research."

His expression suggested he wasn't convinced my parents were studying, as opposed to a more lurid, rich-folks activity, but he let it go. "I see. Where'd you go to school? Before you became a St. Sophia's girl, I mean."

"Upstate New York."

"New York," he repeated. "How exotic."

"Not all that exotic," I said, twirling a finger to point out the architecture around us. "And you Midwesterners seem to do things pretty well."

A smile blossomed on John Creed's face, but there was still something dark in his eyes—something melancholy. Melancholy or not, the words that came out of his mouth were still very teenage boy.

"Even Midwesterners appreciate . . . pretty things," he said, his gaze traveling from my boots to my knot of dark hair. When he reached my gaze again, he gave me a knowing smile. It was a compliment, I guessed, that he thought I looked good, but coming from him, that compliment was a little creepy.

"Cool your jets, Creed," Veronica interrupted. "And before this conversation crosses a line, we should get back to campus. Curfew," she added, then offered Jason a coy smile. "Nice to meet you, Jason."

"Same here," he said, bobbing his head at her, then glancing at me. "Lily."

I bobbed my head at him, a flush rising on my cheeks, and wished I'd stayed in my room.

12

I'd spared myself a confrontation with Scout earlier in the day. Since she and Lesley were playing cards at the coffee table when I returned to the suite, two brat packers in line behind me, my time for avoidance was up.

I stopped short in the doorway when I saw them, Amie and Veronica nearly ramming me in the back.

"Down in front," Veronica muttered, squeezing through the door around me, bringing a tornado of shopping bags into the common room.

Scout glanced up when I opened the door. At first, she seemed excited to see me. But when she realized who'd followed me in, her expression morphed into something significantly nastier.

I probably deserved that.

"Shopping?" she asked, an eyebrow arched as Amie and Veronica skirted the couch on their way to Amie's room.

"Fresh air," I said.

Scout made a disdainful sound, shook her head, and dropped her gaze to the fan of cards in her hand. "I think it's your turn," she told Lesley, her voice flat.

Lesley looked up at me. "You were out—with them?"

Barnaby wasn't much for subtlety.

"Fresh air," Scout repeated, then put a card onto the table with a *snap* of sound. "Lily needed *fresh air*."

Amie unlocked her bedroom door and moved inside.

But before Veronica went in, she stopped and gazed back at me. "Are you coming?"

"Yes," Scout bit out, flipping one card, then a second and third, onto the table. "You should go. You have shoes to try on, Carrie, or Miranda, or whoever you're pretending to be today."

Veronica snorted, her features screwing into that rat-like pinch. "Better than hanging out here with geeks 'r' us."

"Geeks 'r' us?" I repeated.

"She uses a bag with a pirate symbol on it," Veronica said. "What kind of Disney fantasy is she living?"

Oh, right, I thought. *That's* why I hated these girls. "And yet," I pointed out, "you hung out with me today. And you know Scout and I are friends."

"All evidence to the contrary," Scout muttered.

"We were giving you the benefit of the doubt," Veronica said.

Scout made a sarcastic sound. "No, Lively, you felt *guilty*."

"Ladies," Barnaby said, standing up to reveal the unicorn-print T-shirt she'd matched with a pleated skirt. "I don't think Lily wants to be fought over. This is beneath all of you."

I forced a nod in agreement—although it wasn't *that* horrible to be fought over.

"Uh-huh," Veronica said, then looked at me. "We did the nice thing, Parker. You're new to St. Sophia's, so we offered to help you out. We gave you a warning, and because you handled our little game in the basement, we gave you a chance."

"So very thoughtful," Scout bit out, "to make her a charity case."

Veronica ignored her. "Fine. You want to be honest? Let's be honest. Friends matter, Parker. And if you're not friends with the right people, the fact that you went to St. Sophia's won't make a damn bit of difference. Even St. Sophia's has its misfits, after all." As if to punctuate her remark, she glanced over at Scout and Lesley, then glanced back at me, one eyebrow raised, willing me to get her point.

I'm not sure if she was better or worse for it, but the bitchiness of her comment aside, there was earnestness in her expression. Veronica believed what she was saying—really, truly believed it. Had Veronica been a misfit once?

Not that the answer was all that important right now. "If you're saying that I have to dump one set of friends in order to keep another," I told her, "I think you know what the answer's going to be."

"There are only two kinds of people in this world," Veronica said. "Friends—and enemies."

Was this girl for real? "I'm willing to take my chances."

She snorted indignantly, then walked into Amie's room. "Your loss," she said, the door shutting with a decided *click* behind her.

The room was quiet for a moment.

I blew out a breath, then glanced over at Scout. Ever so calmly, without saying a word or making eye contact, she laid the rest of her cards flat on the table, stood up, marched into her room, and slammed the door.

The coffee table rattled.

I undraped the scarf from around my neck and dropped onto the couch.

Lesley crossed her legs and sat down on the floor, then began to order the deck of cards into a tidy pile. "Granted," she said, "I've only known you for a couple of days, but that was not the smartest thing you've ever done."

"Yeah, I know."

She bobbed her head toward Scout's closed door, which had begun to rattle with the bass of Veruca Salt's "Seether."

"How ballistic do you think she's gonna be?" I asked, my gaze on the vibrating door.

"Intercontinental missile ballistic."

"Yeah, that's what I figured."

Lesley placed her stack of cards gingerly on the tabletop, then looked over at me. "But you're still going in there, right?"

I nodded. "As soon as I'm ready."

"Anything you want in your eulogy?"

Lesley smiled tightly. I gathered up my scarf, rose from the couch, and headed for Scout's door.

"Just tell my parents I loved them," I said, and reached out my hand to knock.

13

Four minutes later, when Scout finally said, "Come in," I opened the door. Scout was on her bed, legs crossed, a spread of books before her.

She lifted her gaze and arched an eyebrow at me. "Well. Look who we have here."

I managed a half smile.

She closed a book, then uncrossed her legs and rose from the bed. After turning down the stereo to a lowish roar, she moved to her shelves and began straightening the items in her tiny museum. "You want to tell me why you've been avoiding me?"

Because I'm afraid, I silently thought. "I'm not avoiding you."

She glanced over with skeptical eyes. "You ignored me all weekend. You've either been holed up in your room or hanging with the brat pack. And since I know there's no love lost there . . ." She shrugged.

"It's nothing."

"You're freaked out about the magic, aren't you? I knew it. I knew it was going to freak you out." She plucked one of the tiny, glittered houses from a shelf, raised it to eye level, and peered through the tiny window. "I shouldn't have told you. Shouldn't have gotten you wrapped up in it." Shaking her head again, she put the house back onto the shelf and picked up the one beside it.

"You'd think I'd be used to this by now," she said,

suddenly turning around, the second house in her hand. "I mean, it's not like this is the first time someone has walked away because I'm, you know, weird. You think my parents didn't notice that I could do stuff?"

As if proving her point, she adjusted the house so that it sat in the palm of her outstretched hand, then whispered a series of staccato words.

The interior of the house began to glow.

"Look inside," she quietly said.

"Inside?"

Carefully, she placed the illuminated house back on the shelf, then moved to the side so I could stand beside her. I stepped into the space she'd made, then leaned down and peeked into one of the tiny windows.

The house—this tiny, glittered, paper house on Scout's bookshelf—now bustled with activity. Like a dollhouse come to life, holograms of tiny figures moved inside amongst tiny pieces of furniture, like a living snow globe. Furniture lined the walls; lamps glowed with the spark of whatever life she'd managed to breathe into it with the mere sound of her voice.

I stood up again and glanced at her, eyes wide. "You did that?"

Her gaze on the house, she nodded. "That's my talent—I make magic from words. Like you said, from lists. Letters." She paused. "I did it the first time when I was twelve. I mean, not that particular spell; that's just an animation thing, hardly a page of text, and I condensed it a long time ago. That means I made it shorter," she said at my raised brows. "Like zipping a computer file."

"That's . . . amazing," I said, lifting my gaze to the house again. Shadows passed before the tiny glassine windows, lives being lived in miniature.

"Amazing or not, my mother freaked out. My parents made calls, and I was sent right into private school. I was put in a place away from average kids. Put into a home." She lifted her gaze and glanced around the room. "A prison, of sorts."

That explained Scout's tiny museum—the room she'd made her own, the four walls she'd filled with the detritus of her life, from junior high to St. Sophia's. It was her magical respite.

Her cell.

"So, yeah," she said after a moment, waving a hand in front of the paper house, the lights in the windows dimming and fading, a tiny world extinguished. "I'm used to rejection because of my magic."

"It's not you," I quietly said.

Scout barked out a laugh. "Yeah, that's the first time I've heard that one." She straightened the house, adjusting it so that it sat neatly beside its neighbors. "If we're going to break up, let's just get it over with, okay?"

I figured out something about Scout in that moment, something that made my heart clench with protectiveness. However brave she might have been in fighting Reapers, in protecting humans, in running through underground tunnels in the middle of the night, fighting back against fire- and earthquake-bearing baddies, she was very afraid of one thing: that I'd abandon her. She was afraid she'd made a friend who was going to walk away like her parents had done, walk out and leave her alone in her room. That's what finally snapped me out of nearly forty-eight hours of freaking out about something that I knew, without a doubt, was going to change my life forever.

"It's probably nothing," I finally said.

I watched the change in her expression—from preparing for defeat, to relief, to crisis management.

"Tell me," she said.

When I frowned back at her, she glared back at me, daring me to argue.

Recognizing the inevitability of my defeat, I sighed, but turned around and lifted up the back of my shirt.

The room went silent.

"You have a darkening," she said.

"A what? I think it's just a funky bruise or something?" It wasn't, of course, just a funky bruise, but I was willing to cling to those last few seconds of normalcy.

"When did you get it?"

I stepped away from her, pulling down my T-shirt and wrapping my arms around my waist self-consciously. "I don't know. A couple of . . . days ago."

Silence.

"Like, a couple of firespell days ago?"

I nodded.

"You've been marked." Her voice was soft, tremulous.

My fingers still knotted in the hem of the shirt, I glanced behind me. Scout stood there, eyes wide, lips parted in shock. "Scout?"

She shook her head, then looked up at me. "This isn't supposed to happen."

The emotion in her voice—awe—raised the hair on my arms and made my stomach sink. "What isn't supposed to happen?"

She stood up, then frowned and nibbled the edge of her lip; then she walked to one end of the room and back again. She was pacing, apparently trying to puzzle out something. "Right after you got hit by the firespell. But you've never had powers before, and you don't have powers now—" She paused and glanced over at me. "Do you?"

"Are you kidding? Of course I don't."

She resumed talking so quickly, I wasn't sure she'd even heard my answer. "I mean, I guess it's possible." She hit the end of the room and, neatly sideswiping a footlocker, turned around again. "I'd have to check the *Grimoire* to be sure. If you don't have power, then you weren't really triggered, but maybe it's some kind of tattoo from the firespell? I can't imagine how you could have gotten a darkening without the power—"

"Scout."

"But maybe it's happened before."

"*Scout.*" My voice was loud enough that she finally stopped and looked at me.

"Hmm?"

I pointed behind me. "Hello? My back?"

"Right, right." She walked back to me and began to pull up the hem of her shirt.

"Um, I'm not sure stripping down is the solution here, Scout."

"Prude," she said dryly, but when she reached me again, she turned around.

At the small of her back, in pale green, was a mark like mine—well, not exactly like mine. The symbols inside her circle were different, but the general idea was the same.

"Oh, my God," I said.

Scout dropped the back of her T-shirt and turned, nodding her head. "Yep. So I guess it's settled now."

"Settled?"

"You're one of us."

14

Forty minutes—and Scout's rifling through a two-foot-high stack of books—later, we were headed downstairs. If she'd found anything in the giant leather volumes she pulled out of a plastic tub beneath her bed, she didn't say. The only conclusion she'd reached was that she needed to talk to the rest of the Adepts in Enclave Three, so she'd pulled out her phone, popped open the keyboard and, fingers flying, sent out a dispatch. And then we were on our way.

The route we took this time was different still from the last couple of trips I'd made. We used a new doorway to the basement level—this one a wooden panel in a side hallway in the main building—and descended a narrower, steeper staircase. Once we were in the basement, we walked a maze through limestone hallways. I was beginning to think the labyrinth on the floor was more than just decoration. It served as a pretty good symbol of what lay beneath the convent.

Despite how confusing it was, Scout clearly knew the route, barely pausing at the corners, her speed quick and movements efficient. She moved silently, striding through the hallways and tunnels like a woman on a mission. I stumbled at a half run, half walk behind her, just trying to keep up. My speed wasn't much helped by my stomach's rolling, both because we were actually going into the basement again—by choice—and for the reason we were going there.

Because I was her mission.

Or so I assumed.

"You could slow down a little, you know."

"Slowing down would make it harder for me to punish you by making you keep up," she said, but came to a stop as we reached the dead end of a limestone corridor that ended in a nondescript metal door.

"Why are you punishing me?"

Scout reached up, pulled a key from above the threshold, and slipped it into the lock. When the door popped open, she put back the key, then glanced at me. "Um, you abandoned me for the brat pack?"

"Abandoned is a harsh word."

"So are they," she pointed out, holding the door open so I could move inside. "The last time you hung out with them, they put you in the hospital."

"That was actually your fault."

"Details," she said.

My feet still on the limestone, hand on the threshold of the door, I peeked inside. She was leading me into an old tunnel. It was narrow, with an arched ceiling, the entire tunnel paved in concrete, narrow tracks along the concrete floor. Lights in round, industrial fittings were suspended from the ceiling every dozen yards or so. The half illumination didn't do much for the ambience. A couple of inches of rusty water covered the tracks on the floor, and the concrete walls were covered with graffiti—words of every shape and size, big and small, monotone and multicolored.

"What is this?"

"Chicago Tunnel Company Railroad," she said, nudging me forward. I took a step into dirty water, glad I'd worn boots for my shopping excursion, and glad I still had on a jacket. It was chilly, probably because we were underground.

"It's an old railroad line," Scout said, then stepped beside me. Cold, musty air stirred as she closed the door behind us. Somewhere down the line, water dripped.

"The cars used to move between downtown buildings to deliver coal and dump ash and stuff. Parts of the tunnel run under the river, and some of those parts were accidentally breached by the city, so if you see a tsunami, find a bulkhead and make a run for it."

"I'll make a point of it."

Scout reached into her messenger bag and pulled out two flashlights. She took one, then handed me the second. While the tunnels were lit, it made me feel better to have the weight in my hand.

Flashlights in hand, we walked. We took one branch, then another, then another, making so many turns that I had no clue which direction we were actually moving in.

"So this mark thing," I began, as we stepped gingerly through murky water. "What is it, exactly?"

"They're called darkenings. We all have them," Scout answered, the beam of light swinging as she moved. "All the members of the 'Dark Elite,'" she flatly added, using her hands, flashlight and all, to gesture some air quotes. "That's what some of the Reapers call us—all of us— who have magic. Elite, I guess, because we're gifted. They think we're special, *better*, because we have magic. And dark because the darkenings are supposed to appear when the magic appears. Well, except in your case." She stopped and looked at me. "Still no powers, right?"

"Not that I'm aware of, no. Is that why we're down here? Are you going to prod me or poke me or something, to figure out if I have secret powers? Like a chick on an alien spacecraft?"

"And you think I'm the odd one," she muttered. "No, Scully, we aren't going to probe you. We're just going to talk to the Adepts and see what they have to say about your new tat. No bigs." She shrugged nonchalantly, then started walking again.

Ten or fifteen minutes later, Scout stopped before a door made up of giant wooden beams, two golden hinges running across it, an arch in the top. A large numeral "3" was elegantly carved into the lintel above the door. And on the door was the same symbol I'd seen in the model room—a circle with a *Y* inside it.

This was Enclave Three, I assumed.

Scout flipped off her flashlight, then held out her hand; I pressed my flashlight into her palm. She flicked it off and deposited them both back in her messenger bag.

"Okay," she said, looking over at me. "I suppose I should prep you for this. The other seven Adepts in ET should be here. Katie and Smith are our Varsity Adepts. You remember what that means?"

"They're the college kids," I answered. "And Junior Varsity is high school. You just told me on Friday."

"You've brat-packed since then," she muttered. "Your IQ has probably dropped."

I gave her a snarky look.

"Anywho," she said, ignoring the look, "Katie's a manipulator. Literally and figuratively. You know, in history, when they talk about the Salem witch trials, about how innocent girls and boys were convinced to do all these horrible things because some witch made them?"

I'd read *The Crucible* in English last year (probably just like every other sophomore), so I nodded.

"Yeah, well, they probably *were* convinced. That stuff wasn't a myth. Katie's not a wicked witch or anything, but she's got the same skills."

"Well, that's just downright disturbing," I said.

"Yeah." She nodded, then patted my arm. "Sleep well tonight. Anyway, Katie manipulates, and Smith—and, yes, that's his first name—levitates. He lifts heavy stuff, raises things in the air. As for JV, you know me, Michael and Jason, obvs, and there are three more. Jamie and Jill, those are the twins. Paul's the one with the curls."

"You said you were a spellcaster?"

"Binder. Spellbinder."

"Okay. So what are these guys? Michael and the rest of them. What can they do?"

"Oh, sure, um"—she shifted her feet, her gaze on the ceiling as she itemized—"um, Jamie and Jill have elemental powers. Fire and ice."

"They have firespell?" I wondered aloud.

"Oh, sorry, no. Jamie can manipulate fire, literally—like a firestarter. Set stuff ablaze, create smoke, general pyromania. She can work with the element without getting burned. Firespell is different—it's not about fire, really, but about power, at least we think. There aren't any Adepts with firespell, so we kind of go off what we've seen in action. Anywho, you put Jamie, Jill, and me together, and we're one medieval witch," she said, with what sounded like a fake laugh. "Paul is a warrior. A man of battle. Ridiculous moves, like something out of a kung fu movie. Michael is a reader."

"What's a reader?"

"Well, I bind spells, right? I take words of power, charms and I translate them into action, like the house I showed you."

I nodded.

"Michael reads objects. He can feel them out, determine their history, hear what they're saying about things that happened, conditions."

"Well that's . . . weird. I mean cool, but weird."

She shrugged. "Unusual, but handy. Architecture speaks to him. Literally."

"And for all that, you two still aren't dating."

She narrowed her gaze. "I'm not sure I should let you two talk to each other anymore. Now, are you done procrastinating? Can we get on with this?"

"I'm not procrastinating," I said, procrastinating. "What about Jason?" I already suspected, of course, what Jason's magic was. But he hadn't exactly confirmed it, and my own suspicions—that he had some kind of animal-related power—were strange enough that I wasn't ready to put them out there. On the other hand, how many teenage boys growled when they were attacked?

Okay, when you put it that way, it actually didn't sound that rare.

Scout dropped her gaze and fiddled with her messenger bag. "Jason's power isn't for me to tell. If he's ready for that, he'll tell you."

"I—I have an idea."

She went quiet and slowly lifted her gaze to mine. "An idea?"

We looked at each other for a minute, silently, each assessing the other: *Do you know what I know? How can I confirm it without giving it away?*

"I'll let you talk to him about that," she finally said, raising her hand to the door. "Are you ready *now*?"

"Are they gonna wig out that you're bringing me?"

"It's a good possibility," she said, then rapped her fist in a rhythmic pattern. Knock. Knock, knock. *Bang.* Knock.

"Secret code?" I asked.

"Warning," she said. "Jamie and Paul are dating. In case we're early, I don't want to walk in on that."

The joke helped ease my nerves, but only a little. As soon as she touched the door handle, my stomach began rolling again.

"Welcome to the jungle," she said, and opened the door.

The jungle was a big, vaulted room, of a quality I wouldn't have expected to see in an abandoned railway tunnel far beneath Chicago. It looked like a meeting hall, the walls covered in paintings made up of tiny, mosaic tiles, the ceilings girded with thick, wooden beams. It had the same kind of look as the convent—big scale, careful work, earthy materials. The room was empty of furniture—completely empty except for the seven kids who'd turned to stare at the door when it opened. There were three girls and four guys, including Michael and Jason.

Jason of the deadly blue eyes and currently frigid stare.

The room went completely silent, all fourteen of those

eyes on us as we stepped into the room. Scout squeezed my hand supportively.

Silently, they moved around and formed a semicircle facing us, as if containing a threat. I shuffled a little closer to Scout and surveyed the judges.

Jamie and Jill were the obvious twins, both tallish and lanky, with long auburn hair and blue eyes. Paul was tall, lean, coffee-skinned and very cute, his hair a short mop of tiny, spiral curls.

The guy and girl in the middle, who looked older than the rest of them—early college, maybe—stepped forward, fury on their faces. I guessed these were Katie and Smith. Katie was cheerleader cute, with a bob of shoulder-length brown hair, green eyes, a long T-shirt, and ballet flats paired with jeans. Smith—shaggy brown hair pasted to his forehead emo-style—wore a dingy, plaid shirt. He was the rebel type, I assumed.

"Green," he bit out, "you'd better have a damn good reason for calling us in and, more important, for bringing a *regular* in here."

Okay, so pasty hair was clearly not impressed with me.

Scout crossed her arms, preparing for battle. "A," she said, "this is Lily Parker, the girl who took a hit of firespell to save us and wound up in a paper nightgown in the LaSalle Street Clinic because of it. Ring any bells?"

I actually took a hit because I'd tripped, but since the Adepts' expressions softened after she passed along that little factoid, I kept the truth to myself.

"B," Scout continued, "I have a damn good reason. We need to show you something."

Katie spoke up. "You could have showed us something without her being here."

"I can't show you what I need to show you without her being here." Her explanation was met with silence, but she kept going. "You have to know that I wouldn't have brought her here if it wasn't absolutely necessary. Trust me—it's necessary. The Reapers have already seen her, and they already think she's associated with us. They get ambitious and come knocking on our door tonight, and she's in even more trouble. She's here as a favor to us."

Katie and Smith glanced at each other, and then she whispered something to him.

"Five minutes," Smith finally said. "You have five minutes."

Scout didn't need it; it took two seconds for her to drop the bomb. "I think she might be one of us."

Silence, until Katie made a snorty, skeptical sound. "One of us? Why in God's name would you think she's one of us? She's a regular, and getting hit with a blast isn't going to change that."

"Really?" Scout asked. "You don't think getting hit with a dose of firespell is going to have an effect? Given that we're all bouncing around Chicago with magical gifts, that's kind of a narrow-minded perspective, isn't it, Katie?"

Katie arched an arrogant brow at Scout. "You need to watch your step, Green."

Michael stepped forward, hands raised in peace. "Hey, if there's something we need to figure out here, the fewer preconceptions, the better. Scout, if you have something you need us to see, you'd better show it now."

Scout glanced over at me, nodded her head decidedly, then spun her finger in the air.

"Turn around," she said. I glanced around the room, not entirely eager to pull up my shirt before an assemblage of people I didn't know—and a boy I potentially wanted to know better. But it needed to be done, so I twisted around, pulled my shirt from the waist of my skirt, and lifted it just enough to show the mark across my lower back.

Their faces pinched in concentration and thought, the group of them moved around me to stare at my back.

"It's a darkening," Jason said, then lifted his killer blue eyes to mine. "Is it okay if I touch it?"

I swallowed, then nodded and gripped the hem of the shirt, still between my fingers, a little tighter. He stretched out his hand. His fingers just grazed my back, my skin tingling beneath his fingers. I stifled a shudder, but goose bumps arose on my arms. This wasn't the time or the place for me to get giggly about Jason's attentions, but that didn't make the effect any less powerful. It felt like a tingle of electricity moving across my skin, like that first dip into a hot bath on a cold night—spine tingling.

"It's definitely like ours," Jason agreed, standing again. "Have you developed any powers?" he quietly asked me.

I shook my head.

"I have no idea how she got it," Jason finally concluded, his brow furrowed. "But it's like ours. Or close enough, anyway."

"Yeah," Scout said, "but you nailed it—there's something different about hers, isn't there? The edges are fuzzier. Like a tattoo, but the ink bled."

"What could that mean, Green?" Katie asked.

She shrugged. "I have no clue."

"Research is your field," Smith reminded her. "There's nothing in the *Grimoire*?"

"Not that I could find, and I checked the index for every entry I could think of." I assumed the *Grimoire* was the giant leather-bound book she'd skimmed through before deciding to notify the elders.

Smith raised his gaze to me. "I understand that you've been provided with the basics about our enclave, our struggle, our gifts."

I nodded.

"And you're sure you haven't . . . become aware of any powers since you were hit?"

"I'd remember," I assured him.

"Maybe this is just a symbol of the fact that she was hit?" Jason suggested, frowning, head tilted as he gazed at my back. "Like, I don't know, a stamp of the shot she took?"

"I really don't know," Scout said quietly.

Their conversations got quieter, like scientists mumbling as they considered a prime specimen. I stared at the wall at the other end of the room while they whispered behind me and tried to figure out who—or what—I'd become.

Eventually, Smith straightened and, like obedient pups, the rest of the group followed suit and spread out again. I pulled my shirt back down and turned to face them.

Smith shook his head. "All we know is that she's marked. It might not be a darkening. Anything else is just speculation."

"Speculation?" Paul asked. "She's got a darkening, just like ours."

"Not exactly like ours," Katie reminded him.

I watched Michael struggle to keep his expression neutral. "Enough like ours," he countered, "to make it evident that she's like us. That she's one of us."

Katie shook her head. "You're missing the point. She's already told us she doesn't have skills, magic, power. Nothing but a fancy bruise." As if to confirm that suspicion, she turned her green-eyed gaze on me. "She's not one of us."

"A fancy bruise?" Scout repeated. "You're kidding, right?"

Katie shrugged, the movement and her expression condescending. "I'm just saying."

"Hey," Smith said, apparently deciding to intervene. "Let it go. It's better for her, anyway. Hanging out down here isn't fun and games. This job is dangerous, it's hard, and it's exhausting. This might feel like rejection. It's actually luck."

The room went quiet. When Scout spoke again, her voice was soft, but earnest.

"I know my place," she said, "and we all know this isn't the easiest job in the world. But if she's one of us, if she's part of us, she needs to know. *We* need to know."

"There's no evidence that she's one of us, Scout," Smith said. "A mark isn't enough. A mark won't stop Reapers, and it won't save regulars, and it won't help us. This isn't up for debate. You bring me some evidence—real evidence—that it's a darkening, and we'll talk about it again."

I could feel Scout's frustration, could see it in the stiffness in her shoulders. She looked at her colleagues.

"Paul? Jamie? Jill? Jason?" When she met Michael's gaze, her expression softened. "Michael?"

He looked down for a moment, considering, then up at her again. "I'm sorry, Scout, but I'm with Smith on this one. She's not like us. She wasn't made the way we were. She wasn't born with power, and the only reason she has a mark is because she got hit. If we let her in anyway, if we play devil's advocate, she takes our attention away from everything else we have to deal with. We can't afford that right now."

"Her being damaged isn't reason enough," Katie put in.

I arched an eyebrow. Scout may have had to play nice for hierarchy reasons, but I (obviously) wasn't part of this group.

"I am not *damaged*," I said. "I'm a bystander who got wrapped up in something I didn't want to be wrapped up in because you couldn't keep the bad guys in hand."

"The point is," Smith said, "you weren't born like us. The only thing you've got right now is a symbol of nothing."

"There's no need to be harsh," Michael said. "It's not like she got branded on purpose."

"Are you sure about that?"

The room went silent, all eyes on Katie.

"Are you suggesting," Scout bit out, "that she faked the darkening?"

Katie gazed at her with unapologetic snarkiness. This girl had college brat pack written all over her.

"So much for 'all for one and one for all,'" Scout muttered. "I can't believe you'd suspect that a person who'd never seen a darkening before faked having one forty-eight hours after she was put in the hospital because she took a full-on dose of firespell and managed to survive it. And you know what's worse? I can't believe you'd doubt me." She pressed a finger into her chest. "*Me.*"

The JV Adepts shared heavy looks.

"Regulars put us all at risk. They raise our profile, they get in the way, they serve as distractions." Jason lifted his chin, and eyes of sea blue stared out. He gazed at me, anger in his eyes. My slight at the mall must have hurt more than I'd thought.

"Until we know more, she's a regular, and that's all she is. No offense," he added, his gaze on me.

"None taken," I lied back to him.

"We have other business to discuss," Smith said. "Escort her home."

"That's it?" Scout's voice contained equal parts desperation and frustration.

"Bring us something we can use," Smith said. "Some-*one* we can use, and we'll talk."

Scout offered a sarcastic salute. "Let's go," she said to me, her hand on my arm, leading me away as the group turned inward to begin their next plan.

We were fifty yards away from the room before she spoke. "I'm sorry."

"It's not a problem," I said, not entirely sure if I believed that. I hadn't wanted to be the victim of the firespell attack, hadn't wanted to find the mark on my back, hadn't been thrilled about being dragged to a meeting of Adepts, or becoming one. I knew what Scout went through. Late-night meetings. Fear. Worry. Bearing the responsibility of protecting the public from soul-sucking adults and hell-bent teenagers—and not just your run-of-the-mill soul-sucking adults and hell-bent teenagers. I'd seen the exhaustion on her face, even as I appreciated her sense of right and wrong, the fact that she put herself out there to protect people who didn't know she was burning the candle at both ends.

So even though it wasn't something I'd asked for, or something I thought I wanted, it was hard not to feel rejected by Smith and Katie and the rest of Enclave Three. I was already the new girl—a Sagamore fish out of water in a school where everyone else had years of history together and lots of money to play with. Being treated like an outcast wasn't something I'd signed up for.

"I'll have to keep an eye on you," she said as we reentered the main building and headed across the labyrinth, "in case anything happens."

"In case I get attacked by a Reaper, or in case I suddenly develop the ability to summon unicorns?" My voice was toast-dry.

"Oh, please," Scout said. "Don't take that tone with me. You know you'd love to have a minion. Someone at your beck and call. Someone to do your bidding. How many times have you said to yourself, 'Self, I need a unicorn to run errands and such'?"

"Not that often till lately, to be real honest," I said, but managed a small smile.

"Yeah, well, welcome to the jungle," she said again, but this time, darkly.

It was nearly midnight by the time I was tucked into bed in a tank top and shorts, the St. Sophia's blanket pulled up to my chin. One hand behind my head, I stared at the stars on the ceiling, sleep elusive, probably because I was already too well-rested. After all, I'd spent half the weekend either hunkered beneath the sheets, an ostrich with its head in cotton, or ignoring my best friend by lollygagging on Michigan Avenue. I'd self-medicated with luxury goods. Well, by watching other girls buy luxury goods, anyway.

I wasn't thrilled with what I'd done, with my abandonment. But, whether I was the perfect best friend or not, the sounds of traffic softened, and I finally, oh so slowly, fell asleep.

15

I woke to pounding on the door. Suddenly vaulted from sleep, I sat up and pushed tangled hair from my face. "Who's there?"

"We're running late!" came Scout's frantic voice from the other side.

I glanced over at the alarm clock. Class started in fifteen minutes.

"Frick," I said, adrenaline jolting me to full consciousness. I threw off the blankets and jumped for the door. Unlocking and opening it, I found Scout in the doorway in long-sleeved pajamas and thick blue socks.

I arched an eyebrow at the ensemble. "It's still September, right?"

Scout rolled her eyes. "I'm cold a lot. Sue me."

"How about I just take a shower?"

She nodded and held up two energy bars. "Get in, get out, and when you're done, art history, here we come."

Have you ever had one of those days where you give up on being really clean, and settle for being *largely* clean? Where you don't have time for the entire scrubbing and exfoliating regime, so you settle for the basics? Where brushing your teeth becomes the most vigorous part of your cleaning ritual?

Yeah, welcome to Monday morning at St. Sophia's School for (Slightly Grimy) Girls.

When I was (mostly) clean, I met Scout in the com-

mon room. She was sporting the preppy look today—
Mary Janes, knee-high socks, oxford shirt and tie.

"You look very—"

"Nerdy?" she suggested. "I'm trying a new philosophy today."

"A new philosophy?" I asked, as we shut the common
room door and headed down the hall. She handed over
the energy bar she'd shown off earlier. I ripped down
the plastic and bit off a chunk.

"Look the nerd, *be* the nerd," she said, with emphasis.
"I figure this look could boost my grades by fifteen to
twenty percent."

"Fifteen to twenty percent? That's impressive. You
think it'll work?"

"I'm sure it won't," she said. "But I'm giving it a shot.
I'm taking positive steps."

"Studying would be another positive step," I pointed
out.

"Studying interferes with my world saving."

"It's unfortunate you can't get excused absences for
that."

"I know, right?"

"And speaking of saving the world," I said, "did you
have a call after we got back last night? Or did you just
sleep late?"

"I sleep with earplugs," she said, half-answering the
question. "The radio alarm came on, but it wasn't loud
enough, so I dreamed about REO Speedwagon and Phil
Collins for forty-five minutes. Suffice it to say, I can feel
it coming in the air tonight."

"*Dum-dum, dum-dum, dum-dum, dum-dum, dum,
dum,*" I said, repeating the drum lead-in, although without my usual air drumming. My reputation was off to a
rocky-enough start as it was.

We took the stairs to the first floor, then headed
through the corridor to the classroom building. The
lockers were our next stop. I took the last bite of the
energy bar—some kind of chewy fruit, nut, and granola

combination—then folded up the wrapper and slipped it into my bag.

At our lockers, I opened my messenger bag and peeked inside. I already had my art history book, so I kneeled to my lower-level locker, opened it, and grabbed my trig book, my second class of the day. I'd just closed the door, my palm still pressed against slick wood, when I felt a tap on my shoulder.

I turned and found M.K. beside me—grinning.

"Fell down the stairs, did you?"

Scout slipped books into her locker, then slammed the door shut before giving M.K. a narrow-eyed glare. "Hey, Betty, go find Veronica and leave us in peace."

M.K. looked confused by the reference, but she shook it off with a toss of her long dark hair. "How lame are you when you can't even walk up a flight of stairs without falling down?" Her voice was just a shade too loud, obviously intended to get the other girls' attention, to make them stare and whisper and, presumably, embarrass me.

Fortunately, I didn't embarrass that easily. On the other hand, I couldn't exactly correct her. If I threw "secret basement room" at these girls, there'd be a mad rush to find out what lurked downstairs. That wasn't going to help the Adepts, so I opted to deflect.

"How lame do you have to be to push a girl down the stairs?"

"I didn't push anyone down the stairs," she clipped out.

"So you had nothing to do with my hospital visit?"

Crimson rose on her cheeks.

It was mean, I know, but I had Adepts to protect. Well, one nose-ringed Adept to protect, anyway. Besides, I didn't actually make an accusation. I just asked the right question.

As school bells began to peal, she nailed us both with a glare, then turned on a heel and stalked away, a monogrammed leather backpack between her shoulder blades.

I'm not sure what, or how much, the brat pack had spilled around school about my "fall" and my clinic visit, but I felt the looks and heard the whispers. They lasted through the morning's art history, trig, and civics classes, girls in identical plaid lowering their heads together—or passing tiny, folded notes—to share what they'd heard about my weekend.

Luckily, the rumors were pretty tame. I hadn't heard anything about bizarre rooms beneath the building, evil teenagers roaming the hallways, or Scout's involvement—other than the fact that people "wouldn't be surprised" if she'd had something to do with it. Apparently, I wasn't the only one at St. Sophia's who thought she was a little odd.

I glanced over at her during civics—punky blond and brown hair in tiny ponytails, fingernails painted glossy black, a tiny hoop in her nose. I was kind of surprised Foley let her get away with all that, but I thanked God Scout stood out in this bastion of über-normalcy.

After civics, we headed back to our lockers.

"Let's go run an errand," she said, opening her locker and transferring her books.

I arched a skeptical eyebrow.

"Perfectly mundane mission," she said, closing the door again. She adjusted her skull-and-crossbones messenger bag and gave me a wink.

I followed as she weaved through girls in the locker hall, then through the Great Hall and main building to the school's front door. This one was an off-campus mission, apparently.

Outside, we found the sky a muted steel gray, the city all but windless. The weather was moody—as if we were on the cusp of something nasty. As if the sky was preparing to open on us all.

"Let's go," Scout said, and we took the steps and headed down the sidewalk. We made a left, walking down Erie and away from Michigan Avenue and the garden of stone thorns.

"Here's the thing about Chicago," she began.

"Speak it, sister."

"The brat pack gave you the Sex and the Windy City tour. The shopping on Michigan is nice, but it's not all there is. There's an entire city out there—folks who've lived here all their lives, folks who've *worked* here all their lives, blue-collar jobs, dirt under their fingernails, without shopping for thousand-dollar handbags." She looked up at a high-rise as we passed. "Nearly three million people in a city that's been here for a hundred and seventy years. The architecture, the art, the history, the politics. I know you're not from here, and you've only been here a week, and your heart is probably back in Sagamore, but this is an amazing place, Lil."

I watched as she gazed at the buildings and architecture around her, love in her eyes.

"I want to run for city council," she suddenly said, as we crossed the street and passed facing Italian restaurants. Tourists formed a line outside each, menus in hand, excitement in their eyes as they prepared to sample Chicago's finest.

"City council?" I asked her. "Like, Chicago's city council? You want to run for office?"

She nodded her head decisively. "I love this city. I want to serve it someday. I mean, it depends on where I live and who's in the ward and whether the seat is open or not, but I want to give something back, you know?"

I had no idea Scout had political ambitions, much less that she'd given the logistics that much thought. She was only sixteen, and I was impressed. I also wasn't sure if I should feel pity for her parents, who were missing out on her general awesomeness, or if I should thank them—was Scout who she was because her parents had freaked about her magic, and deposited her in a boarding school?

She bobbed her head at a bodega that sat kitty-corner on the next block. "In there," she said, and we crossed the street. She opened the door, a bell on the handle jingling as we moved inside.

"Yo," she said, a hand in the air to wave at the clerk as she walked straight to the fountain drink machine.

"Scout," said the guy at the counter, whom I pegged at nineteenish or twenty, and whose dark eyes were on the comic book spread on the counter in front of him, a spill of short dreadlocks around his face. "Refill time?"

"Refill time," Scout agreed. I stayed at the counter while she attacked the fountain machine, yanking a gigantic plastic cup from a dispenser. With mechanical precision, she pushed the cup under the ice dispenser, peeked over the rim as ice spilled into it, then released the cup, emptied out a few, and repeated the whole process again until she was satisfied she'd gotten exactly the right amount. When she was done with the ice, she went straight for the strawberry soda, and the process started again.

"She's particular, isn't she?" I wondered aloud.

The clerk snorted, then glanced up at me, chocolate brown eyes alight with amusement. "Particular hardly covers it. She's an addict when it comes to the sugar water." His brow furrowed. "I don't know you."

"Lily Parker," I said. "First year at St. Sophia's."

"You one of the brat pack?"

"She is mos' def' not one of the brat pack," Scout said, joining us at the counter, as she poked a straw into the top of her soda. She took a sip, eyes closed in ecstasy. I had to bite back a laugh.

Lips still wrapped around the straw, Scout opened one eye and squinted evilly at me. "Don't mock the berry," she said when she paused to take a breath, then turned back to the kid behind the counter. "She tried, unsuccessfully, to join the brat pack, at least until she realized how completely lame they are. Oh, and Derek, this is Lily. You two are buds now."

I grinned at Derek. "Glad to meet you."

"Ditto."

"Derek is a Montclare grad who's moved into the wonderful world of temping at his dad's store while working on his degree in underwater basketweaving at U of C." She batted catty eyes at Derek. "I got that right, didn't I, D?"

"Nuclear physics," he corrected.

"Close enough," Scout said with a wink, then stepped back to trail the tips of her fingers across the boxes of candy in front of the counter. "Are we thinking Choco-Loco or Caramel Buddy? Am I in the mood for crunchy or chewy today?" She held up two red and orange candy bars, then waggled them at us. "Thoughts? I'm polling, checking the pulse of the nation. Well, of our little corner of River North, anyway."

"Choco-Loco."

"Caramel Buddy."

We said the names simultaneously, which resulted in our grinning at each other while Scout continued the not-so-silent debate over her candy choices. Crispy rice was apparently a crucial component. Nuts were a downgrade.

"So," Derek asked, "are you from Chicago?"

"Sagamore," I said. "New York state."

"You're a long way from home, Sagamore."

I glanced through the windows toward St. Sophia's towers, the prickly spires visible even though we were a couple of blocks away. "Tell me about it," I said, then looked back at Derek. "You did your time at MA?"

"I was MA born and bred. My dad owns a chain of bodegas"—he bobbed his head toward the shelves in the store—"and he wanted more for me. I got four years of ties and uniforms and one hell of an SAT score to show for it."

"Derek's kind of a genius," Scout said, placing the Choco-Loco on the counter. "Biggest decision I'll make all day, probably."

Derek chuckled. "Now, I know that's a lie." He held

up the front of the comic book, which featured a busty, curvy superheroine in a skintight latex uniform. "Your decision making is a little more akin to this, wouldn't you say?"

My eyes wide, I glanced from the comic book to Scout, who snorted gleefully at Derek's comparison, then leaned in toward her. "He knows?" I whispered.

She didn't answer, which I took as an indication that she didn't want to have that conversation now, at least not in front of company. She pulled a patent leather wallet from her bag, then pulled a crisp twenty-dollar bill from the wallet.

I arched an eyebrow at gleaming patent leather—and the designer logo that was stamped across it.

"What?" she asked, sliding the wallet back into her bag. "It's not real; just a good fake I picked up in Wicker Park. There's no need to look like a peasant."

"Even the humblest of girls can have a thing for the good stuff," Derek said, a grin quirking one corner of his mouth, then lowered his gaze to the comic book again. I sensed that we'd lost his attention.

"Later, D," Scout said, and headed for the quick shop's door.

Without lifting his gaze, Derek gave us a wave. We walked outside, the sky still gray and moody, the city eerily quiet, and toward St. Sophia's.

"Okay," I said. "Let me get this straight. You wouldn't tell me—your roommate—about what you were involved in, but the guy who runs the quick shop down the street gets to know?"

Scout nibbled on the end of one of the sticks of chocolate in her Choco-Loco wrapper, and slid me a sideways glance as she munched. "He's cute, right?"

"Oh, my God, totally. But not the point."

"He has a girlfriend, Sam. They've been together for years."

"Bummer, but let's keep our eyes on the ball." We separated as we walked around a clutch of tourists, then came back together when we'd passed the knot of them. "Why does he get to know?"

"You're assuming I told him," Scout said as we paused at the corner, waiting for a crossing signal in heavy lunchtime traffic. "And while I'm glad he's supportive—seriously, he's *so* pretty."

"It's the hair," I suggested.

"And the eyes. Totally chocolatey."

"Agreed. You were saying?"

"I didn't tell him," Scout said, leading us across the street when the light changed. "Remember what I told you about kids who seemed off? Depressed?"

"Humans targeted by Reapers?"

"Exactly," she said with a nod. "Derek was a near victim. He and his mom were superclose, but she died a couple of years ago—when he was a freshman. Unfortunately, he rushed the wrong house at U of C; two of his fraternity brothers were Reapers. They took advantage of the grief, made friends with him, dragged him down even further."

"They"—how was I supposed to phrase this?—"took his energy, or whatever?"

Scout nodded gravely as we moved through lunch-minded Chicagoans. "There wasn't much left of him. A shell, nearly, by the time we got there. He was barely going to class, barely getting out of bed. Depressed."

"Jeez," I quietly said.

"I know. Luckily, he wasn't too far gone, but it was close. We identified him and had to clear away some nasty siphoning spells—that's what the younger Reapers used to drain him, to send the energy to the elders who needed it. We got him out and away from the Reapers. We gave him space, got him rested and fed, put him back in touch with his family and real friends. The rest—the healing—was all him." She scowled, and her voice went tight. "Then we gave his Reaper 'friends' a good talking-to about self-sacrifice."

"Did it work?"

"Well, we managed to bring one of them back. The other's still a frat boy in the worst connotation of the phrase. Anyway, Derek's one of a handful of people who know about us, about Adepts. We call them the community." I remembered the term from the conversation with Smith and Katie. "People without magic who know about our existence, usually because they were caught in the crossfire. Sometimes, they're grateful and they provide a service later. Information. Or maybe just a few minutes of normalcy."

"Strawberry soda," I added.

"That is the most important thing," she agreed. She pulled me from the flow of pedestrian traffic to the curb at the edge of the street. "Look around you, Lil. Most people are oblivious to the currents around them, to the hum and flow of the city. We're part of that hum and flow. The magic is part of that hum and flow. Sometimes people say they love living in Chicago—the energy, the earthiness, the sense of being part of something bigger than you are."

Glancing around the neighborhood, across glass and steel and concrete, the city buzzing around us, I could see their point.

"There have always been a handful of people who know about us. Who know what we do, know what we fight for," Scout said as we rounded the corner and walked toward St. Sophia's.

And there he was.

Jason stood in front of the stone wall, hands in his pockets, in khaki pants and a navy blue sweater with an embroidered gold crest on the pocket. His dark blond hair was tidy, and his eyes had turned a muted, steel blue beneath the cloudy sky, beneath those dark eyebrows and long lashes.

Those eyes were aimed, laserlike, in my direction.

Scout, who'd taken a heartening sip of strawberry-flavored sugar water after relaying Derek's history, released the straw just long enough to snark. "It appears you have a visitor."

"He could be here for you," I absently said.

"Uh, no. Jason Shepherd does not make trips to St. Sophia's to see me. If he needed me, he could text me."

I made a vague sound, neither agreeing nor disagreeing with her assessment, but my nerves apparently agreed. My throat was tight; my stomach fluttered. Had this boy—this boy with those ridiculous blue eyes—come here to see me?

Right before I melted into a ridiculous puddle of girl, I remembered that I was still irritated with Jason and wiped the dopey smile off my face. I'd show him "distraction."

"Shepherd," Scout said when we reached him, "what brings you to our fine institution of higher learning?" She managed those ten words before her lips found the straw again. I realized I'd found Scout's pacifier, should it ever prove necessary—strawberry soda.

Jason bobbed his head at Scout, then looked at me again. "Can I talk to you?"

I glanced at Scout, who checked her watch. "You've got seven minutes before class," she said, then motioned with a hand. "Give me your bag, and I'll stick it in your chair."

"Thanks," I said, and made the transfer.

Jason and I watched Scout trot down the sidewalk and disappear into the building. It wasn't until she was gone that he looked at me again.

"About yesterday." He paused, eyes on the sidewalk, as if deciding what to say. "It's not personal."

I arched my eyebrows. I wasn't letting him off the hook that easily.

He looked away, wet his lips, then found my gaze again. "When you were in the hospital, we talked about the Reapers. About the fact that we're in the minority?"

"A splinter cell, you said."

He bobbed his head. "In a way. We're like a resistance movement. A rebellion. We aren't equally matched. The

Reapers—*we* call them Reapers—they're not just a handful of misfits. They're *all* the gifted—all the Dark Elite—except for us."

"All except for you?"

"Unfortunately. That means the odds are stacked against us, Lily." He took a step forward, a step toward me. "Our position is dangerous. And if you don't have magic, I don't want you wrapped up in it. Not if you don't have a way to defend yourself. Scout can't always be there . . . and I don't want you to get hurt."

An orchestra could have been playing on the St. Sophia's grounds and I wouldn't have heard it. I heard nothing but the pounding of my heartbeat in my ears, saw nothing but the blue of his lash-fringed eyes.

"Thank you," I quietly said.

"That's not to say I wasn't bitter that you ignored me Sunday."

I nibbled the edge of my lip. "Look, I'm sorry about that—"

Jason shook his head. "You saw the mark, and you needed time to process. We've all been there. I mean, you could have chosen better company, but I understand the urge to get away. To escape." Jason looked down at the sidewalk, eyebrows pulled together in concentration. "When I found out who I was, *what* I was, I ran away. Hopped a Greyhound bus and headed to my grandmother's house in Alabama. I camped out there for three weeks that summer. I was thirteen," he said, raising his gaze again. His eyes had switched color from turquoise to chartreuse, and something animal appeared in his expression—something intense.

"You're a . . . wolf?" I said it like a question, but I suddenly had no doubt, and no fear, about the possibility that he was something far scarier than Scout and the rest of the Adepts.

"I am," he said, his voice a little deeper than it had been a moment ago. Goose bumps rose on my arms, and a chill slunk down my spine. I wondered whether that was a common reaction—Little Red Riding Hood syndrome, maybe.

I stared at him and he stared back at me, my focus so complete that I actually shook in surprise when the tower bells began to ring, signaling the end of the lunch period.

"You should go," he said. When I nodded, he reached out and squeezed my hand. Electricity sparked up my spine. "Goodbye, Lily Parker."

"Goodbye, Jason Shepherd," I said, but he was already walking away.

He'd walked to St. Sophia's to see me—to talk to me. To explain why he hadn't wanted me to sit in on the Adepts' meetings, mark or not.

Because he was *worried* about me.

Because he hadn't wanted me to get hurt.

The moment I'd shared with Jason had been so incredibly phenomenal, the universe had to equalize. And what was the chosen brand of karmic balance for a high school junior?

Two words: pop quiz.

Magic in the world or not, I was still in high school, and a high school that prided itself on Ivy League admissions. Peters, our European history teacher, decided he needed to ensure that we'd read our chapters on the Picts and Vikings by using fifteen multiple-choice questions. I'd read the chapters—I was paranoid enough to make sure I finished my homework, magical hysterics notwithstanding. But that didn't mean my stomach didn't turn as Peters walked the rows, dropping stapled copies of the test on our desks.

"You have twenty minutes," he said, "which means you have a little more than one minute per question. Quizzes will account for twenty percent of your grade, so I strongly recommend you consider your answers carefully."

When the tests were distributed, he returned to his desk and took a seat without glancing up.

"Begin," he said, and pencils began to scribble.

I stared down at the paper, my nerves making the letters spin—well, nerves and the thought of a blue-eyed boy who'd worried for me, and who'd held my hand.

Twenty minutes later, I put my pencil down. I'd filled in the answers, and I hoped at least a few of them were correct. But I didn't stress over it.

Infatuation apparently made me intellectually lazy.

16

Scout waited until dinner to interrogate me about Jason's visit to campus. It being Monday, we'd been blessed with brand-new food. Since I didn't eat chicken, it was rice and mixed vegetables for me, but even simple food was better than dirty rice or stew. Or so I assumed.

"So, what did Mr. Shepherd have to say?" Scout asked, spearing a chunk of grilled chicken with her fork. "Are you engaged or promised, or what? Did you get his lavaliere? Did he pin you?"

"What's a lavaliere?"

"I don't know. I think it's a fraternity thing?"

"Well, whatever it is, there wasn't one. We just talked about the meeting. About the attitude he copped. He apologized."

Scout lifted appreciative brows. "Shepherd apologized? Jeez, Parker. You must have worked faster than I thought. He's as stubborn as they come."

"He said he was worried about me. About the possibility that I'd get wrapped up in a Reapers versus Adepts cage match and wouldn't have a way to defend myself, especially if you weren't there to work your mojo."

"And what spectacular mojo it is, too," she muttered. She opened her mouth as if to speak, then closed it again. "Listen," she finally said. "I don't want to warn you off some kind of budding romance, but you should be careful around Jason. I'm not sure I'd recommend getting involved with him."

"I'm not getting involved with him," I protested. "Wait, why can't I get involved with him?"

"He's just—I don't know. He's different."

"Yeah, being a werewolf does make him kinda unique."

She raised her eyebrows, surprise in her expression. "You know."

"I do now."

"How did you find out?"

"I heard him growl after I got hit with the firespell. I confirmed it yesterday."

"He admitted he was a wolf? To you?"

"He let me see his eyes do that flashy, color-changey thing. He did the same thing again when we talked in the hospital."

"After you made us leave?"

I bobbed my head. Scout made a low whistle. "In one week, you've gone from new kid in school to being wooed by a werewolf. You move fast, Parker."

"I doubt he's wooing me, and I didn't do anything but be my usually charming self."

"I'm sure you were plenty charming, but I just want you to be careful."

"Is that a little were-ism I'm hearing?"

"It's a little reminder that he's not like the rest of us. He's a whole different brand of Adept. And you don't have to buy my opinion. I'm just telling you what I think. On the other hand, in our short but explosive friendship, have I ever steered you wrong?"

"Did you want me to start with the getting hit by firespell or becoming an enemy to soul-sucking teenagers?"

"Did you mean the Reapers or the brat pack?"

I grinned appreciatively. "Ooh, well played."

"I have my moments. Besides, who'd you borrow those kick-ass flats from?"

I glanced down at the screaming yellow and navy patent leather ballet flats she'd let me borrow on our hurried way out the door this morning.

"Fine," I finally said. "Fashion trumps evil and prissy teenagers. You win."

Scout grinned at me. "I always win. Let's chow."

We noshed, said our hellos to Collette and Lesley, and when dinner was done, returned to the suite for our hour-long break before study hall. The brat pack had made camp in the living room, blond hair and expensive accessories flung about as we entered.

Veronica sat cross-legged on the couch, an open folder in her lap and M.K. and Amie at her feet like adoring handmaids.

"It also says," Veronica said, gazing at the folder, "that her parents dumped her here so they could head off to Munich." She lifted her head, a lock of blond hair falling across her shoulders, and gave me a pointed look.

Was that my folder she was reading? Had M.K. taken it from Foley's office while she was on hall-monitoring duty?

"Interesting, isn't it, that her parents left her? That they didn't take her with them? I mean, it's not like there aren't English-speaking private schools in Germany. She's not even *from* Chicago."

"How did you get that?" I bit out. All eyes turned to me. "How did you get my file?"

Veronica closed the navy blue folder, the St. Sophia's crest across the front, then held it up between two fingers. "What, this? We got it from Foley's office, of course. We have our ways."

I took a step forward, anger dimming my vision at the edges. "You have no right to go through my file. Who do you think you are?"

Outside, thunder rolled across the city, the steel gray sky finally preparing to give way. Inside, the room lights flickered.

"You need to back off," Scout said.

Veronica arched an eyebrow and uncrossed her legs. M.K. and Veronica shifted to give her room. She stood up, folder in her hand, and walked toward us, a haughty look aimed at Scout.

"You think you're queen of the school just because you've been here since you were twelve? Being abandoned by your parents isn't exactly a coup, Green."

Scout, amazingly, stayed calm after that outburst, an expression of boredom on her face. "Is that supposed to hurt me, Veronica? 'Cause, if I recall, you've been here as long as I have."

"Irrelevant," Veronica declared. "We're talking about you"—she shifted her gaze to me—"and your new friend. You both need to remember who's in charge here."

Scout made a sarcastic sound. "And you think that's you?"

Veronica flipped up the folder. "The ones with information, with access, always win. You should write that down in one of your little books."

M.K. snickered. Amie had the decency to blush, but her eyes were on the ground, apparently not brave enough to intercede.

"Give it back," I said, hand extended, fingers shaking with fury.

"What, this?" she asked, batting her eyelashes, waving the folder in her hand.

"That," Scout confirmed, reaching out her own hand, and taking a menacing step forward. When she spoke again, her voice was low and threatening. "Keep in mind, Lively, that in all the years you've been here, some interesting little facts have crossed my path, too. I assume you'd like to keep those facts between us, and not have them sprinkled around the sophomore and senior classes?"

There was silence as they faced off, the weirdo and the homecoming queen, a battle for rumor mill supremacy.

"Whatever," Veronica finally said, handing over the folder between the tips of her fingers, lips pursed as if the paper were dirty or infected. "Have it. It's not like I care. We've gotten everything we need."

Scout pulled the file from Veronica's manicured hands. "I'm glad we've concluded our business. And in the future, you might be a little more careful about where you get your information from and whom you share it with, capiche? Because sharing that information with the wrong people could be . . . costly."

Thunder rolled and rippled again, this burst louder than the last. The storm was moving closer.

"Whatever," Veronica said, rolling her eyes. She turned and, like a spinning dervish of plaid, took her seat on the couch again, attendants at her feet, the queen returned to her throne.

"Come on," Scout said, taking my wrist in her free hand and moving me toward her bedroom. It took a moment to make my feet move, to drag my gaze away from the incredibly smug smile on Veronica's face.

"Lily," Scout said, and I glanced over at her.

"Come on," she repeated, tugging my wrist. "Let's go."

We moved into her room, where she shut the door behind us. Folder in hand, she pointed at the bed. "Sit down."

"I'm fine—"

"Sit *down*."

I sat.

Thunder rolled again, lightning flashing through the room almost instantaneously. The rain started, a sudden downpour that echoed through the room like radio static.

The folder beneath her crossed arms, she walked to one end of the room, eyes on the floor, and then walked back again. "We're going to have to put it back." She lifted her head. "This came from Foley's office. We needed to get it out of their hands, which we did—yay, us—but now we're going to have to put it back. And that's going to be tricky."

"Great," I muttered. "That's great. Just one more thing I don't need to worry about right now. But before we figure out how to sneak into Foley's office and drop off a student file without her knowing it was gone, can I see it, please?"

"No."

That silenced me for a moment. "Excuse me?"

"No." Scout stopped her pacing and glanced over at me. "I really don't think looking through this is going to help you. If there's anything weird in here—about your parents, for example, since Foley likes to discuss them—it's just going to give you things to obsess over. Things to worry about."

"And it's better if only Veronica and M.K. have that information?"

Silence.

"Good point," Scout finally said, then handed it over. "You read. I'll plot."

My hands shaking, I flipped it open. My picture was stapled on the inside left, a shot of me from my sophomore year at Sagamore North, my hair a punky bob of black. On the inside right was an information sheet, which I skimmed—all basic stuff. A handful of documents was stapled behind the information sheet. Health and immunization records. A letter from the board of trustees about my admission.

The final document was different—a letter on cream-colored stock, addressed to Foley.

"Oh, my God," I said as I reviewed it, my vision dimming at the edges again as the world seemed to contract around me.

"Lily? What is it?"

"There's a letter. 'Marceline,'" I read aloud, "'as you know, the members of the board of trustees have agreed to admit Lily to St. Sophia's. We believe your school is the best choice for the remainder of Lily's high school education. As such, we trust that you will see to her education with the same vigor that you show to your other students.'"

"So far so good," Scout said.

"There's more. 'We hope,'" I continued, "'that you'll be circumspect in regard to any information you provide to Lily regarding our work, regardless of your opinion of it.' It's signed, 'Yours very truly, Mark and Susan Parker.'"

"Your parents?" Scout quietly asked.

I nodded.

"That's not so bad, Lil—she's just asking Foley not to worry you or whatever about their trip—"

"Scout, my parents told me they were philosophy professors at Hartnett College. In Sagamore. In New York. But in this letter, they tell Foley not to talk to me about their *work*? And that's not all." I flipped the folder outward so that she could see the letter, the paper, the logo. "They wrote the letter on Sterling Research Foundation letterhead."

Scout's eyes widened. She took the folder from my hand and ran a finger over the raised SRF logo. "SRF? That's the building down the street. The place that does the medical research. What are the odds?"

"Medical research," I repeated. "How close is that to genetic research?"

"That's what Foley said your parents did, right?"

I nodded, the edge of my lip worried between my teeth. "And not what they told me they did. They lied to me, Scout."

Scout sat down on the bed beside me and put a hand on my knee. "Maybe they didn't really lie, Lil. Maybe they just didn't tell you the entire truth."

The entire truth.

Sixteen years of life, of what I'd believed my life to be, and I didn't even know the basic facts of my parents' careers. "If they didn't tell me the entire truth about their jobs," I quietly said, "what else didn't they tell me?" For a moment, I considered whipping out my cell phone, dialing their number, and yelling out my frustration, demanding to know what was going on and why they'd lied. And if they hadn't lied exactly, if they'd only omitted parts of their lives, why they hadn't told me everything.

But that conversation was going to be a big one. I had to calm down, get myself together, before that phone call. And that's when it dawned on me—for the first time—that there might be huge reasons, *scary* reasons, why they hadn't come clean.

Maybe this wasn't about keeping information from me. Maybe they hadn't told me because the truth, some-how, was dangerous. Since I'd now seen an entirely new side to the world, that idea didn't seem as far-fetched as it might have a year ago.

No, I decided, this wasn't something I could rush. I had to know more before I confronted them.

"I'm sorry, Lil," Scout finally said into the silence. "What can I do?"

I gave the question two seconds of deliberation. "You can get me into Foley's office."

Fourteen minutes later—after the brat pack had left the common suite for parts unknown—we were on our way to the administrative wing. The folder was tucked into Scout's messenger bag, my heart pounding as we tried to look nonchalant on our way through the study hall and back into the main building. We had two missions—first and foremost, we had to put the folder back. If Foley found it missing, she'd only consider one likely source—me. I really wanted to avoid that conversation.

Second, since my parents' letter assumed Foley al-ready knew about their research—and apparently didn't like it—I was guessing there was more information on the Sterling Research Foundation, or on my parents, in her office. We'd see what we could find.

Of course, it was just after dinner—and only a few minutes before the beginnings of study hall—so there was a chance Foley was still around. If she was, we were going to make a run for it. But if she was gone, we were going to sneak inside and figure out what more we could learn about the life of Lily Parker.

17

Choir practice gave us an excuse to walk through the Great Hall and toward the main building, even as other girls deposited books and laptops on study tables and set about their required two hours of studying. Of course, when we got to the main building, the story had to change.

"Just taking an architectural tour," Scout explained with a smile as we passed two would-be choir girls. She blew out a breath that puffed out her cheeks after they passed, then pulled me toward the hallway to the administrative wing.

I wasn't sure if I was happy or not to discover that the administrative wing was quiet and mostly dark. That meant we had a clear path to Foley's office, and no excuse to avoid the breaking and entering—other than the getting-caught-and-being-severely-punished problem, of course.

"If you don't take the folder back," Scout said, as if sensing my fear, "we have to give it back to the brat pack. Or we have to come clean to Foley, and that means making even more of an enemy of the brat packers. And frankly, Lil, I'm full up on enemies right now."

It was the exhaustion in her voice that solidified my bravery. "Let's do it before I lose my nerve."

She nodded, and we skulked down the wing, bodies pressed as closely against the wall as we could manage.

In retrospect, it was probably not the least conspicuous way to get down the hall, but what did we know?

We made it to Foley's office, found no light beneath the wooden door. Scout knocked, the sound muffled by timely thunder. After a few seconds, when no one answered, she rolled her shoulders, put a hand on the doorknob, and turned.

The door clicked, and opened.

We both stood in the hallway for a minute.

"Way easier than I thought that was going to be," she whispered, then snuck a peak inside. "Empty," she said, then pushed open the door.

After a last glance behind me to ensure the hallway was empty, I followed her in, then pulled the door carefully shut behind us.

Foley's office was dark. Scout rustled around in her messenger bag, then pulled out a flashlight, which she flipped on. She cast the light around the room.

The top of Foley's desk was empty. There weren't any file cabinets in the room, just a bookshelf and a couple of leather chairs with those big brass tacks in the upholstery. Scout moved to the other side of Foley's desk and began pulling open drawers.

"Rubber bands," she announced, then pushed the drawer closed and opened another. "Paper clips and staples." She closed that one, then moved the left-hand side of the desk and opened a drawer. "Pens and pencils. Jeez, this lady has a lot of office supplies." She closed, then opened, another. "Envelopes and stationery." She closed the last one and stood straight again. "That's it for the desk, and there're no other drawers in here."

That wasn't entirely accurate. "I bet there are drawers behind the secret panel."

"What secret panel?" she asked.

I moved to the bookshelf I'd seen Foley walk out of, pushed aside a few books, and knocked. The resulting sound was hollow. Echoey. "It's a pivoting bookshelf, just like in a B-rated horror flick. The panel was open when Foley called me out of class. She closed it again after she came out, but I'm not sure how."

Scout trained her flashlight on the bookshelves. "In the movies, you pull a book and the sliding door opens."

"Surely it's not that easy."

"I said the same thing about the door. Let's see if our luck holds." Scout tugged on a leather-bound copy of *The Picture of Dorian Gray* . . . and jumped backward and out of the way as one side of the bookshelf began to pivot toward us. When the panel was open halfway, it stopped, giving us a space wide enough to walk through.

"Well-done, Parker."

"I have my moments," I told her. "Light it up."

My heart was thudding as Scout directed the beam of the flashlight into the space the sliding panel had revealed.

It was a storage room.

"Wow," Scout muttered. "That was anticlimactic."

It was a small, limestone space, just big enough to fit two rows of facing metal file cabinets. I took the flashlight from Scout's hand and moved inside. The cabinets bore alphabetical index labels.

First things first, I thought. "Come hold this," I told her, extending the flashlight. As she directed it at the cabinets, I skimmed the first row, then the second, until I got to the *P*s. I pulled open the cabinet—no lock, thankfully—and slid my folder in between PARK and PATTERSON.

Some of the tightness in my chest eased when I closed the door again, part of our mission accomplished. But then I glanced around the room. There was a little too much in here not to explore.

"Keep an eye on the door," I said.

"Go for it, Sherlock," Scout said, then turned her back on me, and let me get to work.

I put my hands on my hips and surveyed the room. There hadn't been any other PARKER folders in the file drawer, which meant that my parents didn't have files of their own—at least not under their own names.

"Maybe our luck will hold one more time," I thought, and tucked the flashlight beneath my chin. I checked the *S* drawer, then thumbed through STACK, STANHOPE, and STEBBINS.

STERLING, R. F., read the next file.

"Clever," I muttered, "but not clever enough." I pulled out the file and opened it. A single envelope was inside.

I wet my lips, my hands suddenly shaking, lay the file on the top of the folders in the open drawer, and lifted the envelope.

"What did you find?"

"There's a Sterling file," I said. "And there's an envelope in it." It was cream-colored, the flap unsealed, but tucked in. The outside of the envelope bore a St. Sophia's RECEIVED BY stamp with a date on it: SEPTEMBER 21.

"Feet, don't fail me now," I whispered for bravery, then lifted the flap and pulled out a trifolded piece of white paper. I unfolded it, the SRF seal at the top of the page, but not embossed. This was a copy of a letter.

And attached to the copy was a sticky note with my father's handwriting on it.

Marceline,

I know we don't see eye to eye, but this will help you understand.
    —M.P.

M.P. My father's initials.

My hands suddenly shaking, I lifted the note to reveal the text of the letter beneath. It was short, and it was addressed to my father:

Mark,

*Per our discussions regarding your daughter,
we agree that it would be unwise for her to
accompany you to Germany or for you to inform
her about the precise nature of your work.
Doing so would put you all in danger. That you
are taking a sabbatical, hardly a lie, should be
the extent of her understanding of your current
situation. We also agree that St. Sophia's is the best
place for Lily to reside in your absence. She will be
properly cared for there. We will inform Marceline
accordingly.*

The signature was just a first name—*William.*
That was it.
The proof of my parents' lies.
About their jobs.
About their trip.
About whatever they'd gotten involved in, whatever
had given the Sterling Research Foundation the ability
to pass down dictates about my parents' relationship
with me.

"They lied, Scout," I finally said, hands shaking—with
fear and anger—as I stared down at the letter. "They
lied about all of it. The school. The jobs. They probably
aren't even in Germany. God only knows where they
are now."

And what else had they lied about? Each visit I made
to the college? To their offices? Each time I met their
colleagues? Every department cocktail party I'd spied
on from the second-floor staircase at our house in Sagamore, professors—or so I'd assumed—milling about
below with drinks in hand?

It was all fake—all a show, a production, to fool
someone.

But who? Me? Someone else?

I picked up the envelope again and glanced at the RECEIVED BY mark.

The puzzle pieces fell into place.

"When was the twenty-first?" I asked Scout.

"What?"

"The twenty-first. September twenty-first. When was that?"

"Um, today's the twenty-fifth, so last Friday?"

"That's the day Foley received the envelope," I said, holding it up. "Foley got a copy of this letter the day I got hit by the firespell. The day *before* I went into the hospital, the day before she came to the hospital room to tell me she was wrong about my parents. That I was right about their research. There's probably a letter in here to her, too," I quietly added, as I glanced around the room.

"Foley told you about the genetic research when you came to her office," Scout concluded. "Then she got the letter and realized she really wasn't supposed to tell you. That's why she dropped by the hospital. That's why she changed her tune."

I dropped my gaze back down to the letter and swore out a series of curses that should have blistered Scout's ears. "Can anyone around here tell me the truth? Can anyone *not* have, like, sixty-five secret motives?"

"Oh, my God, Lily."

It took me a moment to realize she'd called my name, and to snap my gaze her way. Her eyes were wide, her lips parted in shock. I thought we'd been caught, or that someone—something—was behind us, and my heart stuttered in response.

"What?" I asked, so carefully, so quietly.

Her eyes widened even farther, if that was possible. "You don't see that?" She flailed her hands in the air and struggled to get out words. "This!" she finally exclaimed. "Look around you, Lily. The lights are on."

I looked down at the flashlight in her hands. "I'm having a crisis here, Scout, and you're talking to me about turning on a light?"

I could see the frustration in her face, in the clench of her hands. "I didn't turn on the light, Lily."

"So what?"

She put her hands on her hips. "The light is on, but I didn't turn on the light, and there's only one other person in the room."

I lifted my head, raising my gaze to the milk-glass light shade that hung above our heads. It glowed a brilliant white, but the light seemed to brighten and fade as I stared at it—*da dum, da dum, da dum*—as if the bulb had a heartbeat.

The pulse was hypnotic, and the light seemed to brighten the longer I stared at it, but the rhythm didn't change. *Da dum. Da dum. Da dum.*

"Think about your parents," Scout said, and I tore my gaze away from the light to stare at her.

"What?"

"I need you to do this for me. Without questions. Just do it."

I swallowed, but nodded.

"Think about your parents," she said. "How they lied to you. How they showed you a completely false life, false careers. How they have some relationship with Sterling that's going on around us, above our heads, that gives the SRF some kind of control over your parents' actions, what they say, how they act toward you."

The anger, the betrayal, burned, my throat aching with emotion as I tried to stifle tears.

"Now look," Scout said softly, then slowly raised her gaze to the light above us.

It glowed brighter, and the pulse had quickened. *Da dum. Da dum. Da dum.*

It was faster now, like a heart under stress.

My heart.

"Oh, my God," I said, and the light pulsed brighter, faster, as my fear grew.

"Yeah," Scout said. "It's strong emotion, I think. You get freaked out, and the light goes on. You get more freaked out, and the light gets brighter. You saw it kind of dims and brightens?"

"It's my heartbeat," I said.

"Well," she said, turning for the door, "I guess you have a little magic, after all."

She glanced back and grinned. "Twist!"

In no mood for study hall, we found a quiet corner of the main building—far from the administrative wing and its treasonous folders—and camped out until it was over. We didn't talk much. I sat cross-legged on the floor, my back against cold limestone, eyes on the mosaic-tiled ceiling above me. Thinking. Contemplating. Repeating one word, over and over and over again. One word—maybe the only word—momentous enough to push thoughts of my parents' secret life out of my head.

Magic.

I had *magic*.

The ability to turn on lights, which maybe wasn't such a huge deal, but it was magic, just the same.

Magic that must have been triggered somehow by the shot of firespell I'd taken a few days ago. I didn't know how else to explain it, and that mark on my back seemed proof enough. I'd somehow become one of them—not because I'd been born into it, like Scout said, but because I'd been running in the wrong direction in the basement of St. Sophia's one night.

Because I (apparently) had magic, and we were out and about instead of hunkered down in the file vault behind Foley's office, I was focusing on staying calm, controlling my breathing, and trying not to flip whatever emotional switch had turned me into Thomas Edison.

When study hall was over, we merged into the crowd leaving the Great Hall and returned to the room, but the brat pack beat us back. I guessed they'd decided that torturing us was more fun than spending time in their own rooms. Regardless, we ignored them—

bigger issues on our plates—and headed straight for Scout's room.

"Okay," she said, gesturing with her hands when the door was closed and locked behind us, and a towel stuffed beneath it. "I need to check the *Grimoire* and see what I can find, but so I know what I'm looking for, let's see what you can do."

We sat there in silence for a minute.

"What am I supposed to be doing?" I asked.

Scout frowned. "I don't know. You're the one with the light magic. Don't you know?"

I gave her a flat stare.

"Right," she said. "You didn't even know you'd done it."

There was a knock at Scout's closed bedroom door. She glanced at the closed door, then at me. "Yes?"

There was a snicker on the other side. "Did you find anything interesting in that little folder?"

I nearly growled at the question. As if on cue, the room was suddenly flooded with light—bright light, brighter than the overhead fluorescents had any right to be.

"Jeez, dial it back, will ya?"

I pursed my lips and blew out rhythmic breaths, trying to calm myself down enough to dim the lights back below supernova.

"What?" M.K. asked from the other side of the door. "No response?"

Okay, I'd had enough of M.K. for the day. "Hey, Scary Katherine," I said, "don't make us tell Foley that you invaded her vault and stole confidential files from her office."

As if my telling her off had been cathartic, the lights immediately dimmed.

Scout glanced over appreciatively. "Why does it not surprise me that you have magic driven by sarcasm?"

There was more knocking on the door. "Scout?" Lesley tentatively asked. "Are you guys okay in there? Did you set the room on fire?"

"We're fine, Barnaby," Scout said. "No fires. Just, um, testing some new flashlights. In case the power goes out."

"However unlikely that appears to be now," I muttered.

"Oh," Lesley said. "Well, is there anything I can, you know, help with?"

Scout and I exchanged a glance. "Not just right now, Lesley, but thanks."

"Okay," she said, disappointment in her voice. Footsteps echoed through the common room as she walked away.

Scout moved to a bookshelf, fingers trailing across the spines as she searched for the book she wanted. "Okay, so it was triggered by the firespell somehow. We can conclude that whatever magic you've got is driven by emotion, or that strong emotions bump up the power a few notches. It's centered in light, obviously, but it's possible the power could branch out into other areas. But as for the rest of it—"

She stopped as her fingers settled on an ancient book of well-worn brown leather, which she slid from the shelf after pushing aside knickknacks and collectibles.

"It's going to take me some time to research the particulars," she said, glancing back at me. "You want to grab some books, camp out here?"

I thought for a second, then nodded. There was no need to add academic failure to my current list of drama, which was lengthening as the day wore on. "I'll go grab my stuff."

She nodded and gave me a soft smile. "We'll figure this out, you know. We'll figure it out, go back to the enclave, get you inducted, and all will be well."

"When you say well, you mean I can start spending my evenings torturing soul-sucking bad guys and trying not to get shot in the back by firespell again?"

"Pretty much," she agreed with a nod. "But think about how much quality time you and Jason can spend together." This time, when she grinned, she grinned broadly, and winged up her eyebrows, to boot.

The girl had a point.

Later that night, when I was back in my room in pajamas, and calm enough to dial their number, I broke out my cell phone and tried again to reach my parents. It was late in Munich, assuming that's where they were, so they didn't answer. I faked cheerful and left a voice mail, still avoiding the confrontation and because of that, almost glad they hadn't answered. There were too many puzzle pieces—Foley, my parents, and now the SRF— that I still had to figure out. And if they thought keeping me in the dark was safer for all of us, maybe letting them think they'd kept their secret was the best thing to do. At least for now.

That didn't stop the hurt, though. And it didn't stop me from wanting to know the truth.

At lights-out, I turned out the overhead lights, but snapped on a flashlight I'd borrowed from Scout, and broke out my sketch pad and a soft-lead pencil. I turned off the left side of my brain and scribbled, shapes forming as if the pencil were driven by my unconscious. Half an hour later, I blinked, and found a pretty good sketch of Jason staring back at me.

Boy on the brain.

"And just when I needed more drama," I muttered, then flipped off the light.

18

Tuesday went by in a haze. My parents had left a voice mail while I'd slept, a hurried message about how busy they were in Munich, and how much they loved me. And again, I wasn't sure if those words made me feel better . . . or worse.

Mostly, I felt numb. I'd pulled a navy blue hoodie, the zipper zipped, over my oxford shirt and plaid skirt, my hands tucked into pockets as I moved from class to class, the same two questions echoing through my head, over and over and over again.

First, what was I?

Let's review the facts: An entourage of kids with magical powers was running around Chicago, battling other kids with magical powers. A battle of good versus evil, but played out by teenagers who'd only just become old enough to drive. One night I was hit by a burst of magic from one of those kids. Skip forward a couple of days, and I had a "darkening" on my back and the ability to turn on lights when I got upset. So I had that going for me.

Second, what were my parents *really* doing in Germany? They'd told me they'd been granted permission to review some famous German philosopher's papers, journals, and notes—stuff that had never before been revealed to the public. It was a once-in-a-lifetime opportunity, they'd told me, a chance to be the first scholars to see and touch a genius's work. He'd been a Michelangelo of the world of philosophy, and they'd been invited to study *David* firsthand.

But based on what I knew now, that story had been at least partly concocted to satisfy me, because they'd been directed to tell me that they were on a sabbatical. But if that's what they were "supposed" to tell me, what were they actually doing? I'd seen the plane tickets, the passports, the visas, the hotel confirmation. I knew they were in Germany. But why?

Those questions notwithstanding, the day was pretty dull. Classes proceeded as usual, although Scout and I were both a little quieter at lunch. It was a junk food day in the cafeteria—corn chip and chili pies (vegetarian chili for weirdos like me)—so Scout and I picked over our chili and chips with forks, neither saying too much. She'd brought a stack of notes she'd copied out of the *Grimoire* the day before, and was staring at them as she ate. That tended to limit the conversation.

As she read, I looked around the room, watching the girls eating, gossiping, and moving around from group to group. All that plaid. All those headbands. All those incredibly expensive accessories.

All those normal girls.

Suddenly, the theme from *Flash Gordon* began to echo from Scout's bag. Putting down her forkful of chips and chili, she half turned to pull the messenger bag from the back of her chair, then reached for her phone.

I arched an eyebrow at the choice of songs, as lyrics about saving the universe rumbled through our part of the cafeteria.

"I love Queen," Scout covered, her voice a little louder than the phone, the explanation for the folks around us. The song apparently signaling a text message, she slid open the keyboard and began tapping.

"*Flash Gordon*?" I whispered, when the girls had returned to their lunches. "A little obvious, isn't it?"

Pink rose on her cheeks. "I'm allowed," she said, still

thumbing keys. She frowned, her lips pursed at the corner. "Weird," she finally said.

"Everything okay?"

"Yeah," Scout said. "We're supposed to meet tonight at five o'clock—we're doing some kind of administrative meeting—but they want me to come down now. Something's gone down with one of our targets. A kid from one of the publics. That means I need to . . . run an *errand*." She winged up her eyebrows so I'd understand her not-so-tricky secret code.

Around us, girls began to put up their trays in preparation for afternoon classes. Scout had never been interrupted during classes, as far as I was aware. "Right now?"

"Yeah." There was more frowning as she closed the phone and slipped it back into her bag. She turned around again, hands in her lap, shoulders slumped forward, face pinched as she stared down at the table.

"Are you sure you're okay?" I asked her.

She started to speak, then shook her head as if she'd changed her mind, then tried again. "It's just weird," she said, lifting her gaze to mine. "It's way early for them to page me. They never page me during school hours. It's part of the whole, 'You need an education to be the best' "—she looked around, then lowered her voice— " 'Adept you can be.' "

I frowned. "That is weird."

"Well, regardless, I need to go back to the room." She pushed back her chair, pulled off her bag, and settled it diagonally over her shoulder, the skull and crossbones grinning back at me. "Are you going to be okay?"

I nodded. "I'll be fine. Go."

She frowned, but stuffed her phone and books into her bag, stood up, and slung it over her shoulder. Then she was off, plaid skirt bobbing as she hustled through the cafeteria.

She didn't come back during fourth period. Or fifth. Or sixth. Not that I blamed her—European history wasn't my favorite subject, either—but I was beginning to get worried.

When I got back to the suite, I dumped my bag on the couch and headed for her door.

The door was cracked partially open.

"Scout?" I called out. I rapped knuckles against the wood, but got no answer. Maybe she was in the shower, or maybe she'd run an errand and didn't want to bother with the lock. But given her collections and the stash of magic books, she wasn't the kind to leave the door unlocked, much less open.

I put a hand on the door and pushed it open the rest of the way.

My breath left me.

The room was in shambles.

Drawers had been upended, the bed stripped, her collections tossed on the floor.

"Oh, my God," I whispered. I stepped inside, carefully stepping around piles of clothes and books. Had this been waiting for her when she'd come back to the room?

Or had *they* been waiting?

"What happened in here?"

I glanced back and found Lesley in the doorway, her cheeks even paler than usual. She was actually in uniform today. "I don't know," I said. "I just got here."

She stepped into the room, and beside me. "This has something to do with where she goes at night, doesn't it?"

"Yeah. I think so."

My gaze fell upon the bed, the sheets and comforter in disarray. And peeking from one edge, was the black strap of Scout's messenger bag.

I picked over detritus, then reached out an arm and pulled the bag from the tangle of blankets, the white skull on the front grinning evilly back at me.

My stomach fell. Scout wouldn't have gone anywhere without that bag. She carried it everywhere, even on missions, the strap across her shoulder every time she left the room. That the room was a disaster area, her bag was still here, and she was gone, did not bode well.

"Oh, Scout," I whispered, fear blossoming at the thought of my best friend in trouble.

The overhead light flickered.

I stood up again, decided now was as good a time as any to learn control, and closed my eyes. I breathed in through my nose, out through my mouth, and after a few moments of that, felt my chest loosen, as though the fear—the magic—was loosing its grip.

"Ms. Parker. Ms. Barnaby."

Jumping at the sound of my name, I opened my eyes and looked behind me. Foley stood in the doorway, one hand on the door, her wide-eyed gaze on Scout's room. She wore a suit of bone-colored fabric and a string of oversized pearls around her neck.

"What happened here?"

"I found it like this," I told her, working to keep some of my newfound animosity toward Foley—who knew more about my parents than I did—at bay.

"She left at the end of lunch—said she had to come back to the room for something." I skipped the part about why she'd come back, but added, in case it was important, "She was worried, but I'm not sure what about. The door was open when I got here a few minutes ago." I looked back at the tattered remains of Scout's collection. "It looked like this."

"And where is Ms. Green now?" Foley finally glanced at me.

I shook my head. "I haven't seen her since lunch."

Foley frowned and surveyed the room, arms crossed, fingers of her left hand tapping her right bicep. "Call the security office. Do a room-to-room search," she said. I thought she was talking to me, at least until she glanced behind us. A youngish man—maybe twenty-five, twenty-six—stood in the doorway. He was tall, thin, sharp-nosed, and wore a crisp button-down shirt and blue bow tie. I guessed he was an executive assistant type.

"If you don't find her," Foley continued, "contact me immediately. And Christopher, we need to be sensitive to her parents' being, shall we say, particular about the involvement of outsiders. I believe they're in Monaco at present. That means we contact them before we contact the police department, should it come to that. Understood?"

He nodded, then walked back toward the hallway door. Foley returned her gaze to the remains of Scout's room, then fixed her stare on Lesley. "Ms. Barnaby, could you excuse us, please?"

Lesley looked at me, eyebrows raised as if making sure I'd be okay alone with Foley. When I nodded, she said, "Sure," then left the room. A second later, her bedroom door opened and closed.

When we were alone, Foley crossed her arms over her chest and gazed at me. "Has Ms. Green been involved in anything unusual of late?"

I wanted to ask her if secret meetings of magically enhanced teenagers constituted "unusual," but given the circumstances, I held back on the sarcasm.

"Not that I'm aware of," I finally said, which was mostly the truth. I think what Foley would consider "unusual" was probably pretty average for Scout.

Then Foley blew that notion out of the water.

"I'm aware," she said, "of Ms. Green's aptitude as, let's say, a Junior Varsity athlete."

I stared at her in complete silence . . . and utter shock.

"You *know*?" I finally squeaked out.

"I am the headmistress of this school, Ms. Parker. I am aware of most everything that occurs within my jurisdiction."

The ire I'd been suppressing bubbled back to the surface. "So you know what goes on, and you let it happen?

You let Scout run around in the middle of the night, put herself in danger, and you ignore it?"

Foleys's gaze was flat and emotionless. She walked back to Scout's door, closed it, then turned to me again, hands clasped in front of her—all business. "You presume that I let these things happen without an understanding of their severity, or of the risk that Ms. Green faces?" She'd spoken it like a question, but I assumed it was rhetorical.

"I will assume, Ms. Parker, that you are concerned about the well-being of your friend. I will assume that you are speaking from that concern, and that you have not actually considered the consequences of speaking to me in that tone."

My cheeks bloomed with heat.

"Moreover," she continued, moving to one of Scout's bookshelves and righting a toppled paper house, "regardless of what you think of my motivations or my compassion, rest assured that I understand all too well what Ms. Green and her colleagues are facing, and likely better than you do, your incident in the basement notwithstanding."

The house straightened, she turned and looked at me again. "Do we understand each other?"

I couldn't hold it back any longer, couldn't keep the words from bubbling out. "Where are my parents?"

Her eyes widened. "Your parents?"

I couldn't help it, potential danger or not. "I got . . . some information. I want to know where my parents are."

I expected more vitriol, more words to remind me of my position: Me—student; Her—authority figure. But instead, there was compassion in her eyes.

"Your parents are in Munich, Ms. Parker, just as they informed you. Now, however, is not the time to be distracted by the nature of their work. And more important, you should put some faith in the possibility that your parents informed you of the things they believed you should know. The things they believed it was safest for you to know. Do you understand?"

I decided that whatever they were involved in was unlikely to change in the next few hours; I could push Foley for information later. Scout's situation, on the other hand, needed to be dealt with now, so I nodded.

"Very well." And just like that, she was back to headmistress. "I cannot forgo calling Ms. Green's parents forever, nor can I forgo contacting the Chicago Police Department if she is, in reality, missing. But the CPD is not aware of her unique talents. Those unique talents—and the talents of her friends—provide her with certain resources. If the state of her room indicates that she is in the hands of those who would bring harm to people across the city, then those friends are the best to seek her out and bring her back." She raised her eyebrows, as if willing me to understand the rest of what she was getting at.

"I can tell them," I said. "Scout said they're meeting at five o'clock."

Foley smiled, and there seemed to be appreciation in her eyes. "Very good," she said.

"The only problem is," I said, "I don't know exactly where they are. I've only been to the, um, *meeting room* once, and I don't think I could find it again. And even if I did," I added, before she could interrupt, "they don't think I'm one of them." That might change once they discovered my fledgling power, but I doubt Scout had had time to update them. "So even if I can get there, they may not listen to me."

"Ms. Parker, while I understand the nature of their work, I, like most Chicagoans, am not privy to the finer details of their existence. I am aware, however, that there are markers—coded markers—that guide the way to the enclave. Just follow the tags. And once you arrive, *make* them listen." She turned around and disappeared into the common room. A second later, I heard the door to the hallway open and close again.

It was three forty-five, which gave me time to get to the enclave, except for one big problem.

"Just follow the tags?" I quietly repeated. I had no clue what that was supposed to mean.

But, incomprehensible instructions or not, I apparently had a mission to perform . . . and I needed supplies.

I grabbed Scout's messenger bag—proof that she was missing—then left the room and shut the door behind me. When I was back in my room, I grabbed the flashlight I'd borrowed from Scout, dumped the books out of her messenger bag and stuffed the flashlight inside. In a moment of Boy Scout–worthy brilliance, I grabbed some yellow chalk from my stash of art supplies and stuffed it, and my cell phone, into her bag, as well.

Hands on my hips, I glanced around my room. I wasn't entirely sure what else to take with me, and I didn't really have a lot of friend-rescuing supplies to choose from.

"First aid kit," said a voice in the doorway.

I glanced back, found Lesley there, already having ditched the uniform for a pleated cotton skirt and tiny T-shirt. In her hands was a pile of supplies.

"First aid kit," she repeated, moving toward me and laying the pile on my bed. "Water. Granola bars. Flashlight. Swiss Army knife." She must have seen the quizzical expression on my face, as her own softened. "I said I wanted to help," she said, then returned her gaze to the bed. "I'm helping."

The room was quiet for a minute as I took it all in.

"Thank you, Lesley. I appreciate it. Scout appreciates it."

She shrugged her shoulders and smiled absently, then moved toward the door. "Just make sure you tell her I helped."

"As soon as I can," I murmured, just hoping I'd have the opportunity to *talk* to Scout again. I stuffed the supplies into the bag, and had just closed the skull-and-crossbones flap when visitor number two darkened my doorway.

"So your weirdo friend's gone AWOL?"

I glanced behind me. M.K. stood in the doorway, arms folded across a snug, white button-up shirt and the key on a silver chain that lay across it. She must have upgraded from ribbon.

"I don't know what you're talking about."

I turned around again, picked up Scout's bag, and slid the strap over one shoulder.

M.K. huffed. "Everyone is talking about it. Her room is trashed, and she's gone. We all thought she was a flake. Now we have proof. She obviously went postal. She's probably tearing around downtown Chicago in that gigantic coat, raving about vampires or something. I mean, have you seen her room? It was practically a fire hazard in there. About time someone cleaned it out."

I had to press my fingernails into my palms to keep the overhead light from bursting into flame.

"I see," I blandly responded, turning and heading for my bedroom door. "Excuse me," I said, when she didn't move. After rolling her eyes, she uncrossed her arms and ankles and stepped aside.

"Freak," she muttered under her breath.

That was the last straw.

With no fear and no thought of the consequences, I turned on M.K., stepping so close that she pressed herself back into the wall.

"I'm not entirely sure how you finagled your way into St. Sophia's," I said, "and I'm not entirely sure that you'll be able to finagle your way out again. But you might want to think about this—threatening the girls you think are freaks isn't really a good idea, 'cause we're the kind of girls who will threaten you right back."

"You can't—," she began, but I held a finger to her lips.

"I wasn't done," I informed her. "Before I was interrupted, I was making a point: Don't mess with the weirdos, unless you want to lie awake at night, wondering if one of those weirdos is going to sneak a black widow into your bed. Understood?"

She made a huffy sound of disbelief, but wouldn't meet my eyes.

I'd actually scared the bully.

"And M.K.," I said, stepping away and heading for the hallway door, "sleep well."

She didn't look like she would.

19

I took the route to the basement that Scout and I had taken a couple of days before. I wasn't sure how many paths led to the enclave, but I figured I had the best chance to get there if I stuck to the one I (almost) remembered.

I found the side hallway and the basement door, then took the steep stairs to the lower level. This part was more of a challenge. I hadn't been smart enough the last time to play Gretel or Girl Scout, to lay down a trail of crumbs or blaze a path back to the railcar line and the Roman numeral three.

But that didn't mean I couldn't learn from my mistakes. And there were plenty of mistakes, my luck having apparently exhausted itself. Fortunately, I'd left early, giving myself plenty of time to get to the enclave, because it took me half an hour to find the metal door that led to the railcar tunnels, and I had to backtrack two or three times. Each time I found the right route (read: eliminated another dead end from my list of routes to try), I made a little mark on the corridor wall with the yellow chalk from my bag. That way, if I made it through the evening without being beaten down by Adepts, I'd be able to find my way upstairs again.

The possibility that I wouldn't be coming back—that I was about to dive into something nasty in order to save my new BFF—was a thought I kept pretty well repressed. The risk didn't matter, I decided, because Scout would have come after me. She'd have come for me.

I'd heard someone say that bravery was doing the thing you were afraid to do, despite your fear. If that was true, I was the bravest person I knew; the lights that flickered above me as I walked through the hallway—an EKG of my emotions—were proof enough of that.

At the metal door, I reached up on tiptoes and felt for the key Scout had pulled down on our first trip to the enclave. I had a moment of heart-fluttering panic when I couldn't feel anything but dust above the threshold, but I calmed down a little when my fingertips brushed cold metal. I grabbed the key, slipped it into the lock, and unlocked the door.

It popped open with a *whoosh* of cold, stale air. My stomach rolled nervously, but I battled through it. I pulled out the flashlight, flicked the button, and took the step.

But I left the door open behind me, just in case.

"All right," I muttered, swinging the beam of the flashlight from one side of the tunnel to the other, trying to figure out the message Foley had given me.

Look for the tags, she'd said.

While I was willing to do a little backtracking in the tidy limestone basement, backtracking through musty, dirty, damp, and dark tunnels wasn't going to happen. I needed the right route the first time through. And that meant I needed an answer.

"Tags, tags, tags," I whispered, my gaze tracking from railcar tracks to concrete walls to arched ceiling. "Gift tags?" I wondered aloud, even at a whisper, my voice echoing through the hall. "Clothing tags?"

The circle of light swung across the curvaceous graffiti that swirled across one of the walls. I froze, my lips tipping up into a smile.

Turned out, Foley hadn't meant the gift kind or the clothing kind or the HTML kind.

She'd meant the spray paint kind.

Graffiti tags.

The walls were covered in them—a mishmash of pictures and words. Portraits. Political messages. Simple tags: "Louie" had been here a lot. Complicated tags: Thick, curvalicious letters that wrapped around one another into amoebas of words I couldn't even read. However abandoned these tunnels seemed now, they'd been the site of a lot of spray painting, a lot of artistry.

I walked slowly down the first section of the tunnel, moving the circle of light from one wall to the other, trying to find the key that would decipher the code. It was hard enough to read them, much less to decipher them, the letters intertwined, the tags overlapping.

My eye caught a short tag in tidy, white letters, which was centered over an arch-shaped opening that led to the left.

MILLIE 23, it read.

I stilled the flashlight and stared at the tag.

St. Sophia's was located at 23 East Erie, and I'd bet money that Millie was short for Millicent—Scout's first name.

I peeked inside the tunnel and aimed the flashlight beam at the arches at the end of that part of the tunnel. One was blank.

The other, the one on the right, was tagged MILLIE 23.

"Very clever, Scout," I said, and stepped inside.

Thirteen tags, thirteen tunnels, and twelve minutes later, I emerged into the final corridor, stopping before the arched, wooden door of Enclave Three.

I wet my lips, tightened my fingers into a hand, and opened the door.

Heads turned immediately, their expressions none too friendly.

Smith stared at me, eyes wide, fury in his face, hair matted to his forehead. "What the hell are you doing here? And where's Scout?"

"She's gone," I said. "And I need your help."

"Gone?" asked a skeptical voice. Katie stepped beside him, her slim figure tucked into capri-cut jeans and layered V-neck T-shirts beneath a leather letterman jacket. "What do you mean, she's gone?"

"She's been taken." I ignored their gazes and looked to the folks more likely to actually believe me.

"She got a page at noon," I told Michael and Jason, both in uniform, both moving closer to me as I began to explain. "She thought it was strange, but she went anyway. Said she had to go back to her room. She didn't come back to class, and when I got back to the suite after school, her room was trashed."

"Trashed?" Michael asked, a pale cast to his face. "What do you mean, 'trashed'?"

"She has all sorts of collections—books and sculptures and these little houses. All of it was on the floor. Her pillows were slashed. Someone tore the sheets off the bed, emptied her drawers. And then there's this."

I rearranged her messenger bag on my shoulder, revealing the skull and crossbones. "It was still in her room. She never goes anywhere without this bag."

Michael slowly closed his eyes, grief in his expression. "They lured her out."

"Wait," Jason said, "Just wait. Let's not jump to conclusions." He looked at me. "She didn't say anything about meeting someone somewhere? About where she was supposed to be going? About what the emergency was?"

I shook my head.

"What about her cell phone?" asked one of the twins—Jamie or Jill, I wasn't sure—stepping forward. She brushed a waterfall of auburn hair over her shoulder, as if preparing to get down to business. "Do you have it?"

I glanced down at Scout's messenger bag. It had seemed empty after I'd taken her books out, but there was no harm in checking. I slipped a hand into the side pockets, then the interior pocket. Nothing, until I heard something clank against the snap that kept the front flap closed. I looked closer, found a small slit in the flap, and when I reached in a hand, touched cold, hard plastic. My heart sinking, I pulled out Scout's cell phone. Too bad I hadn't found it before, but at least I had it now.

"See who called her," Jamie quietly said. "See what the message said."

I slid the phone open and scanned her recent calls, recent texts, but there was nothing there. "Nothing," I announced. "She must have deleted it."

"We usually do," Michael said softly. "Delete them, I mean. To protect the identities of the Adepts, to keep the locations to ourselves. Simpler that way."

Unfortunately, that meant we wouldn't be able to figure out who'd sent Scout the text. But if she'd erased it as part of her standard Adept protocol, then she'd assumed the message was from another Adept.

Had the person who'd sent it, who'd lured her out, been in this room?

"They'll use her," Michael said. "They've taken her, and they'll use her." He walked to the other end of the room, picked up a backpack, and slung it over one shoulder. "I'm going after her."

Smith stepped in front of him. "You will not go after her."

The room got very quiet, and very tense.

"She's *missing*," I interjected into the silence. "Like Michael said, she was lured out of her room, she's been taken by one of the evil Reaper guys, and we need to find her before this messed-up situation gets any worse!"

Smith nailed me with a contentious glare. "*We?* You are not one of us."

"Really not the point," Michael said, stepping forward. "We can debate her membership later."

"She doesn't have *power*," Katie put in. "She's not one of us, and she shouldn't even be down here, much less giving us orders."

Michael rolled his eyes. "Whether she has power or not is irrelevant."

Smith made a disdainful sound. "You aren't in charge here, Garcia."

"If one of our own is in danger—"

"*Hey*," I said, interrupting the fight. "Internal squabbling can wait. Scout's gone, and we need to get her back now. *Now*, and not after you guys have gone a couple of rounds about the enclave hierarchy."

Smith shook his head. "We can't worry about that right now."

Michael made a sound of disbelief, as if words of shock and awe had caught in this throat. I took the lead on his behalf.

"We can't worry about that?" I repeated. "She's one of you! You can't just leave her ... wherever she is."

When no one spoke up, I glanced around the room, from Paul, to Katie, to the twins, to Jason. Guilty heads dropped around the room. No one would look me in the eye.

I put my hands on my hips, the fingers of my right hand tight around Scout's phone, my link to her. "Seriously? This is how you treat your teammates? Like they're disposable?"

"Getting dramatic isn't going to solve anything," Katie said, crossing her arms over her chest. For a cheerleader type, she managed a bossy, condescending stare pretty well. "We appreciate that you care about Scout, but it's not that simple."

I arched my eyebrows. "The hell it's not."

"Katie's right." Those words from the boy I'd almost decided to have a crush on. As Jason stepped forward, I was glad I'd stuck to "almost."

"If we go after her," he said, earnestness in his blue eyes, "we put ourselves, the city, the community around us, at risk. Being a member of the team means accepting the possibility that you'll become the sacrifice. Scout knew that. Understood it. Accepted that risk."

My heart tumbled, broken a little that this boy was so willing to give up our friend for the sake of people I wasn't sure were worth the sacrifice. And that included him.

"Wow," I said, honestly surprised. "Way to play well with others. Your whole existence is about saving people from Reapers, but you're willing to let her be a 'sacrifice'? I thought being Varsity, being Junior Varsity, being an Adept, was about being part of something bigger? Working together? What about all that talk?"

Smith shook his head. "It's just talk—only talk—if we dump our current agenda—the kids who need protecting—to find her. Think about it, Lily—they've managed to lure Scout into their clutches. They're probably using her as a lure for the rest of us. To pull us in." Smith shook his head. "If we're lucky, they'd just try to indoctrinate us. If not"—he glanced over, green eyes slitted shut—"the Reapers would be setting us up for a nasty night. In which we play the role of toast."

I couldn't argue with the logic—it probably *was* a trap.

But still. It was *Scout*.

I shook my head. "I can't believe you. I can't believe this. All that talk, and you bail when someone needs you. Trap or not, you make an effort. You make a plan. You *try*."

Smith looked away. There might have been a hint of guilt in his eyes, but not enough to force him to act. "I'll call the higher-ups and alert them," he said. "But that's all we can do. We aren't authorized to send out a rescue team. It's not done."

"It can't be," Katie put in, this time quietly. "We just can't do it."

Guilt—and maybe grief—hung in the silence of Enclave Three.

"You should probably go," Jason said. He wouldn't meet my eyes. "You know your way back?"

It took me a minute of staring daggers at all of them, a minute to overcome the disappointment that tightened my throat, before I could speak. "Yeah." I nodded. "Yeah. I can find my way back." My way back to the school and straight into Foley's office. If the Adepts wouldn't act, I'd go back to the principal. She'd know something—a source, a contact, a meaty guy with an attitude who could push through surly teenagers to rescue my BFF.

"It was nice knowing all of you," I said, slipping Scout's phone back into her bag, and putting the bag on my shoulder, then heading for the door. "No," I said, glancing back and arching an eyebrow at the blue-eyed werewolf in front of me. "I take that back. It actually wasn't."

I walked out and slammed the door shut behind me, its hinges rattling with the effort.

Time for Plan B.

I was roasting—not because of the heat (the tunnels were rocking a pretty steady fifty degrees or so), but because emotionally, I was livid.

Seven people had the power to help Scout—better yet, the *magical* power to help Scout. What had she called them? Elemental witches? A reader? A warrior?

So far, I wasn't impressed. Granted, I didn't know them very well, and their reticence to help her could have been the impact of poor, emo-inspired leadership, but still.

I stopped in the middle of the corridor, water splashing beneath my feet. These guys—these guys who wouldn't put their butts on the line to save her—they were the best we could do for good and justice? For rebels, they were pretty picky about obeying the rules. Even Smith's first reaction had been to tell me that I wasn't one of them—a rule that meant I didn't have the right to talk to them, much less make demands.

I stopped.

No way was I going out like this.

I turned around.

I went back.

After I pushed open the door, I opened with a biggie. "I can turn on lights."

Silence.

"You can what?"

"I can"—I had to stop and clear my throat, my voice squeaking nervously, and start over—"I can turn on lights. Dim them, turn them on, turn them off. I'm not sure if that's it, or if there's more, but that's what I know now."

Smith, standing before his troops, crossed his hands behind his head. "You can turn on lights." His voice could hardly have been drier—or more skeptical.

"I can turn on lights," I confirmed. "So you can pretend I'm an outsider, look at me like I'm crazy, but I'm not just someone off the street. I am"—I had to pause for a minute to gather up my courage—"an Adept like you. So you might want to pack away the attitude."

"Whatever," he muttered, as if I'd lied about the power thing just to win points with him. Seriously—if I'd been faking it, wouldn't I have faked something a little more interesting?

The rest of these repressed Adepts might have been intimidated by the floppy hair and attitude, but as they'd so recently reminded me, I wasn't one of them. And he wasn't the boss of me.

I held up an index finger. "Yeah, I may be an Adept, but I'm not a member of your enclave, so I'm not really here to talk to you." I turned my gaze to Paul, then to Jamie and Jill, then to Michael, then Jason. "My best friend—your fellow Adept—is missing. Although I'm not entirely full up on the details, I'm betting you all know what could happen to her out there if she's with *them*. She said something about siphoning spells, right? So even if she's only with the teenage Reapers, the ones that still have power, they could be stealing her energy—her soul—for the rest of them to use." I shook my head. "Unacceptable."

They looked at one another, shared glances.

"This is your chance to step forward," I said, my voice low, earnest. "The chance to do the *right* thing, even if it's the *hard* thing."

"The rules—," Katie began, but Jason (finally!) shook his head.

"It's too late for that," he said. "For rules. We're losing this battle. Today, we risk losing a spellbinder. We can't afford that." More softly, he added, "Not as Adepts, not as friends."

He walked to me, then reached out his hand and slipped his fingers into mine. A spark slid up my arm at the contact, and I squeezed his hand. He squeezed back.

"He's right," Michael said, then glanced around from Adept to Adept. "They're both right, and you know it. All of you know it. It's time to do things differently. To do the hard thing. Who's with me?"

Soft sounds filled the room as Adepts looked around, shuffled feet, made their decisions.

"I'm in," Paul said, then smiled cheekily at me. "And, for the sake of having said it, it's nice to meet you."

I smiled back.

Jamie and Jill exchanged a glance, then stepped forward. "We're in," Jamie said.

Hands on my hips, a satisfied grin on my face, I glanced back at Katie and Smith, who now stood together, eyes narrowed, fury in their expressions.

"This is not how we operate," she said. "These are not the rules of the game."

"Then the rules need to change," Jason said, then looked over at me. "Let's go get your girl."

20

"I was going to find you," Jason whispered, his fingers still laced through mine as we left the enclave, two angry Varsity Adepts in our wake. But instead of walking toward St. Sophia's along the Millie 23 path, we moved deeper into the tunnels.

"As soon as I could get away, I was going to find you so we could get Scout together. But I couldn't say that in front of everyone else."

"Mmm-hmm," I vaguely said, not entirely sure I was ready to forgive him for not taking my side the first time around. Of course, I wasn't so unsure that I let go of his hand.

"Okay," he said, "then how about this—if you don't believe me, then consider this my one screw-up." He looked down at me. "I should have—we all should have—stuck up for her like you did in there. So let me make it up to you now. To both of you."

I squeezed his hand.

When we reached a crossroads—a union of four tunnels, the ceiling arched above us—we stopped.

"All right," Jason said, "we're here, and we've got a goal. Now we need a plan."

Paul snorted. "You mean now that we've thoroughly pissed off Varsity?"

"He's right," said the slightly taller of the twins. "We'll get a lecture supreme when we get back."

"If we get back," Michael muttered, then lifted worried eyes to Jason. "How are we going to manage this?"

"I'm still trying to figure that out."

I held up a hand. "First things first. Where are we going?"

"There's a sanctuary," Michael said, hitching a thumb toward one of the tunnels. "It's near here—the Reaper lodge for this part of Chicago. It's also where they store their vessels."

"Vessels?" I asked.

"The people—humans or Adepts—the older ones feed from. The ones the younger Reapers siphon energy from." So a sanctuary was a room of would-be zombies, their lives dripping away because members of the Dark Elite were too self-centered to let go of their magical gifts.

"My God," I muttered, my skin suddenly crawling. I glanced behind me in the direction of the tunnel we'd come from, suddenly unsure if walking into a trap was a good idea, rescue mission or not.

But then I looked down, my fingers skimming the fabric of Scout's messenger bag, and got an idea.

"The Reapers probably think we'll come for her," I said, looking up at Jason, spring blue eyes staring back. "That we'll storm the castle, this sanctuary, to get her back."

"Probably," Jason agreed, then tilted his head, curiosity in his expression.

"Well, if that's what they expect, then we should do the thing they aren't expecting. We flank them—create a distraction. Pull them out and away from Scout. And when they're distracted, we send in a team to sneak her out again."

There was silence for a moment, and I had to work not to shuffle my feet.

"That's actually not bad, Parker," Jason said. "I'm impressed."

"I ate a good lunch today."

"So who does what?" Paul asked.

"I can read the building," Michael said. "I can read it, figure out where she is." I guessed that meant Michael was preparing to use his powers.

"In that case, how about Jamie, Michael, and Parker go in, find Scout, get out." Jason looked at Paul. "You, me and Jill will play the distraction game. Are you guys up for a little snow and ice?"

The twins looked at each other and broke into precocious grins. "Absolutely," said the taller one, her aqua eyes shining. "Snow and ice are right up my alley."

Jason nodded managerially. "Then let's talk details."

Like the enclave, the Reaper sanctuary was housed underground in the cavelike innards of a former power substation, still connected to the tunnels beneath the city. We'd use two entrances—the main door, where Jill, Paul, and Jason would create their distraction—and the back door, where Jamie, Michael, and I would sneak in, hopefully undetected, find Scout, and get out again. I was solely support staff—Michael and Jamie would handle any Reapers, while I'd help take care of Scout and get her safely from the building. We'd all rendezvous in the crossroads again, hopefully with one additional—and healthy—nose-ringed Adept in tow.

The plans and our cues established, we prepared to split up.

"Are you all right with this?"

I looked over at Jason, my heart quickening at the concern in his eyes, and nodded. "Turning on lights isn't much, but it's something. Maybe I can figure out a way to contribute." Assuming I could learn to control it in the next ten or fifteen minutes, I silently added.

He tilted his head at me. "You were serious about that—the lights?"

I smiled ruefully. "Turns out, the darkening wasn't a fake." I raised my hands and shook them in faux excitement. *"Yay."*

"All right," Michael said. "Everybody ready?"

"Ready," Jason said, then leaned down and whispered, his lips at my cheek, "You take care, Lily Parker. And I'll see you in a little while."

Goose bumps pebbled my skin. "You, too," I whispered.

"All right," he said, his voice echoing through the tunnels. "Let's do this." He nodded at Paul and Jill, and they started on their way, moving through the tunnel to the left.

Michael, Jamie, and I shared a glance, nodded our readiness, and headed to the left.

The walk wasn't short, but the tunnels allowed us to move swiftly beneath the hustle and bustle of downtown Chicago to find the place where Reapers conducted some of their soul sucking. A few turns and corridors, and then the tunnel opened onto a platform, a set of stairs of corrugated iron leading up to a rusty metal door.

We stopped just inside the edge of the tunnel—Michael signaling quiet with a raised fist—and stared at the platform. No movement. No sound. No indication of surly, magic-bearing teenagers.

"Let's go," Michael whispered after a moment, and we crept toward the stairs—Michael in front, me in the middle, Jamie behind. Since Jill was going to be making ice for Jason's distraction, I assumed Jamie was the twin with fire powers. I still wasn't sure what a reader or fire witch could do, but I hoped that whatever it was could help us find Scout.

We took the steps to the door, but Michael, in the lead, didn't open it. Instead, he pressed his palm to it, then closed his eyes. After a moment of silence, he shook his head.

"Pain and loss," he said. "All through the building, through the steel, the brick, the city above. The pain leaks, fills the city. All because they won't make the sacrifice."

Another few seconds of silence passed. I stared at

him, rapt, as he communed with the architecture. Suddenly, he yanked his hand back as if the door had gone white-hot. He rubbed the center of his palm with his other hand, then glanced back at us. "She's in there."

Jamie smiled softly at Michael "We'll find her."

At Michael's nod that he was ready to move, we tried the door, found it unlocked. It opened into a hallway that led deeper into the building. The hallway was empty. We stood in the threshold for a moment, gazes scanning for Reapers.

"It's too quiet," Jamie softly said, her tone unconvinced that it was going to stay that way.

"That's the point of distraction," Michael pointed out, "to keep things as quiet as possible for us."

A frigid breeze suddenly moved through the hallway.

"Jill is working," Jamie whispered, the breeze apparently evidence of the ice witch's work. "That's our cue to move."

We walked inside, Jamie lagging behind just long enough to ensure that the door closed silently behind us. "All right, Mikey," she said, "where do we go?"

Michael nodded, then pressed his hand to the hallway wall. "Down the hall. There's a room. Empty—no, not empty. A girl. A soul. Damaged. But she's there."

He opened his eyes again and looked at me, his expression tortured. It wasn't hard to guess how he felt about her, even if she didn't reciprocate those feelings. "She's there."

Jamie looked at me, her aqua irises suddenly swirling with fire. Goose bumps rose on my arms. "Then let's go," she said.

Without warning, a crash echoed through the building, the floor rumbling beneath us. "Alex," I murmured. The bringer of earthquakes.

"And probably her crew," Jamie agreed, taking the lead. "We need to move."

We hustled down the hallway, pausing at each open

door to peek inside, look for Scout, make sure we weren't walking into a bevy of Reapers. But there was no one, nothing. No signs of people—Reaper or otherwise. Nothing but old, industrial equipment and rusty pipes.

"It's too quiet," Jamie said as we neared a set of double doors at the end of the hall. "Distraction or not, this is too quiet."

"Here," Michael said, suddenly pushing through the double doors without thought of what might await him on the other side. "She's . . . here."

I followed him in, lights flickering above us, the rhythm of the lights as quick as my heartbeat. The room was big and concrete, giant tubs and shelving along the sides. It looked like a storage facility they'd tried to turn into some kind of ceremonial hall, a long red carpet running down the middle aisle, a gold quatrefoil on a purple banner hanging from one end. The Reaper symbol, I realized, there for all to see.

And below the banner lay Scout on a long table, her body buckled down with wide leather straps around each ankle and wrist, her arms pinned to her side.

"Oh, my God," I whispered.

She looked pale—even more so than usual. He cheeks seemed sunken, and dark circles lay beneath her eyes. Her collarbone was visible. Her usually vibrant blond and brown hair lay in a pale corona around her head. But for the rise and fall of her chest, I'd have wondered if we'd arrived too late.

I had to bite my lip to keep tears from slipping over my lashes. "What happened to her?" I whispered.

Michael moved around her and began to work one of the buckles around her ankles. "Reapers," he said. "This is what they do, Lily. They steal things that don't belong to them."

Where there had been sadness, fear, trepidation, in his voice . . . now there was fury. Michael tugged at one leather buckle, freed the pin, then pulled loose the strap.

"These kids, these adults, these people, think they have the right to take the lives of others, and for what? For *what*?"

Michael mumbled a string of words in Spanish, and while I didn't understand exactly what he'd said, I got the gist. The boy was *pissed*.

He bobbed his head toward her wrists, which were pinned near her head. "Jamie, keep an eye on the door. Get ready to raise flame if we need it. Lily, get her wrist restraints."

I jumped to the other end of the table and started fumbling with Scout's restraints. She lifted her head as I reached her, blinking with the one eye that wasn't bruised and swollen, but she didn't speak. They must have hit her while she was being restrained. I hoped she fought back. I hoped she gave as good as she got.

"I think you've managed to get yourself into some kind of mess here," I said with a small grin, trying to make her laugh, trying to keep my heart from thumping out of my chest. "I thought you were going to keep yourself safe?"

She tried a smile, but winced in pain. "I'll try harder next time, Mom," she said, her voice cracking.

"You'd better," I said, fumbling with the latch on the first buckle. "We're gonna get you out of here, okay?"

She nodded, then put her head back on the table. "I'm tired, Lil. I just—I think I'll just go home and sleep."

"Stay awake, Scout. We're going to get you out, but I need you to stay awake."

"Hurry, Lily," Michael implored, and I heard the clank as her first ankle restraint was loosed. "I don't know how much time we'll have." He moved around the table to get a better angle on her other ankle.

"I'm going as fast as I can," I assured him.

We'd just managed to untie her, to loosen all her restraints, and help her sit up and swing her feet over the bed when, without warning, the door at the other end of the room, crashed open, falling in on its hinges.

Dark-haired Sebastian, the boy with firespell, walked inside. My breath quickened at the sight of him, and my back tightened at the memory of the pain he'd inflicted. Alex walked in behind him.

"Stay with Scout," Michael murmured. I nodded, and braced my body to help support her as he stepped away and in front of us, a human shield.

"Oh, look," Alex said. "It's an entire band of Buffy wanna-be's."

"Better Buffy wanna-be's than would-be zombies," Jamie said. "You guys are rotting corpses waiting to happen. That's gonna put a hitch in those Abercrombie catalog plans, don't you think?"

Alex growled and tried to take a step toward us, but Sebastian put a hand on her arm.

"I assume the vitriol means you're all acquainted," a third person said. Sebastian and Alex stepped aside, and he stepped into the gap between them.

He was tall, thin, silver haired, distinguished looking. He wore a crisp black suit, with a white, button-up shirt beneath. Every hair was in place, every bit of fabric perfectly creased. His eyes were pale blue, watery, red at the edges. But there was something about his eyes—something wrong. They were empty—dangerously empty.

"Mr. Garcia," he said, his voice flat, bored, as he bobbed his head toward Michael. Jamie moved to stand beside Michael, a supernatural barrier between us and the bad guys. "Ms. Riley," he said. I guessed that was Jamie.

And then the man leveled his watery gaze at me, and I shuddered reflexively.

"I don't believe we're acquainted," he said, just before Sebastian leaned in and whispered something to him.

The man's eyebrows lifted in interest.

My stomach fell, and I hunched a little closer to the table behind me. I was confident I did not want this guy interested in me.

"Aha," he said, sliding his hands into his pockets. "The girl who, shall we say, became closely acquainted with Mr. Born's magic?"

I took a moment to glare at Sebastian, who I assumed had mentioned that he'd hit me with firespell during my fateful trip into the basement.

But more interesting was the look I got back from him. I expected disdain or irritation—the emotions on Alex's face. But Sebastian looked almost ... apologetic.

"I'm Jeremiah," the older man said, drawing my attention away from Sebastian. "And I can't tell you how interested I am to make your acquaintance. I hope you weren't harmed?"

"I'm fine," I gritted out, doubtful that he cared whether I'd been harmed or not. The lights above us flickered once, then twice. When Jeremiah's eyes flicked with interest to the fixtures, I knew I had to tamp it down. I didn't want him knowing that I was now an Adept, thanks to "Mr. Born's magic," and that I was now one of his enemies.

As if she understood the struggle, Scout squeezed my hand. I squeezed back and forced myself to stay calm.

Since Jeremiah was older than the Reapers around him, I assumed he was a leader, one of the self-centered asses who'd decided that taking the lifeblood of others was a cost worth paying to keep his own magic.

He looked from me to Michael and Jamie. "Your distraction was just that," he said. "Merely a distraction. Next time, you might do a little more planning. But, since you're here, what brings you to our little sanctuary?"

As if he didn't know. "You kidnapped my friend," I reminded him.

Jeremiah rolled his eyes as if bored by the accusation. "Kidnapping is a harsh word, Ms. Parker, although given the fact that you've undoubtedly been brainwashed by these agitators, these troublemakers, I'll forgive the transgression. These children don't understand the gifts they've been given. They reject their power. They turn away from it, and they blame us for accepting it. For abiding by the natural order. They cast us as demons."

"The power corrupts," Michael said. "We don't reject it. We give it back."

"And what do you have to show for that decision?" Alex asked. "A few years of magic until you're normal again. Ordinary."

"*Healthy*," Michael said. "Helpers. Not parasites on the world."

Jeremiah barked out a mirthless laugh. "How naïve, all of you." He aimed his gaze at me. "I would hope, Ms. Parker, that you might spend some time thinking critically about your friends and whatever lies they told you. They are a boil on the face of magic. They imagine themselves to be saviors, rebels, a mutiny against tyranny. They are wrong. They create strife, division, amongst us when we need solidarity."

"Solidarity to take lives?" I wondered aloud. "To take the strength of others?"

Jeremiah clucked his tongue. "It's a pity that you've succumbed to their backward belief that the magic they've been given is inherently evil. That it is inherently bad. Those are ideas for the small-minded, for the ignorant, who do not understand or appreciate the gifts."

"Those gifts degrade," Jamie pointed out. "They rot you from the inside."

"So you've been taught," Jeremiah said, taking a step toward us. "But what if you're wrong?"

"Wrong?" Scout asked hoarsely. "How could they be wrong?"

"You steal other peoples' essences," Michael said, pointing at Scout, "from people like her, in order to survive. Does that sound right to you?"

"What is right, Mr. Garcia? Is it right that you would be given powers of such magnitude—or in your case, knowledge of such magnitude—for such a short period of time? Between the ages of, what, fifteen and twenty-five? Does it seem natural to you that such power is intended to be temporary, or does that seem like a construct of shortsighted minds?"

I glanced over at Scout, who frowned as if working through the logic and wondering the same thing.

"We *agree* to give up their powers," Jamie pointed out, "before they become a risk. A liability. Before we have to take from others."

"A very interesting conclusion, Ms. Riley, but with a flawed center. Why should you protect humans who are not strong enough to take care of themselves? What advantage is there in stepping forward to protect those who are so obviously weak? Whose egos vastly outpace their abilities? Those who are gifted with magic are elite amongst humans."

As if bored with the conversation, he waved a hand in the air. "Enough of this prattle. Are you willing to see the error of your ways? To come back to the fold? To leave behind those who would rip you from your true family?"

Reaper or cult leader? I wondered. It was hard to tell the difference with this one.

"Are you high?" Michael asked.

Jeremiah's nostrils flared. "I'll take that as a juvenile 'no,'" he said, then turned on his heel. "*Ad meloria*. Finish them."

21

"Aw, this is my favorite part," said Alex, then outstretched her hands.

But before she could shake the earth, Jamie wound up her left hand as if bracing for a pitch. "Keep your issues," she said, then slung her arm forward, "to yourself." A wave of heat blew past us as pellets of white fire shot from Jamie's hand like sparks from a sparkler.

"Holy frick," I muttered, instinctively covering my head even though the fire wasn't meant for me. But it was enough to temporarily subdue Alex, who drew back her hand and hit the ground, wrapping her arms around her head to avoid the burn.

"Help me off this thing," Scout muttered, grasping my arm. I pulled her to her feet as Michael glanced around at the movement.

"Green," he yelled over the crackle of falling sparks, "get behind the table!"

"Garcia," Scout said, fingers biting into my hand as she kept herself upright, "I'm the spellbinder here. You get *your* ass behind the table."

"They're reloading," Jamie said, turning to grab my arm. She pulled me behind the table, and I dragged Scout with me. "Let's all get behind the table."

We'd just managed to hit the deck when the pressure in the room changed. I knew what was coming, deep in my bones. I clapped my hands to my ears against the sudden ache, as if my blood and bones remembered it, *feared* it.

The air in the room vibrated, contracted, and expanded, and the light seemed to shift to apple green, the table suddenly flying above our heads with Sebastian's burst of firespell. I covered Scout's body with mine and we were both saved the impact, but the move stripped us of our cover. We were all but naked, nothing but air between us and two Reapers who appeared to be better equipped for the battle than we were.

"I'm on it," Jamie yelled, turning from her crouch, fingers outstretched in front of her, her irises shifting to waves of flame again. There was another crackle of sound and energy as a wall of white fire began to rise between us and the Reapers. I kneeled up to sneak a glance and saw Sebastian on the other side, black brows arched over hooded blue eyes. He stared at me, his gaze intense, one arm outstretched, his chest heaving with the exertion of the firespell he'd thrown, lips just parted.

I don't know why—maybe because of the intensity in his eyes, in his expression—but I got goose bumps again, at least until the growing barrier of flame blocked my view. I guessed it was a foot thick, nearly six feet tall, and it crossed the room from one side to the other, a blockade between us and the Reapers.

For a moment, as if entranced, I stared at the wall of white fire, the heat of the dancing flames warming my cheeks. "Amazing," I murmured, turning to gaze in awe at Jamie.

"More amazing if it could withstand that earthquake business," she said as the ground rumbled beneath us. "I braided the strands of flame together. It's hard to penetrate, at least at first, but it won't hold forever. Flame acts like a fluid. It flows, sinks. The strands will separate."

"Scout," Michael called, "can you do anything? Reinforce the wall?"

She squeezed my hand, closed her eyes, and was quiet for a moment. And then she began to chant.

"Fire and flame/in union bound/from parts, a whole/from top to ground." Her body suddenly spasmed; then she went limp. I glanced behind us at the wall. It shivered, seemed to ripple with magic, then stilled again.

She'd tried, but whatever she'd done hadn't quite taken.

Scout tightened her grip on my hand, then opened her eyes and glanced over at Michael. "I can't," she whispered, tears pooling in her eyes. "I'm sorry. I can't. I don't have any mojo left. They took it, Michael."

"It's okay," Michael said, pressing his lips to her forehead. "You'll heal. It's okay."

"I can spark them again," Jamie said, "but I need to recharge for a minute, and the wall isn't going to keep them away for long."

I inched up to peek over the fire, assessed, and quickly sat down again. "There're two more of them. Are we toast?"

"Reaper toast," Scout agreed, then leaned into a fit of coughing.

"Scout?" Michael asked.

When she looked up at him, there were tears in her eyes. "It was a nightmare, a black hole. They trapped me, and they'd have kept going until there was nothing left. No energy, no magic—just a shell."

"They must have doubled their efforts," Michael said, his eyes scanning her face, like a doctor checking her injuries. "Siphoned more greedily than their usual one-day-at-a-time protocol. Probably weren't sure how long they'd be able to keep her." He glanced at me. "Energy taken from Adepts is more potent, more powerful, than energy from folks without gifts, so they'd have taken what they could get while they could get it, passed it on to elders like Jeremiah. You said they trashed her room, right? Maybe they were looking for her *Grimoire*, her spell book, something to try and capture some of her gifts, as well as her energy."

"They'll keep coming," Scout said quietly. "They

won't kill us. They'll just suck us dry until there's nothing left. Until we leave everyone and everything else behind and do exactly what they want."

"Like magical brat packers," I muttered, sarcasm the only way I knew to deal with a future that terrifying.

"What can you do?" Jamie suddenly asked me. "You said something about lights? If we could distract them, maybe we could make a run for the door? Scatter through the tunnels?"

I nodded, my heart pounding, and looked up at the fluorescent lights overhead. I stared at them, concentrating, trying to speed my heart into whatever state was going to trigger the magic. Into whatever state was going to turn off all the lights.

"You can do it, Lil," Scout whispered, leaning her head against my shoulder. "I know you can."

I nodded, squeezing my fingers into fists until my nails cut crescents into my palms.

Nothing.

Not even a flicker, even as my heart raced with the effort.

"Scout, I don't know how," I said, staring up at the lights again, which burned steadily—not even a hiccup—in their fixtures. "I don't know how to make it happen."

"'S okay, Lil," she said softly. "You'll learn."

But not fast enough, I thought.

The ground rumbled again, the flames shaking on their foundations. It was another of Alex's earthquakes, and that wasn't all—the wall vibrated, wavered, at three or four other points along the line. They were hammering at it, trying to break through.

And despite my chest being full of fear, there wasn't so much as a flicker in the lights above us.

Maybe it had been a fluke before, a power surge in the building at the same time I'd been afraid or excited, and not magic after all. Maybe I had been a fluke.

But there was no time to worry about it . . . because the wall began to unravel.

I watched as the strands unbraided, listened as Reapers began to yell around us.

"It's going," Jamie warned over the motion and noise.

She was right, but it had help.

The air pressure changed again, the light turning a sickly green.

"Firespell!" I yelled, both Michael and I hunkering down to cover Scout with our bodies, my arms wrapped around her head.

The very walls seemed to contract, then expand with a tremendous force. The shot of firespell Sebastian threw across the room turned Jamie's fluid fire into a brittle wall that shuddered, then exploded, shards flying out in all directions before crashing to the ground like shattered glass.

When the air was still again, a haze of white smoke filling the room, I glanced over at Jamie. Her eyes were closed, and there was blood rushing from a gash in her forehead.

"Michael?" I asked, shaking white powder from my hair.

He muttered a curse in Spanish. "I'm okay." He sat up again, chunks of white . . . *stuff* . . . falling around his body. "Scout?"

I moved my arms and she lifted her head. "I'm okay, too."

"I think Jamie's hurt," I said.

Michael looked at her, then glanced around. The room was in chaos, Reapers yelling at one another, smoke wafting through the room.

"We've got to make a run for it," he said, "use the chaos to our advantage. It's our best chance."

I nodded, then put a hand on Jamie's shoulder and shook gently. "Hey, are you okay?"

Her eyelids fluttered, then opened. She raised a hand to her face and wiped at the blood streaming from the gash at her temple.

"Here," I said, pulling off my plaid tie and wrapping it around her head tight enough to put pressure on the wound and keep the blood out of her eyes.

"Can you get up?" I whispered. "We're going to try to make a run for it."

She nodded uncertainly, but it was a nod just the same. I helped her to her feet as Michael helped Scout behind me. As stealthily as we could, we began to move through the smoke and back toward the door, picking our way through the remains of the transfigured wall, me trying to hold Jamie upright, Michael all but carrying Scout.

We made progress, the haze aiding our escape, and managed to get halfway closer to the door . . . at least until a voice rang through it.

"*Stop*."

We looked over. Alex emerged from a swirl of white, Sebastian beside her.

She stretched out a hand. "You can come willingly, or I can knock you all on your asses."

Reapers—the ones we hadn't been introduced to—began closing in from the left and right.

"Michael?" I asked.

"Um," was all he said, his own gaze shifting from side to side as he tried to figure a way out.

I'm not sure what made me do it, but I chose that moment to glance at Sebastian, who stood just behind Alex, his hooded gaze on me again. And while I looked at him and he looked back at me, he mouthed something.

Let go.

I frowned, wondering if I'd seen that correctly.

As if in confirmation, he nodded again. "Let go," he mouthed again. No sound, just the movement of his lips around the words.

I stood quietly for a moment as the Reapers gathered around us. Somehow, I knew he was right. And although he was supposed to be kicking our collective butt right now, I knew he was trying to help.

I didn't know why, but I knew it as surely as I knew

that I was standing in the midst of people I wanted to protect.

People I *could* protect.

I took a chance.

"Get down," I told Jamie, Michael, and Scout.

"Lily?" Scout asked, confusion in her voice.

"We know what you've got in store," Alex said. "We know what you can dish out, and I think we've demonstrated that it ain't real much, so it's our turn to teach you all a lesson. To teach you about who matters in this world, and who doesn't."

"Trust me, Scout," I repeated, suddenly as sure about this as I'd ever been about anything else. I was where I should be, doing what I should be doing, and Sebastian had been right.

After a half second of deliberation, Scout nodded to Jamie and Michael. I waited until they'd all crouched down beside me, and then I did as he'd directed.

I stopped *trying* to make magic.

And I let the magic make itself.

I outstretched my arms and trained my gaze on Sebastian, and felt warmth begin to flow through my legs, my torso, my arms.

Firespell.

Not Sebastian's.

Mine.

My magic to wield, triggered by the shot of firespell I'd received a few days ago, but mine all the same.

I held my arms open wide. He nodded at me, then put a hand on his head and crouched down behind Alex.

I pulled the power, the energy, into my body, the room contracting around us as it filled me. My eyes on Alex, one eyebrow arched, I pushed it back.

"Bet you didn't know about *this*," I said.

The room turned green, a wash of power vibrating through it with a bass roar, knocking down everyone who wasn't already crouched behind me.

It took a second to overcome the shock at what I'd

done, at what had seemed natural to do. I shivered at the power's sudden absence, wobbling a little until the pressure in my head equalized again.

The ground rumbled a little, an aftershock; then the room went silent, a spread of unconscious Reapers around us.

Michael stood again and helped Scout and Jamie to their feet. "Well-done, Parker. Now let's get out of here."

I offered an arm to Jamie, then glanced back at the dark-haired boy who lay sprawled on the floor a few feet away. "Let's go," I agreed, positive that I'd see him again.

22

We regrouped in the catacombs, Jason, Jill, and Paul emerging from their tunnel at a run. Jill and Paul both went to Jamie—sisterly concern in her eyes, something altogether different from the brotherly concern in his.

Jason's eyes had shifted again from blue to the green of flower stems, a color that seemed unnaturally bright for a human . . . but better for a wolf. His hair was in disarray, sticking up at odd angles, a bruise across his left cheekbone. His gaze searched the crossroads, then settled on me, ferocity in his eyes.

His lips pulled into a wolfish grin, dimples at the corners of his mouth. I swallowed, the hairs on my neck standing on end at the primal nature of his gaze. I wasn't sure if I was supposed to run and hide, or stand and fight, but the instinct had certainly been triggered.

He looked me over, and once assured that I was fine, checked out Michael and Scout. She was on the ground, sitting cross-legged. Michael sat beside her, holding her hand.

When the two groups had reunited, everyone had made sure that everyone else was okay, and everyone had been debriefed about the rescue, Scout spoke up.

"Thanks, everyone," she said quietly. "If you hadn't come—"

"Thank Lily," Michael said, smiling up at me with appreciation in his dark eyes. "She's the one who led the charge. She did good."

"Parker showed some hustle," Jason agreed, offering me a sly smile, his eyes now back to sky blue. "She'll make a good addition to the team."

Scout humphed. "She'll make a good addition if Varsity lets her join, but that would require Varsity pulling their heads out of their butts. Katie and Smith are being total jerks."

"They'll unjerkify," Jason said confidently. "Have faith."

"I always have faith in us," she said. "It's them I'm not too sure about."

"Have some water," Michael said, passing her the bottle I'd pulled from my messenger bag. "You'll feel better. And when we get back to the enclave, you can tell us what happened to you."

Scout snorted defiantly, but did as she was told.

I stood up and stepped away to a quiet corner and looked down at my hands, still in awe at what I'd managed to do.

And I was still unsure how I'd managed to do it.

Okay, that was a lie. I knew exactly what I'd done, the sensation of doing it somehow as natural—as expected—as breathing. It wasn't that I'd suddenly *learned* how to do it, but more that my body had *remembered* how to do it.

I just had no idea how that was possible.

Jason walked over, pulled a candy bar from his pocket, ripped off the wrapper, snapped off an end, and handed it to me.

I took it with a smile, then nibbled a square of chocolate-covered toffee. I didn't have much of a sweet tooth, but the sugar hit the spot. "Thanks."

"Thank you," he said. "You saved our butts today. We appreciate that, especially since your last visit to the enclave wasn't very pleasant."

"Yeah, I don't think Smith and Katie liked me very

much. And they definitely aren't going to like me now. Not after this."

"Like it or not, you're one of us, so I guess they'll get used to you."

"I guess," I said with a shrug. "The bigger question is, can *I* get used to it? Can my parents"—wherever, whoever they were—"get used to it?"

"My parents did," he said. "Get used to it, I mean."

I glanced over. "They got used to the idea that you're a werewolf?"

He gave me a sly, sideways glance. "Yes," he admitted. "They got used to that. But it's hereditary, so it wasn't much of a surprise when I started howling at the moon."

"They knew, and they sent you to Montclare anyway?"

He nodded. "Montclare was better for everyone."

"Why?"

"The principal knows what I am," he said. "He's a friend of my parents'—grew up with my mother. They shared my secret with him so that someone would understand how to deal with me if something happened."

"If you went all *Teen Wolf*, you mean?"

He grinned at me, his ridiculously blue eyes tripping my heart. "You say what's on your mind, don't you, Parker? I like that."

I rolled my eyes. "You have to stop flirting with me, Shepherd, or we're never going to get anything done."

"Flirting? You're the one who's getting me all riled up."

"Oh, please. You're all, 'Here, Lily, have some candy.' It's obvious who's flirting here."

"Then maybe I should kiss you."

I blinked, my cheeks suddenly on fire. "Oh. Well. If you think that's best."

He smiled softly, then leaned in toward me, smoke over sapphires as his lashes fell. I closed my eyes, blocking out the world around us, my heart pounding as he *almost* pressed his lips to mine.

"Well, well."

Did I mention the "almost"? I mentally cursed my best friend before we jerked apart and sat up straight. Scout stood in front of us, one hand on Michael's shoulder, looking a little better than she had a few minutes ago. The water and few minutes of rest in Michael's company must have helped. And if anyone could summon up a little spirit and energy after a round of soul sucking, it was Scout.

"I assume I'm not interrupting anything?"

"I wouldn't go that far," Jason mumbled.

I snickered and gave him a gentle elbow to the ribs. "You're fine," I told Scout. "We were just taking a break."

"I can see that," she said. "We're ready to hike back, if you want to join us."

Jason turned back and offered me a hand.

"I think I can manage," I said.

"Whatever you need, Parker," he said, offering me a dimple-laced smile.

I had an unfortunate inkling that I knew what that was.

The air in the enclave was thick with tension when we arrived. Katie and Smith weren't thrilled that we'd walked out on them, but they were happy to see Scout. They seemed considerably less happy to see me, and gave me dirty looks as we sat around the table and Michael, Jason, and Scout detailed our adventure.

As it turned out, the message Scout received said that an Adept had been hurt. Scout didn't say which Adept, but given her glances in Michael's direction, I reached my own conclusion. She'd gone back to her room to put up her books and prepare for a trip into the tunnels; that's when they grabbed her. There had been two Reapers, probably college age, but not people she recognized. She had no idea how they'd gotten into the school, but they'd been dressed, she said, like maintenance men—

complete with badges and name tags. They'd already tossed her room when she arrived.

"Why you?" Michael asked, eyebrows furrowed. "If they were looking for a double shot of power, they could have chosen any of us."

Scout dropped her hand, outstretched both of them, and stared at her fingertips. "I think it has something to do with my power," she said, then clenched her hands into fists and raised her gaze to us again. "They kept talking about spellbinders and spellcasters, about the differences between them." She shook her head. "I don't know. I didn't understand most of it. I mean, 'spellcaster' is a made-for-television word as far as I'm aware, not an actual description of power. I'll have to check the *Grimoire*, see what I can find."

"Are you sure you still have it?" I asked. "What if they took it when they went through your stuff?"

Scout grinned widely. "What kind of spellbinder would I be if my *Grimoire* looked like a giant book o' magic? Remember that comic book I showed you the other day?"

"Ah," I said, understanding dawning. "That's sneaky and impressive." She winked back.

"What happened after they grabbed you?" Smith asked, with more concern in his voice than I would have given him credit for.

Scout's voice got softer as she retold that part of her tale, and she gripped my hand as tightly as she had in the sanctuary itself. The Reapers had used siphoning spells to begin the process of ripping away her energy, her will. They'd dispersed to deal with Jason's distraction, and that's when we'd found her.

Jason and Michael replayed their respective parts of the story, the room quieting again when Michael told them I'd used firespell to subdue the Adepts.

But Smith and Katie still looked unconvinced. They apparently didn't buy that I had magic, much less that particular kind of magic.

"It's not possible," Smith said, shaking his head. "A shot of magic, firespell or otherwise, can't transfer magic to someone else. That's not the way it works."

"You're right," Scout said, "but that's not what happened." She pulled a folded sheet of paper from the pocket of her skirt, then spread it flat on the table. "I've done some research. It turns out, there have been a handful of gifted folks whose magic wasn't obvious until something happened, until some act triggered their power."

"So it doesn't just develop on its own," Jill put in, "like you'd normally expect?"

Scout nodded. "Right. Lily didn't get the magic at puberty, unlike the rest of us. It's more like the magic is latent, in hiding, until something comes along and kicks it into gear. And once it's kicked, it's usually pretty big."

"What do you mean 'usually'?" Smith asked, brows furrowed together.

"Lily's not the first," Scout said. "There's an entire line of Contingency Adepts. Twelve of them. Half of them have power magic—the ability to wield electricity."

"Power," I quietly repeated. "That's why I can dim the lights?"

Scout nodded. "Exactly. And like I told you, that's what firespell's made of."

"Well, that sounds okay," I said. I wasn't sure I was thrilled to be an Adept, but there was something comforting about knowing what had happened. I mean, the whole thing was only barely believable, but in the context in which I was currently working—and having shot magic from my fingertips—it was comforting.

But as I scanned the faces around me, which suddenly looked a little peaked, I guessed they weren't as comforted. "Except everybody looks weird. Why does everybody look weird?"

"There aren't any firespell Adepts," Jason said, "at least not that we're aware of. They have an uncanny willingness to stay with the herd."

"To stay evil," I clarified dryly, and he nodded.

"And there is the other catch," Scout said.

"Wait," I said, holding up a hand. "Let me guess. Using this newfound power will slowly make me more and more evil, until there's nothing left of me but a cold, crusty shell of emptiness and despair. Lovely!"

"But we've all got to deal with *that*," Paul said with a grin.

"I mean, there is a benefit," Scout said. "You have a pretty kick-ass power, and you're obvs the only Adept with firespell, so that's awesome for *us*. You're a solid addition to the team."

I lifted my brows. "A solid weapon, you mean?"

"A solid *shield*," Michael said, his voice quiet and serious. "And we can use you."

"Whoa," Smith said, slicking the hair down over his forehead. "Let's not get too excited. So-called contingency magic or not, she's still not one of us. She's not an enclave member until we run things past the supervisors."

I leaned in toward Scout. "Supervisors?"

"The folks with authority," Scout said. "They keep to themselves, and we get their dictates through charming members of the Varsity squad. Lucky us."

"And because of that," Smith said, "there's nothing more we can do tonight. I'm going to make a call to see if another enclave is willing to babysit our targets tonight. Head back home. We'll be in touch."

Not taking no for an answer, he went for the door, six Adepts and one not-quite Adept behind him, heading off to bed before another routine day of classes, and another routine night of battling evil across the city.

Scout yawned hugely, her eyes blinking sleepily when the spasm passed. "I'm about done," she said, then slid an arm through mine after I'd returned her messenger bag and she'd situated it. "Let's go home."

"We should get back, too," Jason said, then glanced warmly at me. "You take care, Parker."

"I always do, Shepherd."

He winked; then he and Michael set off down the tunnels. Jamie and Jill and Paul said their goodbyes, but Scout and I stood in front of the door for a moment. She looked over at me, then enveloped me in a gigantic hug.

"You came after me."

"You're my new best friend," I said, hugging her back.

"Yeah, I know, but still. Weren't you scared witless?"

"Completely. But you're Scout. I told you I'd be there for you, and I was."

Scout released me, then wiped tears from beneath her eyes. Catharsis, I guessed. "I've said it before and I'll say it again—you seriously rock, Parker."

"Tell me again, Green," I said as we switched on flashlights and headed through the tunnel.

"Seriously, you rock."

"One more time."

"Don't press your luck."

It was late when Scout and I returned to St. Sophia's, but while she showered and headed to her room for some much-needed sleep (under Lesley's watchful eye), I plucked my cell phone from her bag and headed out on one last journey I wasn't entirely excited about taking.

Have you ever been in a car or on a walk, and all of a sudden you look up, and trees and blocks have passed you by? When you end up in a spot, but you don't remember much of how you got there? I found myself, a few minutes later, staring at the tidy gold letters on Foley's door. Light seeped beneath it despite the late hour.

I lifted a hand, knocked, and when Foley called my name, walked inside. She stood at the window, still in her suit, a porcelain teacup cradled in her hands. She glanced back at me, one eyebrow arched. "Ms. Green?"

"She's fine. She's back in her room."

Foley closed her eyes and let out a breath of obvious relief. "Thank God for small favors." After a moment, she opened her eyes, then moved to her desk and placed the teacup on the desktop. "I assume you're now interested in discussing your parents?"

I rubbed my arms and nodded.

"I see," she said, then pulled out her chair and lowered herself into it. She motioned toward the chairs in front of her desk. I shook my head and stayed where I was. It wasn't stubbornness; my knees were shaking, and I wasn't sure I'd be able to make it over there without tripping.

"As you know," she said, "your parents are very intelligent people. They are currently working to resolve a somewhat, shall we say, awkward problem. That work has taken them to Europe. I have a personal interest in that work, which is why we're acquainted."

When she suddenly stopped talking, I stared at her for a few seconds, waiting for elaboration. But I got nothing more. "That's all? That's all you're going to tell me?"

"That's more than your parents told you," she pointed out. "Are you asking me to trump a decision made by your parents? Or, more important, have you decided that your need to know trumps their decision not to tell you?"

That made me snap my lips closed again. "I don't know."

This time, I really did take a seat, slinking down into a chair and staring at the desktop. I finally raised my eyes to Foley's. "They're okay, right? Because they're really hard to get in touch with, and their phone keeps cutting out."

"Your parents are safe and sound," she said, her voice softer now. "*For now*. You might consider, Ms. Parker, the possibility that they are safe, in part, because of the current status quo. Because you are safe and sound in this institution, and suspicions are not being raised. Because uncomfortable questions aren't being asked. Because," she added after a moment, lifting her eyes to mine, "the members of a certain dark elite are not aware of where they are, what they're doing, or where you've been placed in their absence."

My heart filled my throat. "They know about the dark elite? About the magic?"

Foley shook her head. "Unfortunately, that is a question I can't directly answer."

My head was spinning and my patience had finally worn thin. "Whatever," I threw out, then stood up and pushed back my chair. "I'll just ask them myself."

My hand was on the office doorknob before she spoke again.

"Is it worth the risk?"

I wet my lips.

"Your trust has been shaken, Lily. I realize that." I glanced back at her. "But if you search your soul, your memories, and you decide that your parents love you, perhaps you'll be willing to give them the benefit of the doubt on this one. You might realize that if they didn't give you all the details of their work, of their lives together, they had a very good reason for it. That the consequences of your knowing might not be worth the risks you'd be creating. The risk to you. The risk to your parents."

I lifted an eyebrow. "And when do I get the benefit of the doubt?"

She smiled, slowly. "You're here, aren't you?"

When I was back in the suite, I checked in on Scout. She was snoring peacefully in Lesley's room, and Lesley was curled up on a sleeping bag at the foot of the bed. I quietly closed the door and slipped into my room, then closed and locked it behind me. I grabbed my cell phone from the top of my bookshelf, sat down on my bed, and dialed.

It took two tries for my phone to actually make a connection to my parents. The third time, my mom answered.

"Lily?" There was a pause, maybe while my mom scanned a clock. "Are you okay?"

I opened my mouth, then closed it again, tears suddenly welling in my eyes. I wanted to yell at her, scream at her . . . and tell her that I loved her. I wanted to rail against her and my dad for not telling me the truth, whatever it was, for holding back so much from me. I wanted to tell her about my classes, about Scout, about the brat pack, about Jason, about firespell. About the fact that I had *magic*, power that flowed from my hands.

But maybe Foley was right. Maybe it was dangerous. Maybe their safety—*our* safety—was somehow dependent on my pretending to be an average high school kid.

Maybe there were more important considerations than Lily Parker getting a chance to throw a tantrum.

"I'm fine," I finally said. "I just wanted to hear your voice."

Smith kept his promise to keep in touch, but it was still two days before Scout got paged again. We walked together into the tunnels, headed for the enclave, the mood very different than the last time we'd taken that walk. Nevertheless, Enclave Three was still quiet when we entered.

Everyone was there. Michael, Jason, Paul, and the twins chatted together. Katie and Smith stood at the edge of the room, unhappy expressions on their faces.

"What's going on?" Scout asked when we reached the knot of JV Adepts.

Jamie and Jill shrugged simultaneously. "No clue."

Smith, a supersnug long-sleeved plaid shirt and skinny jeans all but pasted to his thin frame, opened his mouth, but before he could speak, the door creaked open. Our gazes snapped to the doorway.

A guy stepped inside. Tall, blondish, and well built, he had blue eyes, a dimpled chin, and strong features. He wore a snug U of C T-shirt and dark jeans over brown boots.

"Yowsers," Jill muttered.

"Good evening, Adepts."

"Yo," Scout said, her head tilted to the side, curiosity in her expression.

He shut the door behind him, then pressed his hand to the door. For a second, it pulsed with light, then faded again.

"I think he just warded the door," Scout whispered, awe in her voice. "I've never seen that before. He has got to teach me how to do that. It *rocked*."

"I thought I rocked?" I whispered.

"Oh, you do," she assured me, patting me on the arm. "This is a totally different kind of rockage."

The blond walked to Katie and Smith and shook their hands. They looked none too excited to meet him; Smith's lip was actually curled in disgust. When they'd said their hellos, Katie and Smith stepped aside. The blond stepped toward us.

"I'm Daniel Sterling," he said. "And I'm your new team captain."

That must have meant something to the rest of the Adepts, who exchanged knowing glances.

"New team captain?" Paul asked.

Daniel looked at Paul, hands on his hips. "Your handlers and mine have become aware of a certain lack of . . . cohesiveness within this enclave. I am here to remedy that lack of cohesiveness." He slid a narrowed glance to Katie and Smith, who looked down, rebuked.

Scout and I exchanged a grin.

Daniel glanced at each of us in turn. "We're a team," he said after a minute. "High school or college, human or"—he paused, glancing at Jason—"*other*. All of us, together. Indivisibly."

The Adepts smiled. I appreciated their enthusiasm.

"It has also come to my attention that there's a new Adept amongst you." Daniel moved until he stood directly in front of me, then stared down, one eyebrow arched. "Lily Parker?"

"All day long," I answered.

He managed to stifle a grin, then slid his hands into his jeans pockets. "I understand that you were hit by firespell a few days ago, that a darkening subsequently appeared, and that you then discovered you had some power magic?"

I nodded.

"I further understand that you encouraged these Adepts to enter the sanctuary and retrieve Scout, and that you discovered, while you were there, that you had firespell abilities. I understand that all of you were able to escape largely unharmed?"

My cheeks warmed, and I nodded. Scout gave me a pat on the back.

"Go, you," she whispered.

"That was a completely inappropriate course of action."

That wiped the smile off my face, and put a big grin on Smith's and Katie's.

"This organization works because we have a hierarchy, a chain of authority responsible both for the assignments given to Junior Varsity members and for taking responsibility when those assignments are unsuccessful. You had no right to encourage these Adepts into danger against the express wishes of their Varsity squad. Do you understand that?"

I nodded sheepishly, eyes on the floor, humiliation bubbling in my chest. Nobody liked a dressing-down.

"On the other hand," he said, turning back to Katie and Smith, "you were willing to sacrifice one of the most powerful members of your squad because you were unwilling to take a chance on her extraction. That reeks of cowardice. And cowardice is not why we're here.

"From now on," Daniel said, walking to the end of the room, then turning around again so that he faced all of us, "we work together, as a team, with one goal, and one set of leaders. Is that understood, Varsity?" he asked

Katie and Smith. When they nodded, Daniel looked back at us. "Is that understood, Junior Varsity?"

We all nodded. I wasn't entirely sure if I was supposed to nod, but I wasn't going to risk this guy's wrath again.

"Now that we've settled that, we have some business to attend to."

Despite my attempt to blend in, he looked over at me. "Ms. Parker, you have demonstrated abilities that indicate that you're an Adept. Are you on our side or theirs?"

There was no need to ask which "theirs" he meant. "Yours," I answered.

"Then welcome to the squad." With that, he turned on his heel and walked back to the table, where he, Katie, and Smith began to chat.

I looked over at Scout. "That's it? I'm in?"

"What'd you think—you'd take an oath or something?"

"Something," I said with a nod. "You know, something more symbolic for the fact that I'll be sleeping less and battling bad guys more."

"Two words," she said. "Strawberry sodas."

"Congratulations," whispered a voice behind me. When I glanced back, Jason stood there, a knowing smile on his face.

"I need to go . . . somewhere else," Scout said, bumping me with an elbow. "You two kids have fun."

I made a mental note to talk to Scout later about "subtlety," but smiled at Jason. "Thanks, I think."

"So you're now an official member of Enclave Three. You weirdo."

I snorted. "I'm a weirdo? You're a werewolf."

"I suggest you say that with respect, Parker."

"Or what?"

"Or I'll have to bite you." His lips widened into a grin of heart-stopping proportions. I guessed it would have been pretty effective on him in werewolf form, too.

"I don't think you'll bite me," I offered back, although I wasn't entirely sure about that.

"I guess we'll just have to see what happens, won't we?"

Jason gazed down at me, those ocean blue eyes swimming with promise, at least until a cell phone rang. After a moment of chatting, cell pressed to his ear, Daniel clapped his hands.

"Saddle up, kids," he said. "We've got an assignment."

"We'll finish this later," Jason whispered. "I promise."

I believed him, so I offered him a wink, and we rejoined the others. I took my place at their sides, Scout squeezing my hand when I stood beside her, ready to take on evil in the Second City.

Welcome to Morganville, Texas.
Just don't stay out after dark.

The *New York Times* bestselling Morganville Vampires series
by Rachel Caine

College freshman Claire Danvers has her share of challenges—like being a genius in a school that favors beauty over brains, battling homicidal girls in her dorm, and finding out that her college town is overrun with the living dead.

Glass Houses
The Dead Girls' Dance
Midnight Alley
Feast of Fools
Lord of Misrule
Carpe Corpus
Fade Out

---

rachelcaine.com

Available wherever books are sold or at
penguin.com

Penguin Group (USA) Online

What will you be reading tomorrow?

Tom Clancy, Patricia Cornwell, W.E.B. Griffin,
Nora Roberts, William Gibson, Robin Cook,
Brian Jacques, Catherine Coulter, Stephen King,
Dean Koontz, Ken Follett, Clive Cussler,
Eric Jerome Dickey, John Sandford,
Terry McMillan, Sue Monk Kidd, Amy Tan,
J. R. Ward, Laurell K. Hamilton,
Charlaine Harris, Christine Feehan...

You'll find them all at
penguin.com

Read excerpts and newsletters,
find tour schedules and reading group guides,
and enter contests.

Subscribe to Penguin Group (USA) newsletters
and get an exclusive inside look
at exciting new titles and the authors you love
long before everyone else does.

PENGUIN GROUP (USA)
us.penguingroup.com